BY JOSH MALERMAN

Bird Box

A House at the Bottom of a Lake

Black Mad Wheel

Unbury Carol

Pearl (previously titled *On This, The Day of the Pig*)

Inspection

Malorie

Goblin

DAPHNE

DAPHNE

A NOVEL

Josh Malerman

NEW YORK

Published in the United States by Del Rey, an imprint of Random House, a division of Penguin Random House LLC, New York.

DEL REY and the CIRCLE colophon are registered trademarks of Penguin Random House LLC.

LIBRARY OF CONGRESS CATALOGING-IN-PUBLICATION DATA
Names: Malerman, Josh, author.
Title: Daphne / Josh Malerman.
Description: First Edition. | New York: Del Rey Books, [2022]
Identifiers: LCCN 2022001564 (print) | LCCN 2022001565 (ebook) |
ISBN 9780593157015 (hardcover) | ISBN 9780593157022 (ebook)
Subjects: LCGFT: Novels.
Classification: LCC PS3613.A43535 D37 2022 (print) | LCC PS3613.A43535 (ebook) |
DDC 813/.6—dc23
LC record available at https://lccn.loc.gov/2022001564
LC ebook record available at https://lccn.loc.gov/2022001565

Printed in Canada on acid-free paper

randomhousebooks.com

2 4 6 8 9 7 5 3 1

First Edition

Book design by Caroline Cunningham
Basketball hoop frontispiece: Adobe Stock/alswart

For Allison Laakko and Jason Glasgow

and the summer we spent asking the rim questions

DAPHNE

A tie game with summer-league rivals, friends and family in the bleachers, the ball in your hand at the free-throw line, is no time to ask the rim a question. Yet that's what Kit Lamb does. Even as she lifts the ball, elbow in, left hand supporting, even as it seems like nothing could chop her focus, and nothing has yet, not in this game, not even when she made the and-one that led to this moment. A question for the rim:

Will Daphne kill me?

Kit almost laughs as she releases the ball. There's a hitch in the shot to be sure. She's embarrassed of her own question, even if nobody else could've heard.

The ball leaves her fingertips, the gym is haunted-house quiet. But the question remains suspended in her head. And with it, the image of the woman Daphne, Kit's own idea of her, the horrid centerpiece of Natasha Manska's Samhattan myth; Daphne in denim, Daphne with patches, Daphne the madwoman who smells of smoke and whiskey.

The ball goes through the net.

So, that's a yes. An answer Kit doesn't have time to think about right now.

Chaps inbounds quick from the baseline, but one second is not enough for their star forward to get off a full-court shot.

Samhattan wins.

By one.

Kit is mobbed by her teammates. So many howling voices, so much love. None louder than Dana, who is as sweaty as Kit; Dana, who shot a meager one for eleven but got the steal that led to Kit's game-winning three-point play.

"Legend!" Dana yells. "*Legend!*"

Kit can't stop smiling. As they lift her up, as friends and school-mates rush the floor. As music explodes through the gymnasium PA.

Even as she worries too.

Not about the answer the rim gave her. Not about that *yes*. Not yet.

For Kit Lamb, success never feels entirely *true*. In moments when she's supposed to be the winner, it's more like she's in a theatrical reproduction of someone else's victory.

"*LE-GEND!*" the other ballers shout.

She can see the players from Chaps on their knees, yes, heads hanging, yes. But did this really happen? Did she hit the game-winning free throw with one second to play?

"Holy shit," she says, rising up now on the shoulders of her teammates, her best friends. "Holy *shit*!"

It's all becoming real now. The inviolability of this moment. It's replaying behind her eyes. Or, rather, before them, as if she's home, watching the triumphant sequence on *SportsCenter*. Who cares if there's less than forty people in the gym?

Who cares about absolutely anything else in the entire world?

"*Legend!*" Dana shouts again. Her visage: ardent mirth. Other girls pick up the shout. Even the parents holler. Kit's own looked happily stunned. They even look a little younger. Coach Wanda steps before them and nods Kit's way just as she's interrupted: she's gotta shake the hand of Chaps's head coach. Wanda stresses this all the time: sportsmanship. No matter how much it hurts. But Kit is impressed her coach acknowledged decorum when it feels this *good*.

Who can think of anything else?

The lights look particularly bright in the rafters. The gym feels like a mecca. A heaven. Nirvana. Kit has arrived somewhere. No, she doesn't think this means she'll be playing in the WNBA (though the vision does cross her mind; Betnijah Laney seeing this shot, Sue Bird winking); rather, she's fantasized about this exact scenario a hundred thousand times, as Coach Wanda made the girls shoot free throws after every practice, at their most tired, at their worst, like they would be in a game. The place Kit has arrived is not a location but a goal: she is living a fantasy, and the fantasy is no longer that.

This is true. Every bit of it.

But . . .

. . . is the answer the rim gave her also true?

Will Daphne kill me?

Yes.

And so maybe it's not so improbable, after all, thinking of something else.

"LEGEND!"

Everybody is saying it, in rhythm, a chant. *Le-gend.* As if Kit Lamb at the free-throw line will one day be immortalized in stained glass high up the brick walls of the Samhattan High School gymnasium. The communal word echoes off the ceiling, curls out those open windows, circles Kit's head like cartoon birds in a dream.

LE-GEND

LE-GEND

Like the legend of Daphne, told to the ballers last night, in the dark of Dana's living room. Almost the entire team slept there to ensure nobody would stay up too late before the big game, yet wasn't it Natasha's story of the Woman Who Could Not Be Killed, the lumbering seven-foot colossus in denim, wasn't it that very story that kept Kit up all night, eyeing the darkness, thinking the very question she would eventually ask the rim at the free-throw line tonight?

Will Daphne kill me?

Like she killed so many others . . .

"Fuck this," she says, still held aloft.

Because this is not the time to feel bad. Now is not the time to punish herself for feeling good.

Smiling (tempered now, though, and do her best friends notice?), she tries to remember a phrase she saw online, wrote down in her journal. Strong words that, she's long hoped, might deter the next all-out panic attack.

"Why are you thinking about that?" she asks herself.

No, this is *not* the time to be thinking about panic. Anxiety. Fear.

But she's asked it. And, despite the cacophony in here, she heard herself ask it.

And the tremble she heard in her voice reminds her of the first she ever heard there:

The night she called 911 on herself.

Hello? I think I'm dying . . .

She looks to the gym doors. Sees they're closed. Okay. She breathes a little better. Why? She doesn't know. A feeling. Security. Nobody can get in without opening a door first. She looks to her friends below. Glad for the people she sees. Checks for another. One she might not know.

She wears makeup, Natasha said last night. *To hide her blue face.*

"Aren't you so happy right now?" Natasha asks. She's holding up Kit's right leg. Natasha hasn't made a basket all year. Natasha is one of the funniest people Kit knows. That's why hearing her tell that story last night was so unsettling.

Nothing funny about that one.

"Kit," Natasha says, "they're gonna hang your fuckin' jersey from the rafters."

"Easy," Coach Wanda says, stepping into the crush of players (and friends now, right? Yes, Kit recognizes their faces, all of them; good). Coach extends a hand up to Kit. "Heck of a shot, Lamb."

Kit shakes the hand. Doesn't want to think of the question she asked the rim but thinks of the question she asked the rim.

The rim has never lied to Kit. Not once.

And here the rim said *yes.*

Stop it now, she tells herself. *You fucking won.* Then, to all: "*We fucking won!*"

Coach Wanda is trying to get the girls to stop swearing, but it's no use. Kit Lamb just hit the fucking game-winning free throw with a second to go on the holy-shit clock.

Let the ballers howl. Let them shout *legend* till they're blue in the face.

Kit thinks of that, *blue in the face,* as the world continues to blur with excitement. She thinks of Natasha's story, the seven-footer named Daphne dying in her car, parked in her own garage, her bare hands gripping the wheel long after she died.

They say Samhattan's paramedics pried those fingers loose with wrenches.

They say Samhattan's bogeywoman was blue in the face.

"*Kit!*" someone shouts. Should sound like unbridled joy. Sounds more like warning.

Kit looks to the doors. One is open.

Is she going to have a panic attack . . . *right now?*

"Kit Lamb for the win!"

She might. She knows this amplification well. It comes unannounced, of course. Nobody hears a panic attack coming. Not until it's too close to dodge.

"Kit!" Dana shouts. *"We love you!"*

Kit smiles. Tempered, though.

"You stole the ball!" she calls back. And Dana makes a muscle with one arm. It's funny. Kit should remember it forever. Will she? Or will her memory of this night always be centered on the anxiety she feels, held high in the sky on the shoulders of soulmates?

She wants to cry. So much triumph. So much love.

"KI-IT! KI-IT!"

It's the nature of panic that it is *believed* by the sufferer. Kit's never read about somebody avoiding an attack by telling themselves they'd gotten through the last one.

"Okay, let me down," Kit says. Not loud enough for her friends to hear. There's heat at the base of her neck. Always the place it begins.

She looks to Dana. To Natasha. To Coach Wanda. To the doors. To those windows high up the brick walls.

Will Daphne kill me?

No. She refuses to let this question continue.

"Daphne is a fucking myth," she says.

But she's thinking about her. Thinking about Daphne.

"A *myth*," she repeats. Her voice tiny on the spectrum of sound in the gym. There's Mom and Dad. There's Emily Holt. Beck Nelson. Kennedy Lichtenstein. Tammy Jones.

Friends.

Family.

"Myth . . ."

Something incredible, something unexpected, something rare happens: Kit talks the heat away.

"And this?" she says. "This is real, Kit. This is your life."

The anxiety ebbs. Pride in the shot she made exists alone, untouched, untethered.

As it should.

Now isn't the time for myth.

Now is the time for legend.

She raises her arms and howls, and everybody in the gym are wolves with her.

And soon they lower her back down to the gym floor. The floor on which she just shot the shot of her life.

"Pizza," Natasha says.

"Yes," Kit says.

But first, Kit finds Coach Wanda.

"Thanks for believing in me," she says.

Coach imitates shooting a free throw with perfect form, the same way she'd been teaching the girls to shoot them for years.

"Go eat," she says. "Go be happy."

Kit smiles, but Coach's words feel large.

Go be happy . . .

Is she? Can she be?

No heat at the base of her neck. But a long battle seems to stretch out before her. She sees it extending through the walls of the far side of the gym: all of life, linear, ahead. And anxiety, panic, somewhere in the shadows off to either side of the path. Whatever path she and her best friends take from here.

The question returns, yes:

Will Daphne kill me?

But the question is lost, for now, in the blind bliss of friends unaware of how close they stand to that path. And lost, too, in the sudden mob of teammates pulling Kit across the floor, toward the locker room, toward the rest of the night, what should be the best night of her life.

Just before getting there, she looks to the closest rim, the one she saw the ball, her ball, sail through.

"Yo, cheeseball," Natasha says. "You gonna kiss it? Come on, already. Let's go."

The rim's never lied to Kit Lamb before.

"Coming," she says.

And she follows Natasha and the others into the locker room, where rapid voices discuss big things, even if some of them are disguised as small. And as she approaches the celebration, Kit thinks no, the rim's never lied to her before.

Then, more celebratory howling. Including Kit herself.

And everybody in the locker room are wolves with her.

○ ○ ○

Kit Lamb's Jolly Journal—The Day Before the Big Game

People say you can't leave a paper trail when you're committing a crime, and so this feels like I'm committing a crime. I'm doing it this way, freehand, to hide it (these WORDS, yo) from ever getting out online or anywhere close to that. THAT'S WHY (and this feels big): I'm writing it on actual . . . paper. Amazing, yeah? Yeah. Mom and Dad, if you ever read this, please recognize how backwards the world is: it's now NOT a paper trail when you use paper because nobody reads this shit. Ha. In FACT, if someone were to find my Jolly Journal (oh, how I love that ironic name), they would probably throw it out, thinking it had fallen out of the pocket of the year 1990. So, like I said: hello Journal, I am here to tell you secrets, to hide things, big things, like:

How I really feel about the world.

Okay. Everybody is different and everybody has their own take, their own feelings, their own worldview, but some of us like to keep ours safe. It's not that I don't want anybody to know the real me, it's just . . .

There are parts of me I like and parts I do not and anyway I would like them all kept behind glass before I know exactly what I want to do with them.

Capiche?

What's that, Jolly? What are the parts I like?

HA. We'll get to that. But I can say a couple easy ones for now: I'm a good friend. This is true. And I'm brave. Sort of. Brave insomuch as I'm scared all the time but I keep plugging away and so I must be brave. This is mostly true. I do not hide from my biggest enemy. I face it. Mostly. HELLO, enemy of mine, THY NAME IS:

ANXIETY

Was that supposed to feel good? Writing it down? I think it was. I know it was. That's what I read online. All over the place people tell you it's better to talk about it. They say you'll go mad if you keep it bottled up inside. But here's the thing: if you're not freaking out, the last thing you wanna talk about is freaking out. And if you ARE freaking out, well, ha, then the LAST thing you wanna talk about is freaking out.

You see my problem, Jolly?

Yes. You do.

And it didn't feel good. Writing it down. It felt huge and now I wanna cross it out. Maybe that's because I wrote it in all caps. But hey, that's how I do. If I'm gonna do, I do. That's how I do. That's how we all do. Still, let's try it again, but smaller:

anxiety

Okay. Wow. That looks more like it. Feels more like it too. It's small and lowercase and sneaks up on you and takes you DOWN. Holy shit, does it take you down. And there's no explanation for it, is there?

I saw a ton of that online too. A ton of good stuff about how there is no rational reason and so, Kit? STOP LOOKING FOR ONE. And oh boy, I can relate to that. I've looked for the reason all over my room, all over the house. All over my head. Because how can you expect someone to just . . . take it . . . without knowing why? Hey, look at me, I'm nervous! Why? Well . . . I don't know why. And guess what? What? That makes me . . .

. . . more nervous.

Here's a word that comes up a lot: COMPOUNDS

People love using that word because . . . it's true. It's like cycles, right? One bad feeling comes (anxiety) and then a second bad feeling (shame for feeling anxiety) and then a third round (anger for feeling shame) and a fourth and it feels like you're getting punched in the stomach when all you're really doing is sitting at a table during lunch and listening to your friends and, OH NO, all the bad feelings arrive, they're all here.

In town.

In YOU.

It's infuriating, isn't it? You're not allowed to think about it (anxiety) or else it comes but if you don't think about it . . . it comes.

Not real fair.

Listen, Jolly, tomorrow is a big game. Playing Chaps in the Summer League finale. I can only guess Diana Taurasi doesn't write down how scared she is before the WNBA finals. But I could be wrong. Maybe that's exactly what she does. And maybe that's why she's fearless?

She doesn't let things compound. She gives it all a head fake and all that bad shit goes flying by and she's got an open lane and—

Oh, what do I know about her in real life? She's extraordinary. What do I know about extraordinary?

SECRET: I want to be extraordinary too.

What do I need to do? Sign me up.

Tonight, we're all sleeping at Dana's to "make sure we all get some rest," but really we all just want to hang out and I think maybe it's because we're all actually scared. I like to think I'm not alone on that front. I'm not the only one who lies in bed in the dark and worries that anxiety is gonna come squishing up the stairs like a worm, crawl under my door, crawl up my bed frame, into my bed, into my ear, into my head, into my mind, where it'll lay eggs and then there won't just be this one thought but a thousand of this one thought, like a planet with tons of moons, all in my head, these worms crawling around in the dark while I lie in the dark and the only thing I can do is to wait for them all to die.

That's it, Jolly. The only real cure I've discovered at least.

You just gotta wait for the anxiety to die.

Oy.

Okay. Gonna get ready for Dana's and for the game tomorrow.

Think we'll win?

I wanna say yes.

And so, you know what?

Yes.

But if you say a thing, does that make it so? Or does that make it not so? Does it support it? Or does it jinx it?

Sorry, Jolly. I'm a handful.

But at least I'm trying. And by the next time I talk to you, the game will have been played.

Who knows? Maybe I'll walk out of the gym a hero, my mind empty of all this clutter. Maybe I'll play so freakin' good my enemy will leave me alone, noble in defeat, aware that even someone as ordinary (but potentially extraordinary) as Kit Lamb deserves a break from too much thinking.

We shall see, Jolly. We shall seeeeeeeeee

o o o

The girls ask the rim questions all the time. It's their thing. One of their things. They get together in Garland Park and they saunter over to the crappy, netless rim (bowed, no less), and they ask a question, shoot the ball, and receive answers.

But there are rules.

"You can't ask it the same thing twice," Dana once said, the day they laid down the rules. "Whatever it tells you the first time is the final answer. Any make or miss after that doesn't matter. Not with the same question."

The girls were scared that day; Melanie went white. She'd just asked if her parents would die before she graduated from high school, uncharacteristically morbid. And now . . . maybe true?

Over time, many of the answers have proven true. But like visits to a psychic, it's not difficult, later, to *read* the answers as if they came true, whether or not they did. Except in the case of Kit. Kit, it seems, is special. Her questions have more detail. She does not ask, *Will I find love?* She asks, *Will I be let down by a lover one day?*

The details make it harder to dismiss as coincidence when they come true.

"And you can't ask it about something that's already happened," Natasha said that day, her dark-blond hair not quite yet to its signature shoulder length. "The rim doesn't stoop to proving itself by verifying historical facts. It sees the future and it believes that should be enough."

The future. There seems to be a lot of the future these days. Colleges, yes, love lives, sure, but these friends wonder more about what kind of people they will be, what they will accomplish, what they won't, and when.

Today, a few days after having defeated Chaps in the final league game of the summer season, Kit is still thinking of the question she asked the realest rim, the best rim, the rim inside the gym of Sam-hattan High.

"Come on, All-Star," Dana says, bounce-passing to Kit way out. That's another thing: you have to be careful how far you are when you launch a shot. Nobody wants to ask about their health before firing a forty-footer. What are the chances of good news?

At the same time, if you ask on a layup, how much can you trust it?

It's all about intention, Natasha often says. Natasha who knows tons of weird factoids. Like Ouija-board stuff. Urban legends.

Daphne.

Kit takes a few steps closer to the rim. More like a college three-pointer now. Has her thinking of college.

"Am I going to be accepted to Michigan State?"

She shoots. She misses.

"Fuck," she says. Kit's grades are okay. She's no star in the class-room. But she's also never tried to be.

"Whatever," Natasha says, taking the rebound in stride as she dribbles out for a twelve-footer. Natasha is the worst shot of the group. For this, Kit knows she asks more gentle questions.

Even irreverent Natasha respects the rim.

"Will I throw up from drinking too much before this year is over?" Natasha asks.

She shoots. The ball hits the backboard and goes in. She didn't aim for the backboard.

The girls crack up as Natasha runs the baseline, fists to the sky.

"Of course you will!" Melanie says, her dark bangs hiding the top half of her face. "You're already an alcoholic."

"Fuck you," Natasha says, a bit out of breath from the short run. "Am not. Do you have any idea how much you have to drink to be an alcoholic?"

"No," Melanie says. "I haven't done that research."

"It's like . . . twenty drinks a morning."

The girls laugh again, but they also seem to be considering this information.

"Is Natasha an alcoholic?" Melanie asks.

She dribbles to the rim, goes up for a layup, misses.

Triumphant, Natasha raises her fists once more.

"Told you, scumbag."

Not all questions are created equal. Some are serious, some are not. But up until now, Kit has taken pride in the fact that her streak is intact. She hasn't been lied to yet. And while that makes for a fun afternoon under the Samhattan sun, it's also unsettling. A little bit. As if, whenever she gets the ball, the others get quiet. Like they respect her questions more than they do their own.

"Did you ask the rim anything on your game winner?" Dana asks.

Kit was not expecting this. She's standing at the top of the key, two discolored marks in the pavement. She turns red.

"Me?"

She isn't sure how to respond. Just like the rim doesn't lie, neither does Kit. Not any more than a seventeen-year-old Samhattan High School senior-to-be should.

Natasha faces the rim, ball in hand.

"Did Kit have a question planned in case she ever shot a game-winning free throw?"

She shoots. She misses.

Natasha misses a lot, yes, but . . . see? No lie. It wasn't planned. That's the part that unnerved Kit most for the few days following the huge win. In fact, she hasn't been okay with it at all. That night, Night of the Game Winner, her parents asked if something was bothering her. Both Mom and Dad, at different times. Mom asked at Jenny Will's Pizza, in the middle of the celebration, long after the girls had signed the Spirit of Samhattan, the giant lone rock in Betsy Lure Field, the rock that has been painted over and signed for decades.

You okay?

Mom asked it while everybody else was talking over the sludgy '90s music Jenny's always has playing. The whole team was there, even Coach Wanda. Kit was half listening to Natasha telling a story about Mr. Derringer, Samhattan's physics teacher, when Mom leaned across the table and said:

Hey. Kit. You okay?

What a question, Kit thought then. What an absolutely insane question. How could she not be okay? She'd hit the game winner not two hours before. She was seventeen. Her best friends in the world were beside her. There was a table full of as much pizza as she could ever eat. If she wasn't okay then, in that exact moment, would she ever be?

What do you mean? she asked.

But Mom wasn't a fool. And like the rim never lied, Mom could tell if you did.

Still, Mom didn't press. She nodded and turned her own half attention to Natasha and the others as they broke out laughing, even as Kit busted up, too, despite not hearing the punch line. Thanks to Mom's question.

You okay?

Didn't people know that, whether or not you were okay, the moment they asked if you were, you weren't? And that it was always better not to ask?

Kit wishes she hadn't called 911 the first time she had a panic attack. She worries it's given her a stigma. Do people treat her gently? Different than they do each other? Is Kit . . . damaged in some way?

She felt it then, again: the greasy but vague touch of anxiety at the base of her neck. It always starts there, a small spot of heat, a dull, unsettling sensation she's always seen as being piss-yellow. It lives there; a flock of urine-yellow birds with matted feathers that multiply fast when they want to. They came with their own heat, those birds, and while there was Kit's entire body to attack, they always crawled up the neck first; a straight shot to the head.

Mom squeezed Kit's hand. A small, quick one. Kit almost pulled away. But Evelyn Lamb had a way of knowing when those birds were peeking above their nest, and Kit felt the heat, mercifully, subside.

That made two close calls in one night, Kit noted. And this fact nearly ignited a third. Kit wondered if it would take a lifetime of game winners to avoid panic forever.

Later, home again, Dad asked the same thing. Mom was already upstairs and Kit stood in the living room, the TV controller in hand, the screen still off.

Kit, he said, his sudden voice like brutish bare hands from the doorway over her shoulder. *Everything okay?*

Kit turned to face him. Jason Lamb seemed to stumble upon his daughter's darker moments innocently, whereas Mom always *knew.* Eyeing him, she thought, again: Why ask something like that on a night like this? Were her parents *hoping* she'd freak out?

She only nodded.

Yeah, she said. *Amazing.*

Because it was true.

Dad smiled. He looked up the hall to make sure Mom wasn't listening, then said:

You were fucking *amazing.*

One of their many bonds. When the cat's away, the mice will swear.

Kit smiled. It felt good, a moment of real pride in a night pocked with more inner turmoil than she would've dreamed possible.

Man, if Dad wasn't right: it *was* fucking amazing. Kit had just coolly won the biggest game of her life with a single flick of her wrist, a motion she'd practiced two hundred thousand times, the same fingers that held the TV controller now, the same hands she looked down to, imagining, suddenly, much bigger ones, gripping a steering wheel even in death, like in Natasha's story about the madwoman Daphne.

She doesn't use a knife, Natasha said. *She doesn't use a chainsaw. Not a hook, not a gun, not a rake.*

What does she use? Melanie asked.

When Natasha answered, the ends of her mouth were turned up. Natasha was the kind of person you could hear smiling in the dark.

Her bare fucking hands.

"What up?" Dana asks. She points to the ball in Kit's hands, the ball she forgot she was holding. The sun is hot and it reminds Kit of that heat at the base of her neck.

The sun glares off the backboard and, from this distance—or maybe from any—Kit doesn't think she could make a shot right now.

She looks to the rim. Squints.

"Is Melanie in love with someone?"

The others grunt. These girls, they don't give a shit about crushes.

Kit shoots. Misses. It's a stupid question. She knows. But maybe it'll wipe clean the question Dana just asked her. Melanie quietly says, "I told you guys." But as Dana gets the rebound, she eyes Kit the way close friends do. Like, *Really, what's with you?*

Kit and Dana, thick as thieves. Amongst great friends: the best.

So, shouldn't Dana recognize when it's *not* the best time to flash Kit *that* look?

And there's a lot *with* Kit right now. Or maybe it's a little that feels like it could become a lot. It's not a new feeling (and it's partly why the ice water she discovered in her veins at the free-throw line should be so thrilling), but its mere presence, in any form, eclipses her inner sun. All the ballers deal with *something*. Natasha talks about depression like she's doing stand-up. Dana wishes she looked like someone else. Melanie has insomnia. For Kit, it's anxiety. Yes. And if there's one feeling she knows better than all others, it's the days leading up to an all-out attack. A *panic attackula,* as Natasha joked, leaving Kit with the vision of a bum cloaked in dark clothes planting his hand at the base of her neck. The *Coming Doom,* as she once foolishly called it (foolish because it was too good, too right, and there's nothing fun about it). As if, when she starts to get nervous, a blurry dimension floats toward her, threatens to swallow her, to take her away.

And as far as she knows (and she's done a lot of looking into this), there's nothing she can do about her anxiety. Not entirely. Anxiety may be something she battles the rest of her life. Ice water be damned. Samhattan High's resident hippie, Patricia Maxwell, a classmate who wears tie-dyed shirts and sandals to class, once spoke about anxiety in second-period health. Kit listened close. Patricia said: *You would think that, after one anxiety attack, and after surviving it, you would never fall for it again. But that's the nature of anxiety and depression, isn't it? They fool you into believing them. Every time. Each episode is the real one. Each episode is the actual one you've been fearing the whole time.* Kit had never thought she had anything in common with Patricia Maxwell before, but that resonated. Does Patricia know anxiety like Kit does? Or did Patricia just get lucky with what she said? Like how sometimes you shoot the ball just shitty enough to make it?

Right now it feels like there is not and never was any ice water in her veins. Just regular blood.

The kind Daphne likes to spill.

"Did Kit masturbate to her game winner?"

Dana shoots and makes it.

The others are electric, laughing hard as they slap five. Their laughter should calm Kit down, but she's already thinking about it. The Coming Doom. Panic Attackula. Those yellow birds, learning to fly. And the feeling that more happened at that line than just the shot of her life.

"Guys," she says. She's going to tell them. Let them know she *did* ask the rim a question, the one question she shouldn't have asked.

How do you keep her away, then? Dana grilled Natasha, the night before the game, her voice hopped up with hopeful cynicism. They were all in their sleeping bags in the dark, lights out, supposed to be already asleep.

Only one way, Natasha told them, a theatrical whisper. *You can't think about Daphne. If you think about Daphne too much . . . she comes for you.*

Fuck you, Emily Holt, their starting center, said.

I didn't make the rules, Natasha said.

Are you for real? Beck Nelson asked. She sounded scared. Then she screamed out when a teammate grabbed her ankle in the dark.

You all worry too much, Natasha said. *Just go to sleep.* Then, after a half minute of quiet: *And don't think about Daphne.*

Fuck you, Natasha!

You suck, Natasha!

And all the teammates tossed couch pillows and backpacks at her.

Now, outside, Kit doesn't tell them. She's too embarrassed. Or maybe: too scared. She doesn't want to ruin today any more than she wants to ruin tomorrow. Eventually, she'll be alone tonight.

With her thoughts. *These* thoughts. And nothing more than a journal to grip in the dark.

She lifts the ball to shoot, no question in mind. A car honks. The sound is quieter than if one of their sneakers ground against the pavement. Still, Kit sees a car stopped at the intersection at least two hundred yards from where she stands.

Someone is crossing the street.

Someone tall.

The word "lumbering" crosses Kit's mind. She remembers the way Mrs. Royce used the word in English class, describing a big, merciless man in a book.

Kit shoots. It rattles in.

"You didn't ask anything," Melanie says. She frowns a little. What a waste. Not asking the rim a question. When there are so many questions to ask.

Whoever crossed the street vanishes behind the buildings, the fences, civilization beyond Garland Park. Yet unseen or not . . . it feels like they're still walking this way. Toward the park.

Toward Kit.

Will Daphne kill me?

She smacks herself upside the head. Tries not to think about Daphne.

"Ohhhkay," Melanie says.

"Hey, what up?" Natasha asks.

Her three closest friends. All wondering why she just smacked her own head. Kit Lamb should be in hero mode. Kit Lamb should be a goddess.

Another car honks. This one so close and so loud all four ballers turn to face it. A silver Buick has pulled up onto the grass bordering the pavement. The windows are all rolled down. The car is full of boys. The driver, Stewart Lanse, shoots the girls a cocky smile and says, "You win one fucking big game and now you stand around all lazy?"

Dana tosses the ball his way, it bounces hard off the hood.

Stewart laughs. He looks to Kit.

"Nice shot," he says.

It's the boys' team. Normally, the girls would challenge them to a game. Stewart is a worse shot than Natasha and the girls usually win. But right now, watching her friends approach the car, Kit's just glad for *next*.

It's a word that's become a whole philosophy, the way her mom uses it.

Next is for whenever *now* needs a fucking change.

Kit looks back to the intersection. Cars come and go. Nobody lumbers toward Garland Park.

With the boys, sudden, unplanned plans are made. The girls head to their cars and everybody's going to go to the creek. This is good. If there's one way to undercut the Coming Doom, it's distraction. It's *next*. Kit wanted to say that to Patricia Maxwell that day in health class.

Maybe you can fool it back, she wanted to say.

But she doesn't know if that's true.

"Hurry, Clutch," Dana says.

Kit moves quick to the passenger side of Dana's Pontiac Sunbird. As she grips the door handle, the sun catches her fingers, makes them look bigger, older.

She thinks of bare hands clenched to a steering wheel and the wrenches it took to remove them.

"I'm not gonna ask if you're okay," Dana says, as Kit gets in, "because I know how much you hate that question. *But . . .*"

"I'm great," Kit says. Then, "Better than you'll ever be."

Dana smiles.

"Well, hell yeah," she says. "You should be. You're on top of the world. On top of the *game*."

Dana revs the engine, pulls out of the Garland Park parking lot, and Kit decides, yeah, maybe she *is* on top of the game. Basketball anyway. She works hard at it. So does Dana. They all do. And she just hit a game winner. How many of those does someone get in a lifetime? How many has Candace Parker made? Brilliant as she is, a handful at most.

So okay. Yeah. On top of the game. On top!

And maybe, if she lets herself believe it, on top of living her life too.

But she wonders if you have to be in "believing shape" to believe a thing. Just like you have to be in basketball shape for the season. And she wonders, too, how much work it would take to get in believing shape.

How much thinking would that take? Straight-up, unadulterated *thinking*.

The equivalent of a hundred thousand shots?

So, a hundred thousand good thoughts?

It scares her. Not the work of it. But the idea that you can make a thing true just by thinking about it a lot.

Yeah. That isn't settling right. As Dana drives pell-mell across Samhattan, past "Town Square" (the cemetery built into the center of the city or the city built around the cemetery, she's never sure), past Dawn Pawn and all the rest, even as a Samhattanite in a beige suit steps out of the road, quick, like he's worried the Sunbird was about to mow him down, Kit tries to resist this concept. Despite its upside.

That you might think a thing true.

Just by thinking about it at all.

○ ○ ○

"To the island," Brandon says. "I dare you all."

"Fuck that," Natasha says.

"Why? It's not that far."

"We're not into dares," Natasha says. "We like physical feats. Games. Not dares. We want to live long enough to make terrible decisions in college."

"Dudes," Brandon says. Now he's up, shirtless, wiry, pointing to the island that looks far. The water looks real blue too. "It's not that far!"

"Then swim to it," Dana says. "Douche."

"No dares," Natasha says. "Games, cool. Dares, dumb."

"This is a challenge," Brandon says.

"They're not into it," Ritchie says. Little Richard. That's their nickname for the decidedly not little Richard. "Forget about it."

Brandon eyes his friends.

"Fine," he says. He sits down in the sand again. "Lame."

Nobody disputes this. Brandon isn't scaring anybody.

"Daphne," Stewart says.

"What?" Kit says.

"Half of me," he says, "wants to kiss you right now. That shot was so *dope*."

Kit misses the compliment; she's stuck on how she misheard him. She almost laughs. It's that absurd. She really thought he said—

"Stuff it," Natasha says. "Nobody's kissing Kit without going through me first."

Everyone at least smirk-laughs at this. Kit hears genuine care-free syllables in their laughter.

Why doesn't she hear this in her own?

They're gathered with their shoes and socks off, feet in the creek that leads to the lake that, yes, features a small island, overgrown with thin, half-bare pines, a shoreline of dark, sharp rocks. Not an appealing place. Then again, the creek isn't really either.

"Daphne . . ." Brandon says.

Kit doesn't ask *what* this time. She feels a little heat at the base of her neck.

". . . to think of all the dead stuff in a lake that big."

So, *nasty*, not *Daphne*.

What is Kit doing to herself? Why is she doing this?

Maybe she's not.

"You guys are fucking with me," she says.

She stands up, walks along the creek.

"What do you mean?" Little Richard asks.

Behind her, they're asking one another who's fucking with who? Natasha tells the boys to knock it off, but they sound like they really don't know what she means. And maybe she doesn't either. She's just backing Kit up no matter what.

Kit takes the creek edge toward the lake, alone, careful not to step on any of the angular rocks or roots. Alone now, she thinks of the story Natasha told, how Daphne was a "freak" who was into heavy-metal music. How people in town killed her for being who she was.

Having grown up in Samhattan, Kit has heard the name Daphne before. But it's always been akin to autumn wind: in the name blows, and out by winter. Like those who speak it don't really mean to, and certainly don't want to. Kit's never thought to look into it any more than she would the bogeyman. Before a few days ago, *Daphne* was a word more than it was a name. In fact, part of the reason it bothers her now is that she can't recall anyone ever explicitly saying the name. *Daphne* wasn't a tool used by parents to scare their kids to sleep. *Daphne* wasn't something the bad kids threatened you with on the playground. *Daphne* wasn't even something best friends whispered about at sleepovers.

"Subconscious," Kit says, following the creek's edge. It's a new word for her, insomuch as she's become intimate with it recently, searching for the source of her anxiety. A lot of people say the reason the root is so hard to locate is because it's buried in the subconscious.

And until the night before the big game? *Daphne* was buried too.

Yes, that's right. The two willowy syllables have forever been in the background, Kit thinks. Maybe even the subconscious of Samhattan. This feels true. The way people know the name but don't remember hearing it. The way people say it but don't know why. Before a few nights ago, Kit never had context whatsoever for the name.

Why not?

She tries to remember the first time she heard it. Did her parents speak it? A babysitter? Maybe it was a teacher. A neighbor. A family friend? One of her friends? She doesn't know. And for the first time in her life, she wants to.

"No," she says. "You don't."

That's right. Because Natasha said (in the dark, Kit remembers, can hear the words on Natasha's tongue still) if you think about Daphne . . .

. . . she comes.

Kit looks over her shoulder. Quick. Back to her friends gathered.

She wants to tell herself this is dumb. But just like she can't just tell anxiety to go away, she can't quite get rid of this train of thought. Can't get out from under it. Tied to the tracks, it feels.

When Natasha started her story, nobody on the team said, *I've heard of her.* Nobody said, *Oh, Daphne has a story?* Nobody acknowledged having previous knowledge at all. But also Natasha spoke as if everyone there *had* heard of her. As if . . . as if . . .

"As if Daphne is a Samhattan secret."

That's right. This feels right. In the same way some articles just *feel* right in their description of anxiety and panic attacks, this idea rings true.

A Samhattan secret. A thing everybody knows about but nobody questions. A name familiar to all but with no figure, no features, no face. God, her name really *is* like the wind! Blown into town, crossing the cemetery in Samhattan's center, pulling that graveyard air with it, out into town, through the streets and open windows of the buildings and homes, into the bedrooms of every girl and boy to ever call Samhattan home.

Why hasn't Kit ever thought about this before? Her actual story?

You guys, Natasha had started. It's the way she starts all stories. *So . . . you know Daphne, right?*

And nobody said yes. And nobody said no. And Kit, walking alone now, is afraid of this. Scared by the idea of a whole town shutting out a name.

Well, her story is actually kinda fucked-up. In a really big way.

She has a story? Kit asked. Just a question at the time. It was funny, in a way, to think she had no image, no idea what the name, recognizable somehow, actually meant.

In hindsight, and now that she's really thinking about it, it feels a little . . . crazy.

She sure does, Natasha said.

And it goes a little something like this, Dana said. The others could almost hear her roll her eyes in the dark.

And it goes a lot *something like this,* Natasha said. *Daphne was a woman who lived in Samhattan in the '80s and '90s. She was a seven-foot social freak who had no friends and no family that anybody knew of. She lived alone in Regerton, on Marris Street, and no doubt had to duck every time she stood up in that tiny one-bedroom home. Now, when I say "freak," I don't mean because she was tall. I mean because she'd sit in the food court at Spartan Mall and stare at the little kids as they ate until more than one parent asked her to please stop and others moved to other tables. It was understood that somehow, in whatever way, Daphne's own childhood had been stolen from her.*

What the fuck are you talking about? Emily Holt asked. Emily, who is also tall. But almost a foot shorter than Daphne in Natasha's story too. *Seven feet tall?*

There was a sense that Natasha was making this up on the fly. That she'd simply paid more attention to a name the others had long forgot or had never consciously thought about to begin with. As if all Samhattanites had been bred to *refuse* to think about Daphne.

It's the story I heard, Natasha said, undeterred. *She longed for her own childhood and didn't talk to anybody and kept to herself and lurked about town like a giant pair of pants that came to life. Did I mention that? She only wore denim. Head to toe. Patches of her favorite bands all over. All metal stuff. Hair rock. And she scared the shit out of people, right? I mean, imagine turning the corner downtown and there's this giant standing there, alone, staring at little kids. Oh, and she wore makeup. All painted eyes and tongues.*

Welp, I'm out, Melanie said. *Now you're just making stuff up. Bedtime.*

Now? Emily said. *It's all Natasha does.*

But the ballers sounded uneasy, Kit thinks now. Yes. If she had to define the mood that night, she'd say the ballers were caught off guard.

Surprised.

As if Natasha had suddenly pointed out a thirteenth member of the team, a girl who had always been with them, but they never noticed.

I'm not, though, Natasha said. *I'm really not. She wore makeup because a lot of her favorite bands did. Neighbors said they heard electric guitars blaring from her garage, day and night, Daphne sitting in her car, listening at all hours, but most often at about three in the morning. You know, the Devil's teatime.*

The Devil's teatime? Kit asked.

They all laughed. It was ridiculous. Or, maybe, because they were nervous.

The night, the story, Natasha's voice; it all feels like a bad dream to Kit now. Or even like a close call. Like she'd slept beside a spider that night.

Dark shit, Natasha said. *Loud music, loneliness, anger, all coming from Daphne's house. People steered clear of that place. At seven feet, her nose was longer than our fingers, her head twice the size of ours. And her hands? Fuck, guys, she could palm a basketball like it was a grapefruit.*

Did she play ball? Dana asked. Because someone had to ask it. Everyone in the room wanted to be taller, closer to the rim. Imagine what they could do with that.

No, Natasha said. *And that's the thing, right? From middle school on, the ballers were like, Hey, you should play, join our team, play with us, you could score fifty a game with your size, come on, don't be a loser, don't say no, why are you saying no? Get out here, Kareem Abdul Jabbar. I pick Daphne. What do you mean you're not playing? You better be playing, because you're gonna be the reason we win and if you don't play you're gonna be the reason we lose and one day, when we're older, we're gonna come to your house and kill you because you let us down, Daphne, you fucking loser who won't play ball, yeah, we're gonna come over when you're sitting in your car blasting shitty music and you won't hear us coming and we're gonna knock you over the head and close your fucking garage door and you're gonna die that way from the fumes, alone and huge like you lived your whole pathetic life.*

Jesus, Natasha, Dana said.

Some silence then. Kit tried to visualize the next day's game against Chaps, but the Samhattan High gymnasium felt far out of reach then, and she imagined herself shooting a basketball in a stranger's garage as the stranger gasped for air in her car.

Did someone really kill her? Beck Nelson asked.

They sure did, Natasha said. *Angry ballers who played for Samhattan long before us. They got shitty drunk on wine and went to Marris Street with a baseball bat and found Daphne in that garage and they said something to her and she said something back and—*

What did her voice sound like? Melanie asked. Kit thought it sounded like Melanie was looking for holes. But why? Was she beginning to believe this? Was she also feeling a sense of déjà vu?

Real deep. And slow, Natasha said.

Oh, how would you know that? Emily asked.

You're right, I don't know that. But I know some girls and some guys from the basketball team cracked Daphne on the side of the head and closed the garage and left her there to die. She turned blue from the fumes. And since then? Daphne has killed, like . . . dozens of athletes from our high school. Her ghost. And she still wears makeup. Kiss makeup. To hide her blue face.

Wait, Dana said. *This is the dumbest thing I've ever heard. Why?*

Because we'd know if there was some fucked-up history of athletes dying. We've played sports our whole life, Natasha.

But Kit wondered (and wonders now) if they *would* know.

What else goes as unspoken as the name?

How do you keep her away? Melanie asked.

A heavy, sudden thing to ask. Some belief in the story in that question.

Glad you asked . . . Here Natasha sat up. Her voice was fuller, closer in the dark. *And it'll answer Dana's question too: the reason nobody talks about the ghost of Daphne killing people is because . . . if you think about Daphne . . . she comes for you. So, you wanna keep her away? Easy. Whatever you do . . . don't think about Daphne.*

Now, here where the creek meets the lake, Kit looks up, to the island, to the trees. Thinks of a seven-foot woman living alone out there, banished for her tastes, her size. The way Natasha put it, Daphne was a loner who didn't bother a soul. Nobody liked her, but nobody had any reason to hate her.

She turns at the sound of quick footsteps coming her way. She half expects to see a towering woman, patches adorning a jean jacket.

But it's just Dana.

"Yo," Dana says.

"Yo."

Yes, Dana knows not to ask if Kit's okay, but that doesn't mean she's not going to check on her best friend. And Kit knows she's acted weird since making the shot. She wonders, now, for the first time, if that shot didn't do something bad to her. Something beyond the idea of Daphne. Here, she'd always dreamed of hitting that exact free throw, winning that game, the ball leaving *her* hands, yet . . . now that it's happened, there's a hollowness, a vacancy. Like: *Is that it?* And the answer seems to be: *Yes.* Making the shot didn't change her, not foundationally, not like she'd long imagined a moment like that would. Did she think she'd feel prettier, cooler, smarter? Nobody ever fantasizes about what happens in the days following a game-winning shot; the brooding, the letdown, the realization that if that's as good as it gets, it really wasn't that much after all.

"Daphne," Dana says.

Kit looks to her, real worry in her eyes.

Now Dana has no choice but to ask it.

"What's up, Clutch?"

"Why did you say that name?"

"Name?"

"You're fucking with me."

"Whoa. Easy. You're gonna need a shrink soon if you keep thinking everyone's out to get you."

But Kit's not buying it.

"You just said *Daphne,* dude. You literally just said it. And I know it's because Natasha said we shouldn't think about her. That if we do, she'll . . . I don't know . . . come for us."

Dana's eyes are wide. Her smile is genuine.

"What the *fuck* are you talking about, Kit? I said *laughing.* I said the boys are morons and all it takes is one dumb pun and they can't stop *laughing.*"

She waits for Kit's response.

"But hey," Dana says. "*Are* you thinking of Daphne?"

"Stop it."

"Oh my God. Natasha is going to love this. She freaked you out!"

"No, she didn't." Then, "Dana. Is it weird to you that we've all heard the name before but none of us thought to ask about it? Is it weird that none of us heard that story before?"

Dana looks like she might say yes. But: "No. You're edged."

"I'm *not.*"

"Kit," Dana says. "You pussy!"

"Okay, fine. Yes. I guess it freaked me out. I keep imagining the night they went to her house."

"Yeah, not a nice story. I think you're supposed to listen to Whitney Houston's 'One Moment in Time' the night before a big game, not some story about a freak."

"Let's not call her that."

Dana makes to say something, to make fun of Kit for caring about the fictional bogeywoman.

But she doesn't. She gets it instead.

"Yeah, sure, okay. You're right."

They walk slowly back to the others, the creek running the opposite way.

"Guess what," Dana says.

"What?"

"Daphne."

Kit looks to her just as Dana socks her in the arm.

"I actually said it that time," Dana says. "You haven't gone crazy. Not yet."

But Kit says, "Are you thinking about her too?"

Dana shakes her head. Smiles. But close friends know. And Kit wishes she hadn't asked.

"I'm thinking about how we got a year left together," Dana says. "And it makes me sad as shit."

Kit stops walking. "What are you talking about?"

Dana stops too. But it's not easy, having these conversations, even with best friends. Saying the kinds of things people always wish they'd said to their loved ones before losing them.

"Come on, Clutch. I'm not the college type. My grades are half yours. And yours are shit! I'm not crying, I get it. And who knows what kind of dickheads you'll run into at college and what amazing shit might happen for me back here. Hey, I might even move to Chaps, end up spending my life cheering up all those girls we just totally destroyed."

She smiles but, again, close friends know.

Kit steps closer to her. Dana almost looks frightened by it. But Kit hugs her anyway.

"I love you, dude," Kit says. "And I always will. And you'll always love me. And that?"

Dana has a tear in her eye, but she finishes her best friend's sentiment anyway: "Is fucking *that.*"

They hold their embrace. They both squeeze the extra bit that says this one means something. Their English teacher, Mrs. Royce, once told them it was okay to know when you were inside a memory-to-be, when you were living what would one day be a landmark moment in your life. And they know this is one of those moments. Of course they do.

The friends pull apart and smile and wipe their eyes dry.

"Pussy," Kit says.

"Wimp," Dana says.

Then Kit says, "Well it's nice to think of regular ol' unsettling shit for a second instead of Natasha's insane stories."

Dana looks up the creek.

"Fuck Natasha."

Kit nods and the two friends head toward the others, but it's not completely lost on Kit that, while it is indeed nice to focus on familiar worries, the last thing she referenced, after all, was Natasha's story about Daphne.

Walking, she feels the birds shift at the base of her neck, but the heat of the sun is greater than the heat they produce and the anxiety ebbs.

For now.

It feels good. Because it should. The sun. Being here with a friend. Dana.

But she can't stop herself from asking: How long will it stay away?

Because you're never wrong when you spot it. And it will eventually spot you back.

Daphne, she thinks. She couldn't stop it from coming.

A rumble then, so loud Dana grabs her arm. They're close enough to see the others and see that they're all looking to the sky. But there is no lightning, no dark clouds.

And Kit didn't think it sounded like thunder anyway.

"What was *that*?" Dana asks. One hand to her heart. The other still on Kit's arm.

Kit doesn't know. She looks to the sky, too, then to the island, then to the others. They're talking about it. That sound.

"Sounded like a fuckin' truck falling," Dana says.

But they're far from the road. And besides, that's not what it sounded like to Kit. To her, it was more like an old door opening. A garage door. Unused in years. Nearly rusted to the cement drive.

A garage door as big as the sky.

Opening.

Then? Lightning above, after all.

"Shit," Dana says.

"Come on!" Kit yells.

And the friends race against sudden rain, back to their other friends, back to the cars, both aware that moments like these, the two of them making silhouettes against the distant Samhattan skyline, are fleeting.

o o o

Kit Lamb's "Jolly Journal"—The Day We Went to the Creek

Right, so there's two schools of thought then. Those who believe if you say something or if you write it down, it will not come true. Like you kill it somehow, or you kill the coincidence. For example: someone boarding a flight, they might wanna text their friend: HOPE IT DOESN'T CRASH. Because . . . what are the odds then that it would?

But the other school lives in a darker schoolhouse, I think. That's where you believe it'll come true if you acknowledge it.

I think that's me. But I'm not sure. And either way (and just to BE sure):

I'm not writing her name down.

Nope. Not in here. No way.

And who is "she"? Well, sorry, Jolly. You'll just have to keep guessing and never find out.

Because this isn't the place for that. These aren't my notes for a ghost story. This is where I get real with what I'm dealing with. And what I'm dealing with is

anxiety

Wow, I didn't even know I could write that small. Cool. Maybe that'll come in handy one day if I'm ever kidnapped and need to write a tiny SOS note.

MOM! DAD! HELP!

Listen, Jolly: Dana brought up the fact that we'll be living different lives in a year and it messed me up. Not only because it's probably true and I'm going to miss the living hell out of her, but because I hadn't thought of this once, not once, on my own. What does that mean? Am I so afraid of being afraid that I'm not even thinking of my future? Not planning at all?

HOLD UP. I think I just figured myself out.

Jolly,

I'm afraid of being afraid.

Let's use that airplane example again. We flew down to Florida a couple years ago and I was so nervous, Mom asked them for a paper bag for me to breathe into. I couldn't sit still and I was shaking, and while this wasn't the first time I ran into Panic Attackula in public, it was the first time I wasn't able to run away from it. Where was I going to go? My bedroom? Not likely. And don't you know how it comes, Jolly? How it comes at you? There's no warning. Oh God, no sound at all. You could be laughing, really having a good time, and you suddenly feel this rubbery sensation, like either you're wearing a rubber suit or the person you're talking to is wearing one, and then you can't shake the feeling that we're all just floating minds in these pretend rubber suits and it makes you feel so small and helpless and like you're going to die. But here's the thing: on the plane . . . did I think we were going to crash? Is that what I was worried about? Well, the answer is no. I wasn't worried about dying, Jolly, I was worried about . . . worrying.

YES

I was afraid of being afraid! I remember looking across the aisle at this old woman who was watching a movie before we even took off and I thought to myself, "Am I worried about HER? Am I worried SHE'S gonna crash and die?" And the answer was a solid NO. I knew the woman was going to be fine. So, okay, what did that mean for me? If she was going to be fine, wouldn't that mean I was too? I mean, it's not like one of us could've avoided whatever fate had in store for the other, right?

Right.

CHECK IT: Dad put this stupid magnet on the refrigerator, one of those easy quotes you see in Hallmark stores and you can't really trust that anybody knows who first said it, and so you don't even really think about who said it. But you read it all the time like God said it. It says:

EVERYTHING YOU WANT IS ON THE OTHER SIDE OF FEAR

And I know Dad put it there for me. He never said as much, but I know. It's like the refrigerator is the eye of the house and every time I pass it there's this little wink. Hey, Kit. Don't call 911, because everything you want . . .

Well, is it true? Tell me, Jolly. Are all my dreams just sitting there, ready for me? Are my dreams waiting for me to stop being so afraid? I don't even know what my dreams are anymore. Did I ever have any? I'm so scared of being scared. These days I'm happy if I'm just not unhappy. These days I consider it a success if I just don't freak out. You know, that's kinda like having a tiger in the bedroom with you and you're happy when he doesn't bite you.

Oh, Jolly. I'm trying hard not to sound melodramatic with you: I'm really working on getting something out of this, out of writing this down.

So maybe I'm from that first school after all.

But . . . naw.

Know what I think? I think Dad's magnet is right. I think I need to stop the next time the house winks at me and I need to say: HELL YES, OKAY I AGREE

What do you think, Jolly?

I like it. Because it's true that you can't hear it coming, the thing that comes for you. Nobody hears the beginning of a bad thing. Only when it's already here. So . . . what's already on its way? And how far has it traveled? Does it sleep beneath the stars at night? Does it sleep beside you, waking just before you do so you never know it's there? Or does the thing that comes not need any sleep at all? So that when YOU sleep, it catches up?

I have no idea if I can write once it's here. I can barely speak. I mostly stand still and freeze up and wish it away.

The Coming Doom.

Panic Attackula.

Such dumb names for such serious things. That's Natasha's doing mostly. But I guess everything evil has a name.

Even the one I won't write down.

But if I write it down . . . maybe then . . .

I can always cross it out later.

Ready, Jolly? I'm gonna see how the other school lives. I'm gonna believe that saying it makes it not real.

Ready? Here I go.

Oh . . . never mind.

I did write it. But I erased it.

And that'll have to be that.

For now.

And hey, maybe that means I'm from both schools? Or just superstitious and nervous enough to hedge my bets.

Ugh.

Goodbye, Jolly.

For now.

Maybe this entry was all just a lesson for me. Just like that old woman across the aisle on the airplane.

Which reminds me for whatever reason of the unsane thunder we heard by the creek today. The sound of an airplane twisted into a corkscrew.

By giant hands.

And with that . . .

I HOPE I DON'T CRASH

○ ○ ○

Tammy Jones is rare, and she knows it. It's not just that her hair is short, cropped to the skull; it's that her hair is red. Cardinal red. The only one in her family with it, one of those recessive-gene things, though Tammy likes to think it has more to do with being touched by an angel just before she crawled out of her mother. And crawled she did, she believes, just as she believes she is personally responsible for everything she's got so far in life, from her middle school grades to her handle. Yep. That last thing is a big deal to Tammy Jones and most of the people she hangs out with these days. *Game recognizes game,* Dad loves to say, especially after a good player or coach tells his daughter how impressed they are. Her handle was unrivaled in middle school (shit, the other girls couldn't even use their left), and she's discovered the same mostly holds true at the high school level. It's only been summer league so far, true, but she's heard the hot months are actually harder; ballers say the real stuff comes out in June, July, and August, when the players and coaches are looser with their games and girls like Tammy Jones have more freedom than they ever will in the rigid regular-season schedule. She can tell the older girls know how good she is. Just like she knows Coach Wanda didn't play her as much as she should have because coaches have minute limits on the young ones. And even if you're the best freshman-to-be to step foot in Samhattan High School in a decade, you still have to earn your keep.

That's fine. Tammy wants to earn hers.

Her parents have schooled her hard on this. Just like they school her hard on everything, from God to grades. She understands that, by the end of her freshman season, she's going to be starting alongside Kit Lamb and Dana Berger and she's probably going to be the leading assister, even if she is only half their size.

Nobody has a handle like my girl, Dad says.

But Mom tries to keep everyone cuffed to the Earth. It's the pious thing to do, she says. *Michael Jones,* Mom says, *what do you know about dribbling a basketball? You played power forward, for crying out loud.*

That's right, I did, but I could bounce it. I had more moves than my number.

What was your number? Tammy once asked him.

Mom and Dad laughed then. They laughed so hard it was difficult for Dad to spit out the answer. But he got to it:

One.

"Wanna hang downtown?" Felicia says. Felicia is one of Tammy's closest friends. Marnie, making up the trio today, is the other. Neither of them are ballers. But Tammy Jones is only at the beginning of a relationship with the game that should (if all goes right) begin to suffocate the rest of her life, whereas close friends and grades will suffer, until all is eclipsed by the Great Game itself.

"Sure," Tammy says. And why not? They're suddenly old enough, it seems, to wander Samhattan without their parents glued to their wrists. "Where to?"

"Coffee," Marnie says. Marnie is small, even half the size of Tammy, who is half the size of Kit Lamb, who hit that game-winning free throw like she was made of glacier ice.

Tammy smiles. Good for Kit. That ball almost didn't even touch the net, it went through so smooth.

The trio take Steinman Street toward the semi-tall buildings beyond. Not much reaches higher than six or seven stories in this city (this isn't Chaps, after all, and absolutely nothing like Goblin), but to a trio of fourteen-year-olds, downtown is downtown.

That's another reason Tammy Jones is rare. At fourteen, she's way beyond her years. So are Felicia and Marnie. It's why they're friends and why they've always been friends. Hell, they can't believe it's taken their parents this long to set them loose in a city with only so many streets.

Yet there *are* mean streets in Samhattan. Fifth Street is particularly notorious for ne'er-do-wells looking to scam. Tammy has yet to walk that street alone, but she's not afraid of it either. She's seen her share of shady, and while she understands that a grown man with a knife renders her ability to no-look pass meaningless, she's also an athlete with a mind as sharp as that knife.

She can take care of herself.

Up ahead, it's the Samhattan Steak House. The girls eye it like they would a man or woman in a suit. These kinds of places are cheesy to them. Overblown. Obvious. Why spend so much money when you can get rice and beans for three dollars at Hi-Fi Grocery, and get fitter at that? These people. These high-priced Samhattan people. Tammy doesn't think she'll ever get it.

But still, passing the fabled restaurant, she does wonder if one day she'll be the toast of the town. Scoring, what, thirty a game by the time she's a senior? Twenty-nine-point-six almost has a better ring to it. Like she *could've* scored thirty, but she likes to pass it too.

"Think they allow shorts and sneakers?" Felicia asks. She's wearing neither. But Tammy is.

"They should," Tammy says. "If I ran a place? The more the merrier."

"Let 'em bring in their own kitchen table to eat at," Marnie says.

"No," Felicia says. "The living-room couch!"

They laugh. They're fourteen. It's cool to poke fun at adults, even as adulthood creeps up on them like ghosts.

Ghosts?

The name *Daphne* crosses Tammy's mind. She shakes her head, or rather, she tilts her head to the side, like the letters could fall out her ear.

"What's up?" Marnie asks. "You did that thing you do."

"What's that?"

"You had an idea that sucked."

"Yeah, well." Tammy makes to play it cool. But why? She grew up on Crain Street with these two. She sharpened her mind, her eye, and her mind's eye with these two. Tell them: "You know that older girl Natasha Manska? Strong. Dirty blond?"

"No," Marnie says.

"Yeah," Felicia says. "Funny girl."

"Yep. And that's just it. She was trying to scare the hell out of all us ballers at that sleepover. Told us some spooky stuff."

"Like what?"

Up ahead, Dawn Pawn. The girls know it's named after the woman who owns it.

"Con Pawn, more like it," Tammy says.

"Yawn Pawn," Marnie says.

"What was the story?" Felicia asks. "Come on, don't hold out."

"Oh," Tammy says. She tilts her head again. But the name doesn't fall out. "Just stupid stuff. Ghosts and . . . whatever."

But her friends are already uninterested. It's not really their thing; ghosts and horror. There were some kids in middle who swore by it. But Tammy, Felicia, and Marnie are more into music than they are monsters.

To them, the graveyard in the center of Samhattan is just a shortcut on the way across town.

They head that way now.

"I like those girls, though," Tammy says. She's talking about the team. "They take it seriously. I like that. I can learn a lot from them."

"Even as they learn from you," Marnie says.

"Now you sound like my dad."

"Well, maybe I *am* your dad."

They laugh as they cross the street. Farther south, smoke billows from the dual factories, both surrounded by chain-link fences and boom barriers requiring ID. The bricks on the buildings downtown are off-white, bordering on gray. With the gray Michigan clouds, downtown is uniform, not unlike the horizon where an ocean meets the sky. Only here it feels finite. Like the muted color doesn't go on forever, only as far as Samhattan. And for the people who work in those factories (and line up every morning with their IDs to prove they do), the color seems to follow them home.

But there is no security gate on the front of Steinman Cemetery. The fence is open as long as the sun is up. And while it is indeed located in the very center of town, it's large enough to get lost in, like Central Park in New York City, Tammy imagines; a place inside a place. Or, in this case, just enough of a place inside just enough of a place.

Samhattan isn't much to write home about. Even if it's home.

"Cool trees," Marnie says. Because she likes them. Because, like most industrial towns, Samhattan isn't overflowing with foliage. Isn't overflowing with much of anything.

Yet the city does have its share of stories. Some that took place in this very graveyard. Like when the men and women who used to run things intentionally buried the town's only known serial killer alive. Or when the Samhattanite Ben Evans dug up his own parents and filmed their dead bodies.

The girls don't even bring this stuff up. They're not interested.

In fact, they don't talk much at all as they take the one-way gravel road past the first of the many headstones. From here, they can still see the storefronts, the wacky Third-and-Fourth-Eye Books with its window displays of cosmic-self-help that once scared them silly as toddlers. And Otto's Auto, where the windows are gray with exhaust.

"These store names," Tammy says. "You'd think business owners only know how to speak in nursery rhyme."

They're deeper now, where the trees block out most of the city and some even curl in over the graves closest to the fences. A lot of green now against that slate sky. At the first fork in the gravel, they turn right, wanting to get to the diner before it closes its doors, along with its coffee.

Fourteen years old. Walking alone and seeking out coffee.

Rare kids, indeed.

"You guys won that game?" Felicia asks.

"Yep. I told you so already."

"I guess so. And, hey, so long as you keep up the grades, I don't care how many games you win or lose."

"Shit, now you *really* sound like Dad."

"That's because your mom would rather you win those games than those grades," Marnie says.

They laugh. A little. 'Cause it's true.

At the second fork, they make to turn right again but Tammy eyes a long rectangle of clean dirt at the foot of a cluster of red maples.

Big trees. Angels, the Third-and-Fourth-Eye bookstore employees might call them.

"Hold up," Tammy says.

Felicia and Marnie don't ask why. Whatever's caught Tammy's eye might be cool. So, they follow her off the gravel, up the thin dirt path between headstones, old and only getting older.

"Dirt," Marnie says. For fresh graves.

But is it? Tammy doesn't know. It's not positioned like a pile of dirt they'd shovel into barrows. In fact, it looks more like its own long grave.

The three friends eye it with the same quiet intensity.

"Big enough for Brittney Griner," Tammy says. She doesn't need to explain who that is. Her friends know.

And they don't refute her either. Up close like this, it really does look like a grave for a giant. Only, less cared for. Unmarked.

"Kinda makes you wanna dig," Marnie says.

"That's like the Call of the Void," Felicia says. "Like when you look over the second-floor balcony at the mall and you kinda feel like jumping."

"Or when you're standing at the edge of traffic," Marnie says, "waiting for the light to change."

"And you kinda wanna step in it," Felicia ends the sentiment for her.

"The Call of the Void," they both say together.

"You two," Tammy says. She shakes her head. This time her friends think it's because they're talking morbid and she's brushing them off. But that's not it. She's shaking her head for the same reason she did minutes ago. Because, as she looks at this thus-far-hypothetical grave, the same name pops into her head again.

Daphne.

Enough dirt here for a woman her size.

Tammy doesn't look away. Doesn't look over her shoulder, though the name (and the feeling, right? The clear realization that the name has been on her mind since it left Natasha Manska's lips) sends a cold wind blowing from nowhere. Maybe it's imagined, that wind. But some things become real when you think about them too much.

Daphne.

Why does it feel like Tammy is examining for the first time something that's always been there? That name, heard now and again in life, but like when her parents have the TV on in the other room: faint, suppressed. Like when a friend uses a word you think you know the meaning of, but you don't, not really, and you never think to ask.

It's almost like Natasha was examining it for the first time, too, as she said it out loud.

"Come on," Tammy says. "They're gonna close."

"Well, it's your fault if we miss out on coffee," Marnie says.

But they don't really care. These three, they're smart. They adapt. Other places in Samhattan have coffee too.

So, the girls continue toward their goal. Three lifelong friends with impending high school and entire lives to ponder. So much to pick apart, unpack, talk about. So, Felicia and Marnie do. But Tammy can't bring herself to join in yet. With all the world to think about, she's only got one thing on her mind.

And it's like a worm, this thought, like when someone can't quit the chorus of a hit song.

And it's not pretty either.

It's the bones of a seven-footer, buried in a back corner of a city graveyard, unmarked and uncelebrated, uncared for and ignored. And yeah, it sounded to Tammy like the woman didn't deserve whatever she got. But it's not exactly empathy she feels right now.

It's fear.

Felicia takes her hand, a gesture Tammy assumes is meant to comfort her. But when she looks down, there is no hand in her own.

She stops.

"Yo," Marnie says. "What?"

Tammy looks over her shoulders, looks everywhere, says, "Did you . . ."

But she can tell they didn't touch her.

No, this is not pretty.

She tilts her head once more. Tries to shake these thoughts out.

"I got bad news for you, Tam," Felicia says, the cemetery gravel crunching beneath her shoes. "I don't think head-fakes work on bad thoughts."

o o o

The problem, Natasha said, the whole team on their backs in the dark, the night before the big game, *is that once one friend starts thinking about her, they all do.*

By then, some of the ballers were asleep.

That makes no sense at all, Dana said.

But it does, Natasha said. *Because if one friend thinks about Daphne too much, then Daphne comes and gets her, right? And so, once the one friend has been got . . .*

Got? Dana asked. *You're fucking nuts, Nat.*

Once one friend is killed, Natasha said, *the others start thinking maybe Daphne did it. See?*

If that was true, then the whole world would be thinking about her, Melanie said.

And all the ballers felt like they had been thinking about her. Or, rather, *not* thinking about her. Their entire lives.

What might someone call the opposite of déjà vu? A sense of having intentionally *not* been there before.

Not true, Natasha said. *Daphne works faster than the spread of her story. Because pretty soon people catch on.*

To what? Kit asked.

To the fact that they better shut up about Daphne.

"Kit," Dad says, waving a hand across the kitchen table. "You get too much sun today?"

"Jesus," Kit says. "You guys seriously need to stop asking me if I'm okay."

Mom and Dad exchange a look.

"Okay," Dad says. But he doesn't let it go. "Now we're the bad guys for noticing you've been staring into space for five minutes?"

"You're thinking about something," Mom says. "Have you entered a drug phase we need to know about? It's okay. But tell us."

It's funny, but it's not. Mom's funny, but Kit's not in the mood. Mom knows Kit and her friends well. Mom is cool. So is Dad. Yet what she's asking is real. Like: *What's up with you and your friends?*

"We were out by the creek," Kit says. "Hot day. I'm tired."

"It rained," Dad says.

Mom's cellphone rattles on the kitchen counter.

"So, sue me," Kit says. She rolls her eyes but when she looks back to Dad, he's smiling. These two, their fights don't last.

The phone rattles on the counter.

"Not getting that," Mom says. "Hate that phone."

She says this a lot.

"Dad," Kit says, "what's kiss makeup?"

"Kiss and make up?"

"No . . . maybe?"

Natasha said Daphne wore *kiss makeup*.

"It's just a phrase," Dad says.

Mom's phone rings again.

"Man, do I miss the days before cellphones," she says. "Know what we used to do? We'd say, 'Hey, I'll see you Thursday at seven,' and then wow, we saw them Thursday at seven." Then, to Kit, "Do you mean the band?"

"What?"

"KISS. KISS makeup."

"Oh." *Is* that what Natasha meant? "Are they metal?"

Mom and Dad laugh because it's funny, the way she asked it.

The phone stops ringing.

"Naw, I wouldn't say that," Dad says. "But I guess some people would. They wore makeup, yeah."

"They were called Kiss?"

"KISS. Yeah. You don't know them? That makes me feel old."

"They're before our time too," Mom says. "Why do you ask, Kit?"

Kit should've been expecting this follow-up, but she wasn't. She was thinking of what Natasha said.

She wears KISS makeup, but not like a star man or a cat or any-thing . . . it's all eyes and long tongues. Her whole face. I'm not even sure it's makeup.

"Kit?"

"Oh . . . I . . . Natasha was talking about that band, I guess. I didn't realize that's what she was saying."

Dad looks out the kitchen, to the living room where the vinyl collection is.

"I don't think we have any of theirs."

"We don't," Mom says. "And thank God for that."

"Are they bad?" Kit asks. But she doesn't mean to ask if they're not any good; she means to ask if they're evil.

It's like an earworm, she thinks. The way this name is rolling about her mind.

"I mean, no," Dad says. "I wouldn't say *bad*. They're just not . . ."

"They're whatever," Mom says. "They're no Iron Maiden, if that's what you mean."

Dad winks at Mom.

"But people liked them?"

"They still do," Mom says.

"Metal people?"

Again, Mom and Dad laugh. What a silly way to ask it.

"You wanna hear some KISS?" Dad asks. "Let's look 'em up on—"

Mom's phone rings again. She groans and gets up from the table.

Dad says, "We'll look up some of their songs. They could be your favorite band of all time, just waiting to happen."

KISS makeup. All eyes and long tongues.

Kit imagines a tall figure outside the front door. Someone that would have to duck to enter.

"Look," Dad says. He's holding his phone for Kit to see. It's not what she expected. All black-and-white makeup mostly. They look like they're part of a musical. A Broadway show.

"I don't understand," Mom says into the phone.

The way she says it, Dad and Kit shut up and turn to her. Mom doesn't do drama. Evelyn Lamb is always Evelyn Lamb. Something's wrong on the phone.

"Okay," she says. "But . . . how is this possible?"

Her voice is level. Too level.

Dad and Kit wait. Mom turns to them. No, not *them*, just Kit. The phone to her ear, she looks concerned. It's not good. Whoever's talking, whatever they're saying, it has something to do with Kit. Kit doesn't even consider she might've been "caught" doing anything because she doesn't do anything to get caught at. Even if she took a hit off a joint with the boys' team, her parents wouldn't be angry. They'd tell her to make sure it was safe.

"What's going on?" she asks.

But Mom's still listening.

"Okay," she says. "Yes. Thank you. I just . . . Okay."

She hangs up.

The kitchen is silent in a bad, expectant way.

"Oh, Kit," Mom says. Now she does look to Dad, the way she does when she's silently saying, *Be ready: we need to parent.*

"Mom?"

Mom walks over to the table. She looks to Kit and says:

"Tammy Jones was killed."

"What?"

"What are you talking about?" Dad says.

Kit stands up. Like she might do something about this news. This unfathomable news.

"Sit down," Mom says. Not a demand. More like Kit's going to need to be seated for the rest.

"That was Helen." Mom's closest friend in Samhattan. Helen Martin. "She said Tammy Jones was found dead in her bedroom. Her . . ."

"Her what?" Kit asks. *"Mom.* What?"

She thinks of her journal. Thinks she's just writing this down. Whatever this is, it can't be anything more than that.

"There was trauma to her face. To her head."

But it is more than that.

"I don't understand," Kit says. "Trauma?"

Mom looks to Dad. But Dad is as stunned as his daughter.

"Her head and face," Mom says. "Oh, Kit."

"*Mom!* What happened to Tammy?"

"Hang on," Dad says. He stands up too. "Are you saying . . . someone hurt her?"

"Killed," Mom repeats. "That's what Helen said. That's the word she used."

"Evelyn," Dad says. But it's not like using her first name is going to make sense of what she's saying.

Killed. Tammy Jones. A freshman-to-be at Samhattan High.

Kit feels dizzy. Weak.

Already Tammy Jones is (*was*) one of the better players on the Samhattan basketball team. Kit and Tammy weren't close, but Kit respected the hell out of her game.

"Oh my God," Kit says. "But she's so . . . young."

Then she does sit down. Because if she doesn't, she might fall.

"What else did she say?" Dad asks.

At first, Kit thinks he's asking what else did Natasha say.

"She didn't know much," Mom says. "Just . . . Okay. Helen said Tammy's parents believe someone snuck in through her bedroom window. Someone broke in somehow." She's holding back tears. Tears for Tammy, tears for Kit. But Mom is tough like that too. Then, to Kit, she says, "I imagine you want to talk to your friends."

Mom is hip, yes. She speaks the language of youth, of her daughter.

Kit gets up again, looks for her phone. It's on the table in the living room.

She feels dizzy again.

"Mom . . . did Helen mention a name . . . Daphne?"

She didn't mean to ask it. It just came out.

"No," Mom says. "What do you mean? Do you know something about this?"

"No," Kit says.

"Daphne?" Dad asks. And he has a look in his eye, Kit thinks. Probably how she looked when Natasha said it the other night. Did Dad think of a local legend (*le-gend*) when he spoke her name?

"Hey, don't fuck around, Kit," Mom says. Not with anger. With practicality. If Kit knows something, say something.

"Honestly, no."

"Why'd you ask that, then?"

"Because," Kit says. But her voice doesn't sound entirely like her own. And the heat at the bottom of her neck is spreading up to the base of her skull. "Natasha told us a story . . . oh who the fuck *cares*."

Dad goes to Mom's phone, scrolls through the numbers. Calls someone.

As he begins talking, asking questions that sound like impossible riddles to Kit, Kit reaches her own phone in the living room. There are seventeen missed texts. She knows what they're all about. Yet, through the dizziness of this news, the horror of imagining a teammate's face smashed in, she cares less about what Dana and the others have written and much more about the fact that the heat has reached her ears.

Is she short of breath? She might be. She might need to do one or more of the many routines she's learned through the years. Breathing in for four and out for three is one. So is standing in a doorjamb and pressing both palms out as hard she can, using all her strength. So is walking up and down the block. Should Kit walk up and down the block? Out there in the big world where someone lives and breathes, someone who just came through Tammy Jones's window and bashed her freshman face in?

"This is so bad," Kit says. "So, so bad."

Dad's voice rises in the kitchen. Mom is talking to someone too. Is there a third voice? Are they using speakerphone? Jesus, it feels like all of reality, the parts people take for granted, are gone.

"The police *have* to have more to say than *that*," Dad says. He sounds pissed. It's heavier, darker than scared.

"Jason," Mom says. "It just happened."

"Yeah, well . . ." He looks across the room to Kit and Kit looks away. She can't stand the terror in his eyes. The fear for his own daughter's safety.

Weren't they *just* looking up a rock band from the '70s? Grown men in makeup? Weren't they *just* having a moment?

KISS makeup.

But all eyes and tongues.

Yes, Kit recalls what Natasha said. Of course she does. It's all she can focus on. You think about her, she comes. And once one friend conjures Daphne, the others can't stop thinking about her coming for them.

Out of earshot of her parents, she tells herself, "You weren't the only one who was thinking about her."

The thought is almost too complex to consider. And somehow it belittles Tammy Jones. Renders her part of a dumb myth.

But Kit can't stop herself from imagining Tammy Jones as the first domino. Falling.

She remembers a documentary she watched about mushrooms. How mushrooms actually think, like people, how they send signals to each other, an underground communication.

She imagines the way she feels, right now, sees it traveling to Dana. To Natasha. To Emily Holt.

"Tammy's just the first," she says.

Is this what Kit really thinks?

She sits quick on the couch. Feels like she could implode with the anxiety that's coming. But is it coming from within or without?

She stands up again.

She tries to find the ice water she felt at the free-throw line.

But it's not there. And it never was.

Sometimes you shoot so wrong, you end up making a shot Fate called a miss.

A baller on the other team once said that to Kit in a game.

She lifts her phone. Scrolls. First text is from Dana. It says exactly what Kit knew it would. Exactly what she doesn't want to see, read, hear, think about right now.

It says:

Is this real?

"Kit," Mom says. "Sit down."

She's scared. Mom is. Not of any local legend, of course not. And is this even a local legend? It's more like a local secret. A Samhattan subconsciousness. Do Mom and Dad even know who Daphne is? Have they ever heard a story, any story, about the woman?

Have they been hiding her from Kit?

Has everybody?

She thinks about the time she called 911 on herself. How the ambulance came. How the paramedics actually took Kit to the hospital because she was short of breath, kept saying she was dying.

Kit looks from Mom to Dad. He's not talking into the phone now. He's looking at her. Both of them. Worried.

"It's gonna be okay," he says. But Kit is past okay right now.

"I need . . ." she says. "I need . . ."

"Kit," Mom says. "Hey, honey."

"I need to go upstairs."

"Okay. You can do that. I'll walk you—"

"I need to . . . write this down."

Mom and Dad exchange a look and between them seems to be a road at night, upon which an ambulance travels, Kit hyperventilating in the back, not yet knowing she'd met Panic that night, first time, not yet knowing they'd become so close.

She walks, dizzy, to the stairs. Mom comes to her as Dad starts whisper-yelling into the phone. Mom touches her elbow and Kit pulls back. It felt, for a second, like Mom's hands weren't Mom's hands. Like they were twice the size.

"Upstairs," Kit says. Is she breathing right? She's trying. She doesn't know. "Write it down."

Mom follows her up the first few steps. But soon Kit is in the hall upstairs, alone, brushing that feeling from her elbow, the feeling of greasy fingers upon her, no warning.

"Kit," Mom calls from downstairs. There's a crack in her voice. "We love you, Kit."

Kit nods. I *love you too. Okay, Mom.* Nods. Makes it into her bedroom. Thinks of Tammy Jones in hers. Thinks of Tammy Jones's young face. Different now.

Did she turn blue?

Did she wear makeup?

"We love you, Kit," Dad yells upstairs.

As if this might save the moment. As if this might calm her down.

As if these words could possibly stop what's coming.

○ ○ ○

Kit Lamb's Journal—Tammy Jones Is Dead

I can't think straight. Are these sentences making sense? I read about a man who shoved a woman in front of a train and when the cops asked him why he did it he said, "Sentences stopped making sense."

Am I going mad?

Can I hear it now? Oh my God. I can feel it. All over me. ALL OVER. All over the bedroom, all over the bed. I tried closing my eyes and that just made me sick. I can't sit still. I'm standing while I write this. I'm burning up.

Is it here? Am I under attack?

Fuck, I'm hot.

Oh, Jesus. Jolly. Help me. Mom and Dad are screaming into phones downstairs. The whole city must be screaming into their phones. I think I can hear them!

It's teasing me: panic.

It's not here. It's not. HOW IS IT NOT? Is it because there's actually something to be scared of? Something to be sad for?

My phone keeps buzzing. They're all writing me. They all don't know if I know. Are they writing me because they think I could have an attack? Am I that to them? The friend who could lose her mind? Is that why they lifted me on their shoulders after I made the shot? Because they were relieved their damaged friend might've lost her mind if she missed it?

Oh, fuck I'm hot.

Is it here? Or is it not?

I want a rim to talk to. Oh, Jolly, HELP.

I'm sitting on the floor. I'm up again. I'm sorry, Tammy. I'm so, so sorry.

What HAPPENED?

HOW COULD THIS HAPPEN

I don't wanna think about my desk drawer. I don't wanna turn to that. Not yet.

Is it here? Is it in the room with me? Am I going to die of fright? Can anxiety kill a person?

Tammy Jones is dead.

She wasn't and now she is.

What am I doing? Why aren't I talking to my friends? Who is Dad yelling at? Is someone outside? I'm too afraid to look.

I'm going to look.

Nobody outside. Why did I think there was?

Oh my God, it's happening isn't it I'm freaking out, aren't I?

This is so terrible, Jolly.

This is terrible.

THIS IS

o o o

"This is terrible," Dana says.

Five of the girls and two of the boys are zooming, each as pale as the next. Usually, when they do this, it's all jokes, rips, barbs, stunts, and dares.

Not tonight.

"I can't believe it. I almost . . . don't," Melanie says. "Tammy Jones . . ." Her eyes are as vacant as when she first appeared in the meeting. Her dark hair hides most of the rest of her face.

"I cannot wrap my head around this," Stewart says. "How can this happen in Samhattan?"

"Randy Scotts," Natasha says. Because she's the one who said it, it sounds like a joke.

"Come on, Natasha," Dana says. "That's fucked-up. He's been dead a long time."

Natasha shrugs. She wasn't joking. She also wasn't serious about the ghost of Samhattan's only known serial killer rising from his grave to do this. Yet isn't the idea of Daphne just as insane?

Kit is fully aware that nobody has mentioned Daphne's name. Not yet. She grips her journal in her lap and tries not to think of the pill bottle in the desk drawer.

"I'm scared," Emily says. Her blond hair is white in the illumina-tion of the ring light she uses for Zoom.

"Of what?" Dana asks.

Kit sees it. All the way across town, through the screen; Emily is thinking of Daphne.

But so is Dana.

Isn't she? Aren't they all?

Kit is.

"If it could happen to Tammy," Emily says, "it could happen to—"

"No," Brandon says. "This had to be some family thing."

"Family?" Kit asks. Hope in her voice. As if Tammy dying by her parents' hands is a better world.

Brandon, shirtless, paces his bedroom, where posters of basket-ball stars adorn the walls. All of them are dunking. He's taped pho-tos of his own face over theirs.

"*Yes*," he says. "An uncle. A family friend. A boyfriend. There's gotta be a link. There always is. And it's almost always family."

"What are the chances of some random psycho breaking into Tammy's house and hurting her like this?" Natasha asks.

For the first time, Kit eyes her like she would a danger. A threat. Natasha started this. Didn't she?

She almost asks, *Where did you hear that story?*

But Dana talks first: "Well, if it's random, then it *can* happen to any of us," she says. She's wearing a tank top and her hair is in braids. As if they had a game in an hour. Kit feels these two worlds grating: basketball . . . but a baller now dead.

"The police will find him," Stewart says.

"Him?" Kit asks.

"Oh, it's a man *for sure*. You think a woman just . . . did that to Tammy?"

They all go quiet for a second. Some of their faces suggest, yeah, Stewart's probably right. But they stare off into space, too, and Kit imagines a seven-foot woman standing in that space.

"Hey, I don't wanna sound crazy," Kit begins. She feels crazy. Feels close to the night she called an ambulance on herself. Yet these are her closest friends in the world. And the looks on their faces are not very different from her own.

"Don't even do it," Natasha says. "Don't belittle Tammy's death by suggesting a fucking ghost killed her, Kit."

"I know," Kit says. "But—"

"Ghost?" Brandon asks.

"I love ya, Kit," Natasha says. "But let's not go there."

"Go where?" Brandon asks.

"Brandon," Dana says.

"No, seriously. What do you mean?"

It's impossible to tell on Zoom, but it feels like they're all looking at Kit. Waiting for an answer.

She gives them one.

"Daphne."

She looks down to her journal. Then to the desk drawer.

Natasha drops her head into her hands.

"Daphne?" Stewart says. He looks clueless. But he also seems to consider the name. As if . . .

As if he's heard it before and never stopped to think about it.

"Wait," Brandon says. "Who's Daphne? The fuck are you guys talking about?"

Melanie signs off without a word. Emily shakes her head before doing the same.

"Jesus, guys," Dana says. "Tammy died. This is serious."

"Kit?" Brandon asks.

It's the word "snuck" that wasn't sitting right with her. Based on the story Natasha told, Daphne wouldn't *sneak* anywhere. Kit suddenly wonders if there isn't a hole in the Joneses' front door, a silhouette like in the old cartoons: the shape of a seven-foot woman in denim having busted straight through.

No, Daphne wouldn't sneak anywhere.

Kit looks over her shoulder. Looks to her bedroom window.

She's gotta stop thinking about Daphne.

"Kit?" Brandon asks again. "Who is Daphne?"

She looks to her desk, to where the Xanax Dana snuck her (she was worried about Kit; took it from her own parents; no parents needed to know, right?) is hidden at the bottom of a small pill bottle stuffed with cotton.

Does she need one? Even a tiny piece? She's never taken more than a quarter before, and even that only twice. She's heard about athletes getting addicted to pain pills. She knows the same can happen for medicine of the mind.

"I don't know," she finally answers. "I'm not saying anything. I'm sorry."

"You can't do that," Brandon says.

Stewart doesn't speak, and Kit sees some recognition in his eyes.

Hasn't everyone at least heard her name? In the wind? In the echo of a word, even if not in the word itself?

"I told a ghost story the other night," Natasha says. "It got to Kit. That's all."

Kit looks to Dana. But on Zoom, Dana could be looking anywhere.

"You told her?" Kit says.

"I'm out of here," Dana says. "Peace and love. Life is short. Act like it."

She signs off.

Kit can't tell if that was directed at her. Was it?

She looks to the drawer.

The problem with drugs, she knows, is that drugs *work*.

"Same," Stewart says. "We'll get through this." He gives the others a solemn peace sign and vanishes.

Brandon eyes the camera sadly and signs off too.

Leaving only Natasha and Kit.

"I'm gonna go," Natasha says.

"Hang on."

"Kit."

"Listen . . . what do you really know about that story?"

Why is she asking this? Doesn't she know how dumb she sounds? Doesn't she know she's just scared of where her mind may go and *wants* to blame it on something, anything, *wants* there to be an object so she doesn't get lost in the blameless, rudderless confusion of panic?

"Aw man, Kit. I know as much as I said. It's no different than a story about a creepy janitor who works at a camp or a crazy patient in a mental home. Honestly, it's not like I'm holding out."

"But where did you hear the story?"

"Man . . . I don't even remember."

But does she?

"When you told the story, I felt like I'd heard about Daphne my whole life but never thought to look into it."

Natasha eyes the camera. Is Kit crazy, or is Natasha hiding something from her?

"Hey," Kit says. "I'm not gonna freak out."

Just saying it makes her feel like she might. Right here. Right now.

"Seriously," she says. "You heard of her before, too, right?"

"Her name. Sure. Haven't we all?"

"But can you remember what the context was? Why you heard it? What it was about?"

"Kit . . ."

"I just don't like the part about not thinking about her. That . . . that . . ."

"*Kit.*"

Some force there. Natasha has never spoken to her like that. At the same time, she's relieved to hear it. Natasha is insisting.

"Honestly, Lamb," Natasha says. "It was just . . . me fucking around."

"Okay."

"Okay?"

"Yeah, okay."

"You good?"

"Me?"

"Yeah. You."

"Yeah."

"Okay."

"Okay."

"Good night, Kit. And God rest Tammy's soul."

Natasha signs off, leaving only Kit on the Zoom.

She stares at herself, sees the sadness in her eyes, sees the fear there too. There hasn't been word of the Samhattan police catching whoever did this. No news of a lead at all. Mom and Dad are downstairs, on their phones, talking nonstop to other parents, Coach Wanda, the police.

Kit eyes herself. She knows what it's like to be an outsider. Like Daphne was.

It was just me . . . fucking around.

And it probably was.

But man, if that story isn't an earworm.

She looks to her bedroom window. Thinks of Tammy's.

She wonders what it would be like to be seven feet tall. A quiet fan of loud music. She wonders if she, Kit, could pull off wearing a jean jacket to school, patches of her favorite bands stitched all over. She imagines face paint, imagines herself wearing it.

She googles images of the band KISS.

What is she doing? But she's doing it.

And the images, in context, frighten her. She imagines each of the band members brutalizing Tammy Jones. She thinks of that bottle in her desk again. She doesn't want to need to take one. Doesn't want to become someone who does.

Is it here? Is she in the throes of an attack?

She's so scared, so sad, she can't tell.

"KISS," she says.

One's a cat, a couple are stars, one could be a demon. She wonders if Daphne looks like a demon.

Just fucking around . . .

Yes, yes. Natasha was probably just fucking around. It's likely the story has nothing to do with Tammy's death. Wait: more than likely.

"Natasha's story has *nothing* to do with Tammy's death," she says. Because she needs to say it.

It's a coincidence, is all. And just like when the others ask the rim questions, coincidences start to look like prophecies made true. People can find links wherever they want to. It literally happens all day every day. How many times has Kit heard someone talking about the death of a family member only to say they dreamt of it beforehand? Or they had a sense, a feeling . . .

Yes, a lot like the rim. Like the time Dana asked if she was going to pass her trig test and then she kind of did, but only because the test was canceled, and oh how they all thanked the rim.

But that's just it, isn't it? The rim is like that for everyone else but Kit. The rim doesn't lie to Kit.

And the rim said Daphne is real.

Said more than that.

Dad's voice comes loud from downstairs. Kit listens for news. Hears none. Just variations of *We need to know our daughters are safe.*

She opens YouTube, plays a KISS song. The first one that comes up. "I Was Made for Loving You." It doesn't sound like metal at all. Sounds like disco. It makes her nervous. The music sounds like the heat she feels at the base of her neck. One of the star men sings, turns out. Kit listens to a third of it, then turns it off, closes out the window.

Behind her, in the Zoom video of herself, a woman stands in her bedroom.

Kit turns, arms up, expecting hands like the hands playing those instruments in that video to explode out, to grab her face, to crush it.

"Kit," Mom says.

"Oh, shit," Kit says. "Oh my God. You scared me."

"Listen," Mom says. "The police wanna talk to you girls. The team."

"What? Why?"

"Because . . ." She hesitates. "Because you were Tammy's friends."

"Right . . . Okay."

She's hot. Too hot.

"They wanna know if you guys knew of anyone who might've known her. A boyfriend. Something like that."

"Is there more, Mom? You're acting like there's more."

"Yeah," Mom says. Because she doesn't lie. Can't.

She steps farther into the room. Places a hand on Kit's shoulder.

"What?"

"Tammy had a team photo in a frame on her wall. It's not there anymore. The police think the person who murdered her stole it."

Kit feels heavier, colder, farther from that desk drawer.

"I'm sorry," Mom says.

"I don't understand. What's happening?"

"Dad is talking to the police about security for tonight. It looks like they're sending someone. You're going to be fine."

"Why would the photo be missing?"

Is her voice shaking? Are her hands?

She feels like she might not survive tonight.

"I really don't know, Kit."

"I'm freaking out, Mom."

"I know. I am too. A terrible thing happened tonight. In our city. To a friend." Then: "Sleep with us tonight."

"I don't know if I can sleep at all."

"Then stay awake in our room. I don't want you out of my sight until they catch this sick fuck."

Sick fuck.

It brings to mind a gibbering, unshaven man. But Kit instinctively resists this idea. Instead, she pictures a tall woman, dead behind the wheel of her car, asphyxiated by the fumes in a closed garage.

She imagines Daphne's eyes opening. Gray holes in a blue face.

Will Daphne kill me?

The song she just heard, KISS, plays in her head as she takes her mom's hand, as she nods, saying, *Yes, yeah, I'd like to sleep with you and Dad tonight, every night, until they catch the sick fuck who killed Tammy Jones, because I can't stop thinking of her, Mom, I can't stop thinking of the one person I'm not supposed to think about.*

"Hurry up, then," Mom says. "Get your stuff and meet me in there. We'll put a movie on."

"I don't wanna watch a movie."

"I don't either."

They hold each other's eyes a beat before Mom exits Kit's bedroom to the sound of Dad fuming downstairs into the phone. The music has long gone quiet below. But the streets are coming to life with distant sirens. Police arriving at each of the ballers' homes.

Kit opens her desk drawer. The bottle is right there. Looks harmless. A little piece of plastic. Yet it harbors such dilemmas.

She doesn't let herself think on it any longer. Tammy Jones is dead. Killed.

Kit opens the bottle, quickly pulls out the cotton, finds the blue Xanax, sets it aside, just as Mom calls out from down the hall, but close: "Come on, Kit."

The heat has risen past Kit's ears. She thinks of an interview she saw with Tina Franklin when Franklin was a rookie in the WNBA. Franklin said the game moved at a faster speed at this level. She kept saying *at this level*. Then she joked and said it felt like her entire life was now moving *at this level*.

Kit understands. What's anxiety when there's no calm to offset it?

She cracks the pill in half, makes to break it into quarters, hears Mom in the hall again, downs one half without water.

It's okay. She's got ice water in her veins.

Doesn't she?

"Coming," she says.

She puts the bottle back into the drawer and closes it just as Dad appears in the doorjamb and says, "Sleep with us tonight. I don't trust a goddamn person in this city right now."

o o o

Sitting on a cold green chair in the Samhattan High School gym, lined up with the entire (remaining) team, some parents, and Coach Wanda, too, with an actual detective standing before her, it strikes Kit how right she was to be up last night, up all night, in Mom and Dad's bedroom, listening for sounds in the hall.

This isn't a game. In fact, she's seen more than one WNBA star comment on how what they do, what they play, is, in fact, *only* a game. And meaningless, at that, in the face of what troubles society, what troubles the world.

Here, something troubles Samhattan.

Kit hasn't slept. But she's not exhausted. She's piqued in a way she hasn't been before. Ghosts or no ghosts, legend or reality, Tammy Jones was killed, a team picture was taken, and the gym she finds herself in is no longer a place of cheer, triumph, joy.

This is the same floor on which she just hit the shot of her life. And now?

Now it's an interrogation room. The bright lights in the rafters might as well be a single bulb in a stone room deep in the belly of the Samhattan Police Department.

There isn't a shred of humor on the face of the detective, Carla McGowan, who gives off the energy of a tire too full of air, the pump still motoring beside it.

Kit senses a similar acceptance, a gravity, from the others. Most of them are dressed in sneakers and shorts, tank tops and braids, as if they're unable to divorce the outfit from the gym, the place they were summoned, a place Detective Carla McGowan no doubt believed they'd be more comfortable. But of course they're not. Nobody speaks unless spoken to. Nobody offers up information. Because nobody has any. All the ballers sit quiet and listen to the serious woman as she explains how important it is that any information, *any at all,* could be the very bit she needs to solve what's happened here.

It's clear she has no leads.

"The metrics," McGowan says, "are the usual. Though this man seems bigger than most." She clears her throat. "He's probably between the ages of twenty-five and thirty-five. Single, most likely. A loner, probably. But big. The marks on your friend indicate a very strong man, indeed." Then: "Have any of you girls seen a man like this around the city? Around the gym? Maybe he was talking to Tammy after games? Outside the locker room? Maybe you saw him after school last year? Saw her interacting with a man taller than I am?"

Carla McGowan is tall too. And she carries every inch of it with confidence. Yet Kit senses something there. A commonality.

Game recognizes game.

Coach Wanda leans forward and looks all the way down the line of girls.

"If you saw something, say something," she says. "No use protecting anybody now. And any trouble you know of isn't as bad as the trouble he's already caused."

But the girls remain silent.

"Nobody?" McGowan asks. "I guess I believe that. It would be pretty remarkable if a thirty-five-year-old man was lurking about the school. Coach Wanda woulda probably already been told." She eyes the team close. They eye her too. "How about Tammy's family? Do you know of any uncles, older brothers, someone maybe her family didn't tell me about?"

This question rattles Kit. It reveals, for her, a depth she wasn't fathoming. Brandon had suggested something like it, but Tammy's family *hiding* information from the police?

"Girls?" Coach Wanda says. "Speak up. Now or never." Then, to McGowan, "Have you checked all the employees of the local hangouts?"

"Well, I'm not sure," McGowan says, obviously not wanting to give away everything she knows. "What places do you have in mind?"

"I think she once worked at the Rickshaw Inn," Dana says.

"Bussed tables," Natasha says.

"We know that much," McGowan says. "But go on."

"Maybe someone from there," Wanda says. Her short brown bob and large glasses give her the look of a coach from the 1970s, not 2022. Kit thinks of a tall, dead woman in a car from the '80s or '90s too.

"We've certainly checked her former place of employment," McGowan says. "And while we're not closing any doors, nobody there fits the bill. Not this bill."

She seems to stare into the space of the gym for a beat and Kit knows she's seeing what she saw at what must have been the crime scene. Tammy's death isn't just news for Detective McGowan; it's a memory.

"Who else . . . ?" McGowan asks. She lets the question linger, doesn't rush anybody.

Melanie raises her hand.

"Yes?" McGowan says.

"Tammy lived at the far edge of town."

"Yes."

"Maybe someone from out of town was watching her in town."

"Watching her?"

"Yeah, like, from out of town."

Some of the girls snicker nervously. It's a ridiculous idea. An outsider stopping at the town border, looking across it like they would through a window.

"That's not such a bad theory," McGowan says, helping her, it seems. "An outsider seems reasonable. Maybe you'll be doing work like I do one day."

Melanie reddens. Kit knows it was hard enough for her to talk in front of everyone like that. It must be unbearable to think everyone is imagining her as a police officer.

"But what I'm looking for here is any concrete instance, a time you actually saw her talking to somebody who fits that bill. Even if it was just a man asking for directions on the street."

"Why a man?" Natasha asks.

Kit shifts on the green chair. Thinks of a tall woman. Taller than McGowan.

McGowan says, "Like I said, the strength—"

"Yeah, but women are just as strong as men these days," Natasha says. "We beat the crap out of the boys' team every time we play them."

Coach Wanda makes to scold Natasha for the language, perhaps. Then she seems to find nothing to disagree with. She looks to McGowan for her response.

Natasha speaks again first.

"I mean, you could be limiting your search, right? If you rule out women. That's, like, half the town, half the world. You could be looking all over for a man and the killer could be standing right next to you. You could be asking the killer if she knows any man as big as you and here, that woman is even bigger."

Kit shifts again. Is Natasha just flat-out suggesting Daphne?

McGowan holds Natasha's gaze before finally nodding her agreement.

"All right," she says. "Any of you girls see Tammy Jones interacting with any women who might've been about my size or bigger?"

"Yes."

It isn't one girl who says it. It's like seven at once. Kit is one of them. Because it's true. In summer leagues, in the fall, too, the ballers come in contact with all types of coaches and former players. Sports-medicine people, parents, more. A player as good as Tammy Jones even had a few scouts.

"Well," McGowan says, pulling out a notepad and a pen from her blue police jacket pocket. "Let's start with you."

She looks to Beck Nelson, who sits first in line, next to Coach Wanda.

"Well, don't just sit there like a ninny," Wanda says. "Talk to the woman. And tell her everything that comes to mind. All of you, talk."

And Beck does.

They all do.

And as Detective McGowan writes, Kit senses that commonality again. As if the woman is not jotting down important notes about a horrific case but rather writing in her journal, like Kit does, doing all she can to stave off what feels like the inevitable.

Yes, she thinks. McGowan writes the same way she does. Under different circumstances, this might bring Kit comfort. But today, under the same lights that illuminated her game-winning shot, and not twenty feet from the rim she silently spoke with, it worries her to think the person in charge of ending this nightmare could be as rattled as her.

Is this it? Is this woman their hope? Their defense? Is this woman whose hand shakes as she writes, whose eyes have seen Tammy Jones's incurvated face, is she going to stop what's coming?

Kit looks down the row to Natasha. Recalls Natasha saying the story was just a story. She believes her. Believes Natasha believes that anyway. Mostly. But how much of that was Natasha worrying about her imperfect friend? How much of what anybody says to Kit right now includes the fact that she called 911 when her mind ran away with itself? Like she needs protecting . . .

And the way Natasha watches the detective . . .

Is she debating whether this woman can provide that protection and more?

Kit looks to McGowan too.

Wonders what she knows, what she doesn't. Wonders what she's seen, what she hasn't.

Wonders what's imperfect inside this woman too.

Because, after all, game recognizes game.

And Kit's hands move involuntarily in her lap as if she, too, is writing in her journal, attempting to stave off the inevitable, even as McGowan scribbles in hers.

o o o

Interviewing high schoolers is no different from asking kids what they learned at elementary school on any given day. They always respond with a variation of *nuthin'*. It's partly the reason Carla McGowan hasn't had kids. Another reason is that love hasn't been very good to her. And maybe that can be explained by how often she's moved around the state, city to city, working her way up the ladder in a nonlinear way, never having held the same position in any two. She was a beat cop in Detroit; community support officer in East Kent; scenes of crime investigator in farmland Chowder; fingerprint officer (briefly, one week) in Goblin; civilian investigation officer in Chaps; and now, detective in Samhattan. Not much time for roots, living a life like this, though even she recognizes some degree of making excuses, as she's been in Samhattan close to two years now.

Still: even if she had found love, she sure as hell didn't want any kids. There's a long period of their lives in which they either don't listen to you or subconsciously rebel against you, and it's not until they're about thirty that they realize how good you really were to them. That's the arc Carla took with her own parents, and that's the arc she sees all day every day, interviewing the people of Samhattan. Teens don't know what's important yet and so they worry more about how they look while answering than they do the actual answers. It's all right. Carla gets it. The world doesn't have to be perfect, all her questions don't have to be answered in a linear way.

And often people reveal things without meaning to. But if there's one thing that revs her up, one thing that brings her close to her own breaking point, it's wasting time. And while this current case isn't one of a missing person (boy, is it ever *not;* Carla has the death photos on the phone in her blue jacket pocket; all of Samhattan knows exactly where the girl is now), she still feels an urgency some might call anxiety.

It's one of the reasons she's been moved around the state as much as she has: Carla McGowan has a tendency to cross legal lines when she panics.

Often, with crimes like these, McGowan, daughter of a deeply unsettled Cuban woman and an unknowingly neurotic Irish man, wishes she could pull the cruiser over and freak the fuck out. It seems there used to be time for doing things like this. It used to be you could go out drinking and vent about school, your job, the world, your place in it. Yes, back in high school and college: You felt shitty? You found a corner of the world to cry in. You felt like crying? You cried. You felt like dying? You put on some emotional music and you curled into a ball and you waited to see if it happened and it never did, so you got back up and faced the world again.

But gradually, over decades now, she's felt that era end. Whether it's the professionalism that's expected of her or the fact that the world is actually moving at a faster clip, she doesn't know. But if there's one improvement to the Samhattan police force she'd like to recommend to Chief Barbara Pollen, it's that officers (and detectives) ought to be given baseball bats and private rooms where dozens of breakable objects waited to be destroyed.

Venting is good.

Getting things off your chest is good.

But breaking things is often best.

And she still feels this way, despite what happened in the interrogation room in Chaps, the reason she was transferred to Samhattan in the first place.

Hell, she doesn't want to think about that today. She can't. Not with what happened to fourteen-year-old Tammy Jones last night. And while murder isn't the rarest of city crimes (even in a smaller city like Samhattan), the early reports from the coroner's office are baffling.

Bare hands.

No time for old regrets with potential fresh ones on the table.

McGowan needs to act fast. She understands this clearly. Faster than she's ever worked before. And as goes the report: Well . . . no. Right? There's simply no way what she saw, in person, and still carries now in her jacket, was the result of bare hands. Still: no evidence of any weapon at all. She stood in the same room Jones was killed. Stood above the mess that was made.

"Not unless her head was dropped from the parking structure by bare hands," she says out loud, taking a left on Stein Street.

McGowan mostly works alone. It's not that she prefers it that way (in fact, she dreams of an assistant, anyone to take care of the administrative duties while she focuses on connecting the dots), it's just that Samhattan is only so big. Sure, it's got rich areas and poor areas and a reasonable downtown and dozens of different restaurants with cuisine from around the world, but it's also got a cemetery smack dab in the center of it, and no city with *that* could ever boast to be much of a vacation destination. There seems to be one of everything in town: one mechanic, one doctor, one basketball coach, one big, fat cemetery.

And one detective.

She passes the graveyard now. Thinks of the impending funeral of a fourteen-year-old girl with a ton of promise both on and off any court.

"Tammy Jones," she says. "I'm so sorry."

Passing the trees that block the view of the tombstones, she's infused with a sudden urge to solve the case *now,* this second. Immediacy, she believes, is what an artist means by "inspiration." It's not pretty. The unsinkable drive to get a thing done.

This is what got her to cross that line in Chaps.

"I'm gonna do it, Tammy," she says, almost in rhythm with the blinker as she approaches Fifth Street. It's no small thing to her: the fact she's maintained her enthusiasm for this job two years in means a lot to Carla McGowan. The way other officers talk (and you ought to hear Chief Pollen), it's as if nothing matters, nothing gets solved, the sun will one day die, the world is going to turn to ice, and hey, it's just one little case in one little town in one little country at one meaningless moment in time. It's dispiriting as hell, truth be told, and it gets under her skin, makes her want to bust desktops in the precinct, pull ribbons from the typewriters, grab her co-workers by their badges.

"Hey, hey," she says. "Easy."

She's piqued. But McGowan has learned to fortify herself. It's not all psychotherapy and meditation either: she's found some solace in the spirituality books on the shelves in Samhattan's own Third-and-Fourth-Eye Books. The girls she questioned today, local jocks, would jeer if they knew how often she frequented that weird little store. But do they know what lessons are shelved there? And do they know that one day they will invariably need lessons of their own?

What lines will each of them cross one day, when the way things should be grate against the way they are?

Kids today, she believes, might not be any different from kids yesterday, but it sure wouldn't hurt for them to grow up a little faster. A teammate of theirs was murdered last night. Did McGowan really need to go through the rigmarole of politely extracting answers?

Still, the girls did bring up an idea she hadn't considered.

She turns right on Fifth Street.

It's almost embarrassing, how little she has to go on. Driving the city's blocks of ill repute (worst repute) feels something like going to an ex-boyfriend's house late at night when nothing else worked out at the bar. Can't find a criminal? Go to Fifth Street! They wear ribbons around their neck for first, second, and third place! Park and point out the window and you'll finger a petty criminal or an eventual white-collar horror just beginning his climb up the shit-soaked ladder of "respectable" crime.

"Why do you think all criminals are men?" she mockingly asks herself. She shakes her head.

That was really something today, wasn't it? The way those teens kept hammering home the idea it could've been a woman who did that to Tammy Jones. McGowan had to hold herself back from showing them the pictures, asking them if they ever heard of a woman doing anything close to *that* in their entire lives. But that's how things were these days, she supposed. And she didn't think it was so bad a thing either: people were fighting for a new perception out in the streets, out in the world. Women, this new generation was saying, are capable of anything men are.

Still, she senses hastiness in the distance. A feeling she knows intimately and one that has not served her well. If she's not careful, if she takes her eye off it, things could go south in this case quickly. A murderer loose in Samhattan. A dead teen. *Hey girls*, she thinks, *this might not be the best time for sociological arguments.*

Yet . . .

As she passes the litter-strewn sidewalks and overgrown weeds at the base of these buildings, she thinks maybe these kids aren't "arguing" after all; maybe they already *see* things this way. It's possible McGowan is a dinosaur at forty-one and these teens are the new prism through which the world is seen. They want equal-opportunity everything, including the bad stuff. *A murderer on the loose, you say? Don't rule us out.* Because, you know what? It means more to them that someone like Carla McGowan, a detective, has an open mind than that their suggestions are plausible.

McGowan understands. She even almost applauds it. Only, in this case . . .

"No fucking way."

Those pictures are burning a hole in her jacket pocket, straight through her phone. They're filling that pocket with the impossible shapes a face could become if enough pressure is applied.

Bare hands.

"No way."

She instinctively looks to the bare hands of Samhattan's worst as they jaywalk without looking either way, as they smoke who-knows-what on apartment stoops, as they clasp hands and look over their shoulders and have no idea the unmarked car riding slow is the very thing they're hoping to avoid. But Carla McGowan doesn't have time for the petty right now. It's that goddamn team photo, is what it is, taken from the wall in Tammy Jones's bedroom. That's got her worried in a way she hasn't been worried for some time.

Hastiness.

She can smell it. It's not upon her yet, no, but it's come to Samhattan.

And with it: cold, fast concern. Hurry worry. She better find out who did this *right now,* or something like it is going to happen again.

To another member of the team.

She thinks of the most recent book she bought at Third-and-Fourth Eye. *Your Mind, Your Land* suggested thinking of your mind as a dry-erase board. How no thought is permanent and therefore no thought is ultimately destructive. There's a long passage where the author equates anxiety with an unwanted houseguest and how it's okay, even prudent, to ask certain guests to leave.

McGowan tries to wipe her mind clean, to cancel the party before the guests arrive.

Up ahead, Chuck Larson lumbers up the street in his Samhattan blue. Chuck's the oldest cop on the Samhattan beat. The poor man has been up and down Fifth Street for some thirty years and probably should have retired half that ago. But she thinks he must get something good out of it. And she knows him well enough to look past the set jaw and cold-eyed mask he wears as he patrols. Most of the locals probably see through it too. The Samhattan Police put Larson here for the exact reason one would guess: with so much shit going down on Fifth Street, you've got to at least pretend to be doing something about it. Whether Larson actually is, that's another matter. McGowan believes he means well. He's single. And probably has nowhere else to be. Hell, she's the same way.

"Yo, Chuck," she says, pulling up to the curb. The old-timer carries his club like he's patrolling 1940s Chicago. His faux toughness softens as he looks over his shoulder and sees who it is.

"Carla McGowan," Chuck says. "I've always loved your name. It dances with itself."

He steps to the passenger window and bends at the waist. Chuck is a tall man. Easily six-foot-four. Carla thinks of Tammy Jones and the size of the bare hands that could have done that to her. The word "pumpkin" comes to mind. Like when Carla left her pumpkin on her porch all the way into February and the pulpy, rotting remains froze in the form of a battered face for weeks.

"Pretty shitty thing that happened," Carla says.

Chuck nods.

"The worst," he says.

He looks up the street, and when he looks back at her, it feels, to Carla, like it's only him and her in the entire city. Then: a memory. For her. Something meaningful—no, something bordering on profound. It's like déjà vu but less vague. Whatever memory she's attempting to retrieve is a big one. Or maybe it's just that thoughts carry more weight when they're still out of reach.

She reaches this one, grabs it, and thinks:

When you started, two years back, Chuck Larson mentioned something about something happening to the girls' basketball team. No shit. He did. He said something about it being swept under the rug. Do you remember? Yes, you were at one of those awful police parties at Dander Hall and he said something about how there was only so much room for files and so much time for studying them and then he said something you've never forgotten, Carla McGowan, he said:

"Some crimes are better forgotten."

Chuck eyes her funny.

"What's that, Carla?"

"Chuck," she says. And she wonders if running into this man is why she took Fifth Street today at all. Subconscious, indeed. "Do you know of any history with the girls' basketball team? Anything that happened a while ago? Anything funny like that?"

Chuck stands up straight enough so that part of his face is obscured now. McGowan leans forward to get a better look at him. Is Chuck Larson about to lie to her? Why does it feel like he is?

She feels that rush again. That urgency. That artist's inspiration.

"Chuck? Why do I get the idea I've made you nervous?"

Chuck looks to her and a quick splash of anger crosses his face.

The look of someone who knows more than you do, McGowan thinks. The look of someone who's dealt with whatever this is a lot longer than you have.

"Easy, Carla. Just because you're good at what you do doesn't mean I'm not."

"Didn't say that. Asked if you knew about anything tied to the girls' team. Samhattan High basketball."

She recalls the interrogation light hanging in that Chaps station. The feeling of urgency then too. She can almost see the line she crossed, now, but at the time, lines ceased to exist.

"Something, maybe," Chuck says. He says it quick. Like he'd decided it was now or never. And how close was he to never? And how close was McGowan to never hearing it?

"Maybe?" she asks. "How much of a maybe? Is that 'maybe' a fifty-one percent yes?"

"Yes," Chuck says. Quick again.

McGowan reaches across the car, opens the passenger door.

"Get in, Chuck," she says.

He looks up and down the street.

"If there's one street that isn't going to change with or without you for ten minutes, it's Fifth," she says. "Get in."

And so the oldest member of the Samhattan police force seems to shrink in size, to give in to something, as he folds up on himself, and gets into the car.

"Now, Carla," he says. And now he sounds less like a police officer and more like her old man. Buried, yes, in a different city. "This story is something of a sticker."

"What does that mean exactly?"

Chuck shakes his head, having no idea he's doing the very thing young Tammy Jones did the day prior; attempting to get rid of an unwanted thought.

"That means it sticks. You know how some songs stay in your head and you can't get 'em out?"

McGowan doesn't answer. She only stares, alert, ready, and not a little baffled by what Chuck is saying.

"Well, this is like that," Chuck says. "Only, there's no sound to this earworm. This worm doesn't come with any music at all. Though she liked music quite a bit."

"She?" McGowan asks.

And as Chuck begins, she thinks of the girls' basketball team, all seated in the Samhattan gymnasium.

Next to Chuck Larson, McGowan should feel young. But she doesn't. She thinks of people younger than her, of the girls, the ballers, and the new prism through which the world is seen.

The new prism through which maybe she needs to start seeing the world. And through that prism, color, light, and lines.

Lines she shouldn't cross.

o o o

Kit Lamb's Journal—We Were Questioned by Police Today

Read the entry title again.

Read it.

We were questioned by police today. The Samhattan police. A big, strong woman whose roots were showing and whose detective pants were all wrinkly and everything about her told me she takes what she does so seriously she doesn't give a care about anything else. She was sweating with panic.

She scared me, Jolly. So, so much.

Not because we did anything wrong. Not because we could go to jail. But because of how scared SHE was. Does this make sense? The whole team was sitting in the gym, THE SAME GYM WHERE I

MADE THE SHOT, and all of us had to listen to the woman and had to respond to the woman and Coach Wanda looked as nervous as the detective. This was no joke, Jolly. This was no lie! This wasn't some free-floating feeling that frightens you because you can't pinpoint where it came from. This was right in front of us.

WE WERE QUESTIONED BY THE POLICE TODAY

And you know what I did? You know where I kept looking?

Yep. At the rim.

Eyed it like it was a psychic who could tell me our future.

There were moments I wanted a ball in my hands so I could just ask it, you know? Will this woman catch who did this? Will Tammy's killer go free?

There were other times, too, where I didn't want a ball anywhere NEAR me. I fantasized about smashing the rims with hammers so nobody could use them, so nobody could ask them questions ever again.

But then . . . I started asking questions of things, other things, things that weren't the rim.

Like: If Natasha responds first, no matter what she says, then this detective will solve this case. And like: If one of us ballers raises a hand before speaking, Tammy's killer will never be found.

I saw questions in everything, Jolly. If the detective's shoe squeaked against the gym floor, then THIS will happen. If Coach Wanda calls my name, then THIS. If someone interrupts someone else, if there's a moment of silence longer than three seconds, if the power goes out, if Principal Taylor enters the gym, if the door opens, if Melanie coughs, if Emily swears, if THEN if THEN if THEN, yes no yes no yes no, over and over, until literally nothing was done or said that wasn't preordained by Fate.

I felt like if I didn't leave the gym in minutes I was going to lose my mind. In front of everyone. Including the detective. And she would see how troubled I am and she would suggest I stick around for further questioning and she'd have me locked up for being insane because, while she went out looking for a killer today, she couldn't willfully ignore the maniac girl she'd met on the way.

YOU CALLED THE POLICE ON YOURSELF BEFORE? OH! TELL ME MORE

It's her job, after all.

And everything about this woman spoke of JOB.

And the others were asking questions and giving answers and giving theories and I just keep seeing questions in everything, as if a game was being played on the same floor we were using as an interrogation room, ghosts of other games, and girls from every era since the school opened, all of them shooting, and they made some and missed some and every single flick of the wrist was a question that would and could affect the rest of their lives. There were girls from the '60s, '70s, '80s, '90s, 2010s, and each had their own style and their own form and the game changed with them, BASKETBALL THEATER: from the below-the-rim fundamental bounce-pass and set-shot to the behind-the-back pass, the no-look pass, hardcore defense where you could swarm 'em, followed again by an era where you couldn't even hand-check and the scores almost doubled. Still, in every era, no matter how the ball was shot, a question came with it, spun in the air, went in YES or did not NO and the future was either cast or revealed and I couldn't tell which was which.

And in the bleachers?

HER

Yep. Jolly, listen to me: I imagined her sitting in the blue bleachers behind us. HER with her denim jacket and pants. HER knees almost to HER chin she's so tall, watching the ghosts of the game, watching history unfold, watching the players and hearing their questions even as I did. She didn't talk, no: she was like a breathing ledger, all those *answers lodged into her big head, her eyes and face blocked by black-and-white makeup that could've been tongues and could've been faces and could've been her actual skin.*

She towered over me, us, even as she sat, and every time Natasha reminded the detective that a woman could've killed Tammy Jones, I wanted to turn and point to the bleachers and say

HER

It was HER

Jolly!

Daphne

there

Daphne

there

DAPHNE

THERE I wrote her name.

IT WAS DAPHNE!

I'm on edge, Jolly. Thee edge.

I'm scared.

We should be. All of us.

We're in danger.

And that detective, McGowan, if she doesn't solve this . . . who will?

And can she?

I'm going to crumple up this piece of paper and shoot it into the little garbage can in my bedroom. Okay? I'm gonna write down my question and I'm gonna ball this paper up and I'm gonna shoot and I'll have my answer.

All right, you ready?

Because if you're going to ask the questions, you gotta be ready for the answers.

The question:

Am I next?

And . . .

. . . the answer is . . .

○ ○ ○

Melanie stands before her bedroom mirror, taking out her braids. After the interrogation (it's the word she uses, it's how it made her feel), the girls got together and talked about Tammy Jones, talked about Detective McGowan too. There was a majority sense this was an isolated incident, a thing from Tammy's past they know nothing about. That's how it works, Melanie knows. The darknesses of other people's lives. It's always a little nice to hear other people have problems, big problems, but it's downright shocking when those problems are bigger than your own.

Still, despite the talk about the detective (God, the woman seemed clueless) and Tammy's family, Melanie can't stop thinking about Natasha's story.

She can't stop thinking about Daphne.

Silly to worry, she knows. Insane in its way.

But there's just something to the story, her name . . .

Melanie unbraids her hair.

Truth is, she'd heard of Daphne, and heard Daphne's story, before. Only, she hadn't thought of it since then. Kinda like when a friend tells you a dream, Melanie thinks. Yeah. How you might remember a sentence or two, but really, if it was all just a dream, where's the weight? Where's the part of it that *matters*?

Melanie thinks maybe the minds of people hold on to the stuff they think matters. And before Natasha's story . . . Daphne simply did not matter.

"Quit thinking about this," she tells her reflection. She's good at talking to herself. Because, normally, she listens.

Daphne isn't even as fictional as the tooth fairy. At least with *that* story you found some money under your pillow. But this one? The one she heard? At best it would've been a story meant to get kids to do something, feel something, brave something. Melanie thinks she first heard the name on the playground in elementary school. She recalls a vague unease at a name anyway. Still, at some point since then the quiet storms of memory took the name away. *Daphne.* When Natasha said it, Melanie almost said, *Oh yeah!* The way someone would if they remembered something from their youth, for the first time in a decade or more. But there was something else about it too: it was as if the name (and the story) were out of reach, and that she actually *had* been trying to recall it. Like, Natasha's story did a little more than just remind Melanie: it suggested something had been stopping her from totally recalling the story, something outside of herself.

Now, in front of her mirror, she remembers a recess aide, a woman in thick glasses and a puffy brown coat, leaves swirling in a small triangle of wind behind her.

The aide said:

Don't say that name, kids. Don't ever say that name again.

And a look, too, right? In the eyes of that aide, just after she delivered her command.

"It was like she forgot what she was talking about right after she told us to forget it," Melanie says now. "Like she literally didn't know what she just said."

If Melanie's honest with herself (and this is not an easy admission), she felt some measure of relief when she heard Tammy Jones was killed. Tammy and not Melanie. Because it sounded like a scene straight from the stories (she now clearly remembers) about Daphne.

And if the woman comes for those who think too much . . .

Well, thank God she wasn't the only one thinking.

But can she stop?

She untwists a braid, combs it out, notes how half her head is untwisted and the other is not. Makes her look like two people; a member of the basketball team on one side, a crazed overthinker on the other.

Criminally insane.

Like Daphne.

See?

Melanie steps away from the mirror and walks over to her bed-room window. No matter how honest the revelation was, the relief at discovering someone else died was short-lived. Because now what? She knows Kit is thinking of Daphne too. That's plain as yogurt. Is everyone?

Don't ever say that name again.

It's an impossible situation, of course. That's how her aunt Paula put it when she was wasted, when she told Melanie her version of Daphne's story many summers ago, as the two sat in lounge chairs, their feet getting wet from the rotating sprinkler.

Melanie marvels at the story now. And how she hadn't thought of it, not once, since that day.

It's a crazy story, Paula said, her accent full Michigan. She was way into the gin at this point. Melanie, only thirteen at the time, wasn't far behind. *I guess it happened thirty-something years ago? I'm no good with dates. Not with dates with men and even worse with dates in history. I didn't even know it was Saturday till your mom said so a few minutes ago. Or maybe it was ten minutes ago.*

She laughed. Melanie smiled, sipped more gin. Maybe Paula thought it was water.

So, there was this huge girl . . . like . . . NBA tall . . . and she was weird . . . not because she was big . . . but because she was quiet. Not like you. Or maybe yes, like you. I don't know. This Daphne . . . does she have a last name? I don't have a clue. I'm bad with names. She was big and weird and these assholes in town, they came and killed her.

Melanie squinted at the ice in her glass.

Killed her?

So, it's like this, Paula said, exactly as the sprinkler sprayed their feet again. *Daphne drove a muscle car, whatever year it was. And she had it running in the garage and these murderers, they came by her place with a mind to toss eggs at her door. But they saw the car running and they thought, Hey, let's close the garage and maybe Daphne will back up into the door. A prank. Nasty, but small. They closed the garage door, but they had no idea Daphne had fallen asleep in the car, listening to a heavy-metal band. Like Rush. She was taking a nap after a long drive from who-knows-where to see a band. Maybe Rush. So, you see, these mean people, they killed her. She died like people who commit suicide die, but she didn't commit suicide. See? Dark matter. It's all dark matter. And so now she haunts Samhattan like a white sheet in chains.*

Haunts?

You sound spooked, Mel. Did I freak you out? I'll take that as a win. Anytime I can get anybody to feel anything, I'll take that as a win.

Haunts though?

The sprinkler got their feet again. Paula gulped more gin.

I guess the legend is she comes around if you talk about her too much. She comes and strangles you or beats you up. 'Cause she's angry, see? 'Cause she didn't deserve that, see? And also maybe because she was killed in her sleep and so her ghost doesn't know if this is a dream or not.

Melanie went quiet. Like she does. That's her thing. The other girls call her shy, but really, most of the time, she feels she chooses silence. She doesn't talk because she doesn't need to constantly express herself like Natasha does. Hell no. Like when Nat was telling her Daphne story, Melanie didn't say, *I know about Daphne, too,* because then everyone would be all *Oooh, what do you know?* And she didn't feel like talking about it. Not because Paula said that's what draws Daphne to you. No. That's not why.

Right?

Outside, below, a white van passes. A heating and cooling logo on its side. An older woman walks her dog. The streetlamps are on.

Natasha's Daphne story was different from Paula's. That's true. In Natasha's, the "assholes" were high school ballers, not mean, vague entities. And the way to bring her about was to think of her. Not just talk about her like Paula said.

That's the part that bothers Melanie.

She doesn't like talking much anyway, so she was safe from someone she wasn't supposed to talk about.

But thinking?

Shit. Melanie thinks as much as Stephen Hawking did.

She heads back to the mirror, starts taking out the braids on the other side of her head. She thinks of Tammy Jones's face caved in, imagines her looking like one of those rubber Halloween masks when you toss them on your bed, when they fold up, how the eyes get closer together, the nose gets longer, how the ends of the mouth curl in a way to suggest inevitable speech.

But what's bothering her more than the story itself is the feeling that Natasha somehow pried something loose from Melanie's subconscious. Yes. Without permission.

And against all advice.

She feels a breeze, looks to the window. Goes to it, closes it. Looks through the glass and sees, a dozen blocks up, a silhouette pedaling a bike.

"Mel," her mom says, behind her in the doorjamb.

Melanie, startled, looks to her.

"You talked to a cop today?"

"I did."

"You didn't say we have weed here, did you?"

"What do you think I am? A narc?"

"You didn't though?"

"It wasn't about that, Mom."

"Still. I got worried, is all."

"That's insane. A friend died."

"You said you didn't know her."

"I didn't," Melanie says. She crosses the room, back to the mirror.

"Well, if police are going to be coming around, be careful, is all."

"Mom. There's a cop in the street outside. And nobody cares about grass anymore."

Mom smiles.

"Where'd you get a word like that? Is that what kids are calling it today? Has it come full circle like that?"

Melanie rolls her eyes, untwists new braids.

"And talking to a cop is different than them outside watching the house."

"I know, Mom."

"You doing okay?"

"Yeah."

"Yeah, you always do well."

"Yeah."

"Okay. Let me know."

"Let you know what?"

"Let me know how things turn out with all of this."

"I don't know what there is to tell."

"You know what I mean."

But she doesn't. Or doesn't care. Mom leaves and Melanie works at her hair. She hears an owl-like screech outside, a shriek that ripens into a tire on the street. Comb in hand, she goes to the window.

A dark Samhattan night. The police are parked somewhere down the block out front. Out of view. From Melanie's window: a man takes his trash out even though trash day is tomorrow. A teen younger than Melanie sits on the stone steps of her brick home.

There's that figure on the bike again. Many blocks up. From this distance, it's hard to make out the details.

Melanie heads back to the mirror.

She thinks of the seven-footer asleep in her car. Thinks of the fumes rising from the pipe, gas snaking in the garage, fumes slinking up into the car, up the length of her face, up her nose, to her brain that's taking in the sound of a purring engine and hard music.

Her ghost doesn't know if this is a dream or not . . .

"Quit it," Melanie says.

But wow if that phrase of Aunt Paula's isn't crystal clear in her head. After so long of not having thought of it at all.

"Ugh . . ."

She's glad there's nobody to talk to in her bedroom. It's so much better when you don't have to. *So* much better. Natasha, she's at the opposite end of the spectrum. She talks like it's a city ordinance. *Shit, did you see her telling the policewoman who she should be going after?*

She sets the comb on her dresser, heads back to the window.

Outside, the biker again. Under a lamp. Back into the dark. The wheels spin slow by a pair of men talking on the sidewalk. The men don't acknowledge the rider. This bothers Melanie.

Maybe it's the hair, the jacket, the fact that it feels like the biker is pedaling in slow motion even as the men gesture at a regular speed. Like something impossible in a dream.

Why didn't the men look at her?

"Her?" Melanie asks.

She steps from the window, crosses her bedroom, hesitates at the bedroom door. Calls out:

"Mom?"

Mom's downstairs. Melanie can see the bottom of the curved staircase. Can see the front door. Can hear the TV is on in the kitchen.

"Mom?"

"What's up, Mel?"

Melanie doesn't know what's up. She hurries back to the window.

"Mel?"

Mom's at the foot of the stairs now, calling up. Melanie knows. She's heard Mom's voice from that very spot a thousand times. Through the glass, that person on the bike, too big for the bike, that same slow-motion way. She (it's a woman, Melanie knows this for sure now) rides through the intersection, crosses the street, is illuminated by a streetlamp.

Then, into the darkness again.

"Mel?"

Melanie leans closer to the window, cups her hands to see better. Nothing. Is the biker still in the darkness? Melanie squints. She can't tell.

But directly below her window on the lawn, an impossibly tall woman looks back up.

Melanie steps back.

"Oh God . . ."

The front door to the house opens.

Closes.

"Mel?"

Melanie thinks of the face she saw, looking up at her.

Her room feels hot. Crawling heat. She hurries out into the hall, stops at the top of the stairs.

There's a seven-foot woman in denim crossing the foyer, climbing the first step. Her hair hangs greasy, her fingers black with oil. She steps by Melanie's mom, Mom, who looks up to Melanie as if to ask, *You okay, Mel?*

Melanie raises a shaking hand, points at the woman who is now halfway up the steps.

It's Daphne, yes. Her head grazes the ceiling as she comes.

"MOM!"

But Mom only looks confused.

"Mel, what is it? Is there news? Did they find who did it?"

Melanie smells smoke and alcohol.

"Mel?"

She turns and runs for her bedroom. Slams the door behind her. Rushes to her desk and opens the top drawer and hears her bedroom door open and turns to face Daphne with a pair of scissors that feel too small. She cries out as she stabs the space between them, as two bare hands cover that space, one taking Melanie by the upper arm.

The sound is clean, quick. Melanie can smell the grease, the oil.

Daphne has torn off Melanie's arm.

Melanie opens her mouth to scream, to speak, to say anything, but Daphne swings the arm against the side of her head and the world goes black. Yet Melanie takes with her into that darkness the makeup, the face that is not Paula's story, not Natasha's, nobody's.

On the floor, blacked out, there is still some life in her. Enough to feel the giant boot upon her head.

"Mel?" Mom calls from below.

Then, footsteps, ascending, even as Daphne, finished, enters the hall.

Mom passes, without seeing the woman responsible for the death of her daughter, doesn't hear her, but will later tell Detective McGowan it smelled strong of smoke and whiskey, yes, it smelled of the bar. Search the bars for who did this. Search them *now*.

At the doorjamb, Mom sees her Mel, though it takes her moments to believe the split face on the floor belongs to her daughter. At first, she mistakes it for a basketball jersey the girls wore when they played for the middle school team.

At first she thinks her daughter's folded face is only discarded clothes on the floor.

But the blood pouring from it is unmistakable. And the closer she gets, the more she sees of Melanie. The more she sees of the anarchy that is all that remains of her daughter.

o o o

The first thing Carla McGowan thinks as she takes a seat in the main office at Samhattan High School is that the principal, Janice Taylor, is smaller than she thought she'd be. Taylor looks much bigger on TV and even in print, she comes off as twice as big.

McGowan seems to be measuring everyone by size these past two days.

Principal Taylor is also the first woman principal in the high school's history, and it has McGowan thinking of those girls again, insisting the killer could be a woman, and would she, Carla, please quit counting out half the population just because she was raised to do exactly that?

All this leads to thoughts of Chuck Larson's story, told to McGowan in her unmarked squad car:

A local legend McGowan hasn't heard before. A story about a woman named Daphne.

"I don't like conducting business anywhere but at the school," Taylor says. She's so small that even her ordinary glasses look big. So do the glasses Coach Wanda wears, Wanda, who sits beside McGowan in a matching yellow chair, facing the seemingly huge administrative desk.

"I wouldn't call this business," McGowan says. She feels a bit overwhelmed. Not only because this meeting is already different from her idea of what it would be, but because Larson's poorly articulated tale included a former player from the Samhattan High School girls' basketball team, a young woman who might've sat in this very seat, faced this very desk, as city officials began worrying about her obsession with Daphne.

"Well, whatever it is," Taylor says, "it's not for the bar, not for the public. And certainly not for the home. I work very hard to keep my house clean of all dirt. Thus"—she fans her hands outward—"the office at night."

"Dirt . . ." McGowan says. As if Tammy Jones's death is a stain on the school. She suddenly wants very badly to show the woman the pics on her phone. The stains on the floor in Tammy Jones's bedroom.

Why does it feel like Taylor has prepared her defense for this meeting? And more: why did it feel like Chuck Larson was relieved to tell his story?

"I just need a little help," McGowan says.

"Well," Taylor says. "You're not gonna characterize me any old way you please. I know how these situations can go. Schools can be blamed. And foremost those who run them. I doubt I can help you locate anybody at large, so I'm not entirely sure *why* we're here. But you said you wanted to talk. So let's talk."

McGowan has little trouble seeing how a person like Janice Taylor has succeeded in her field. On the wall behind her is a framed slogan:

YOU SHOULD BE ABLE TO TAKE CARE OF THIS YOURSELF

"Tammy Jones was a student here," McGowan says.

"A student-*to-be*, yes."

"Yes. About to be a freshman. Already making friends with girls much older on the basketball team."

"I don't know of any rivalries, jealousies, motives at all."

McGowan looks to Coach Wanda, because it's a little nuts, the way Principal Taylor just bulls through things. And if McGowan doesn't look at someone else, she might say something she regrets.

At the same time, a fourteen-year-old was killed. Who has time for protocols?

"All right," McGowan says. She thinks of Chuck's voice in the cramped car, describing a basketball player killed in 1998. A senior named Belinda, who had been ostracized for going about town, talking about . . . Daphne. She was obsessed, Larson said, though nobody could rightly tell if the girl was enamored with the local legend or if she was scared. And if she *was* scared, how scared? And why? Larson suggested the girl was "troubled," which McGowan recognized as conveniently dismissive.

But there was empathy in his voice. More than him simply feeling sorry for the girl. Almost like he had endured something in this story too.

"Do you have any reason to believe one of your male teachers was interested in any way in Tammy Jones?"

The question lands with a thud. Taylor looks to Wanda and holds her eyes for a solid few seconds before her face cracks into a faux smile.

"Excuse me, Detective?" She finally says. But McGowan holds her ground. She doesn't repeat the question. And after adjusting her blazer, Janice Taylor speaks: "No. I have absolutely zero reason to believe one of our male . . ." She trails off, as if McGowan's question is ultimately not worth answering.

"What happened to Tammy Jones was a brutality beyond anything I've ever seen in Samhattan," McGowan says.

"Well, you should've been here during the Randy Scotts years."

"I'm here now."

"You sure are."

"And if the coroner is telling me Tammy was killed with bare hands . . . I need to find a man strong enough to do that. I need to find one who might be connected to her in the first place. How soon are the students assigned counselors?"

"Not before school starts, if that's what you mean. Bare hands?"

McGowan hesitates before responding. What does Principal Taylor know of bare hands? Something. Yes.

"Yes."

"Well . . . no counselors before school starts."

It's clear what Taylor is saying: Tammy Jones wasn't yet enrolled at Samhattan High. So, no counselor for her. And subtext: *Tammy Jones wasn't technically one of ours yet.*

"I think possibly someone with an intimate relationship got into her bedroom," McGowan says. She turns to Coach Wanda, "And no male assistants? Even a guest for a single practice?"

Wanda considers this.

"We've had parents come and watch practices from time to time. Tammy's own did that."

"Her father isn't employed by Samhattan High School," Principal Taylor says, not without triumph.

"Okay. Look," McGowan says. Because sometimes the moment calls for a reality check. Even as she sees a line again, one she shouldn't cross. Like the one in an interrogation room in Chaps. In some ways, that room was no different from this one. Four walls. Questions and unsatisfactory answers. "I'm not much for sparring. If you wanna feel like you're winning this talk . . . then, great. You won. Let's award you the prize *first* so we can just get that out of the way. I asked to talk to you because I'm looking for the killer of a young woman in this town, our town, and it's *my* job to find him.

I'm questioning everybody I can think of, and I have zero desire to make you or your school look bad. People get hurt all the time, yes, but if we can do something about even a small percentage of those, if we can put any killer behind bars, then we're doing something pretty fucking amazing with our lives. So, let's drop the boxer stances and talk. Woman to woman. Samhattanite to Samhattanite. Pretend you and me . . . we're at the bar . . . and we're just talking over a drink, discussing what we think could've happened to Tammy Jones. Because, who knows, Janice, we might just solve it."

Principal Taylor doesn't immediately react, and her expression is difficult to read. Will she make this easy? Or was her steel façade forged so long ago there's no chance of uprooting?

"I *thought* you wanted to talk to me about a very specific *thing,* Detective. A thing you *might* want to talk to me about, considering you're a detective and you live in Samhattan."

"What do you mean?"

But Taylor is already lifting a box from beside her chair and placing it on the desk.

"Oh God," Coach Wanda says, pain in her voice.

"We *could've* talked about this other stuff over the phone," Taylor says. Triumph in her voice yet. "I could've told you I didn't know of any males who might've done this and *that* would've been *that.* But *this*"—she taps the top of the box with a single blue fingernail—"this is the file on the last time something bad happened to a member of the girls' basketball team."

McGowan looks to the box. Looks to Wanda. She thinks of Chuck Larson's story about the baller Belinda in 1998. Thinks how her ears perked up when he said there was no weapon found. No, he hadn't said the girl was crushed to a pulp, but he did suggest the killer used his bare hands.

That was twenty-four years ago.

"Twenty eleven," Principal Taylor says. "Two girls, Kell Darren and Nicole Welsh. Both members of the basketball team. Both now buried in the center of town."

Is there relief in Taylor's face too? Mirroring the empathy McGowan saw in Chuck's?

"This is what you should be focused on," Wanda says. Her voice cracks with the memory of what must be described in the box.

"How could I have known to ask about this?" McGowan says. She feels ambushed.

"Because it's not that different than what happened here."

"Then why don't I know about it already?"

"*That*," Taylor says, "is not my jurisdiction." Then, "I brought this box up from storage myself. So, don't you dare imply I don't care."

McGowan imagines the look Taylor gives her is the same one she scolds students with.

"Thank you," McGowan says. And she means it.

She stands up to take the box.

"I do have my theories *why* you wouldn't have heard about these two murders," Taylor says.

"Murders," McGowan repeats. She sits again with the box and removes the top.

Wanda says, "It's disturbing, Detective."

"But that's not why people shut up about it," Taylor says.

McGowan sees a small stack of typed pages.

"The reason is because they don't think they *should* talk about it," Taylor says.

McGowan's heart picks up speed at two words on the top page: "bare hands."

She thinks of Chuck Larson, folded up on himself in the passenger seat of her car, mumbling mostly disconnected facts about the city and its history like a schoolkid telling ghost stories during a power outage.

Daphne

McGowan wrote it off as Larson told it. Only using it for clues, links, to Tammy Jones. But now . . .

Is Joyce Taylor telling her the entire city has been quiet about this ghost story . . . intentionally?

Taylor says:

"They worry that if they *do* talk about it, and word spreads, then one person, two persons, three persons, four will be talking, writing, singing, and *thinking* about . . . her."

"Her?" McGowan asks, her eyes still on the page. But she knows now who Taylor means.

"Don't think for one second the people of Samhattan aren't quiet about it on purpose, Detective." And Taylor looks a little self-conscious for the first time since McGowan sat down. A little self-aware. "Don't think for one second all the people you know, the people you see every day, don't think for *one second* they don't believe in the power of talking about—"

The phone erupts on the desk. Taylor gets it before the second ring. McGowan feels disoriented. So many questions.

Why do you look scared, Janice?

Taylor speaks into the receiver:

"Who's calling the principal's office when everybody knows the principal isn't supposed to be in her office on a summer night?"

McGowan and Wanda watch as Taylor's face goes from smug to curious to—

Scared, McGowan thinks again.

She closes the lid on the box. Knows she's going to be reading it later. She stands up. Knows she's going to be rushing from this office in seconds.

Taylor looks to her. Nods.

"At her home?" Taylor says into the phone. "I see."

McGowan is already at the office door.

Principal Taylor cups a hand over the receiver and looks to McGowan with a wholly unguarded expression for the first time tonight.

"A second girl from the team," she says. "Melanie Jack."

But McGowan hears the name as she's exiting the office.

She rushes up the tiled halls of the high school, the same halls the ballers walk as they dream of big games, big shots, big futures. She hears the name again, coming through the static of her CB: *Melanie Jack,* again, echoing in these halls, as if Melanie Jack were already, unfairly, part of a myth, and no longer (and never-again-to-be) real.

○ ○ ○

Kit Lamb's Journal—I'm Shrinking

I'm nervous. I feel it everywhere in my body. Any part of me I think of, I feel it there. My waist. My stomach. Tingling. Hot. My elbows, my fingers, my neck. My joints don't feel right. Somebody's replaced my joints with water. There's nothing holding me up, nothing holding me together.

And I'm shrinking.

I'm getting smaller. The more that happens, the less I can do.

Jolly, I'm so nervous I can't speak. Mom and Dad aren't yelling into the phone this time. This time they're silent. Dad is sitting on the edge of their bed in his shirt and jeans. Looks like he's lost something key to who he is. Mom is standing in the hall just outside their bedroom door. She doesn't know where else to be.

Melanie . . .

Oh, I can't even write it down. I don't WANT TO. I want whatever is coming for me to just COME ALREADY, because I can't stand the waiting and I can't stand the cold freeze of shrinking. I'm so scared. I saw this woman online teaching people to replace the word "nervous" with "excited." She said, "Now watch how amazing your life becomes!"

Jolly, help.

I'm so nervous it's all I am.

Am I having an attack? Am I under attack? That's what's happening, isn't it? I think this is as big as it can get, this feeling, but I don't know how big it can get because it's never gotten bigger than this before.

Am I going to die of fright? Am I slowly being scared to death?

Jolly?

Talk to me. You do the writing.

I'm shrinking.

When your parents go past fear and stand still in the halls, when they can't even stand up off the bed they're so scared, there's no longer anybody to protect you.

Melanie had police at her house.

I do too.

Parents, police. Warnings. What more can we do? Distance? Yes, we need to leave Samhattan. Maybe that's what Mom and Dad are thinking about right now. I bet they're so EXCITED about it. I bet they're so EXCITED about the fact that a killer is picking off their daughter's friends. Two now. Two from the team.

It's her. You know it. I know it. Mom and Dad might be knowing it as we speak, slowly, stupidly, knowing it. Remembering her name just like we all did when Natasha spoke it.

Oh God, it was like being reminded of something terrible in your past.

Did we all suppress her together? Is it possible for an entire city to suppress a memory, a story, a name?

I wonder if everybody's as EXCITED about her as I am. I wonder if everyone in Samhattan is thinking about

DAPHNE

I'm so EXCITED, Jolly.

I'm shrinking and I'm so EXCITED because the smaller I get, the less I can do.

What can I do against someone so big?

Isn't it EXCITING, Jolly? Isn't it?

Isn't my life amazing now?

I'M SHRINKING, JOLLY.

I'm shrinking.

I'm shrinking.

And Daphne

gets

bigger.

○ ○ ○

Dana bought a gun.

The girls (Kit, Natasha, Emily, Dana, Beck) are behind Samhattan High when Dana shows them.

"I'm not fucking around," she says. "This is a pattern now."

It is. Detective McGowan called it the same thing when she spoke to their parents. Said that between the two basketball players and the stolen team photo, all members of the team (girls, for now) are on complete lockdown. Curfew. All *must* be watched until this man is caught.

Detective McGowan still thinks it's a man.

Melanie's mom, Julia Jack, has no answers for what happened. She told McGowan and the other officers she'd heard Mel calling from upstairs and so the man must've already been up there. Julia has no idea how this happened. There is no sign of a break-in, no sign of a struggle, except, of course, her daughter, whose arm was removed and used against her own head. The window in Melanie's bedroom wasn't even opened.

McGowan, the girls can tell, is lost. They don't need to see her face to know so.

"We can't look to the police for security," Dana says. "Look how easily we got together, here, now."

"Okay," Emily says. "Listen, I get that. But this . . . this is dangerous too."

"Is it?" Dana asks.

They're all eyeing the gun she holds. It looks different from how they thought it would. And it's impossible not to imagine it going off.

"What are you going to do with it?" Kit asks.

"I'm gonna go to sleep with it," Dana says. "And I'm gonna wake up with it too."

Someone's coming from around the corner of the school.

Dana bobbles the gun. The others don't know if she's thinking to hide it or use it.

Stewart, Brandon, and Little Richard step into view.

"Who the fuck told you we'd be here?" Dana asks.

Stewart looks to Beck. The lanky sophomore-to-be averts his eyes.

"For fuck's sake," Natasha says. "You didn't think we could handle a conversation about protection without them?"

"Dude," Beck says. "We need everyone we can get."

"Fuck that," Natasha says.

"Hey," Brandon says, uncharacteristically (and for that, frighteningly) serious. "We're freaked out too."

"If you don't want us here, we can go," Stewart says. He means it. Dana eyes the boys. Gives in.

"Whatever."

"Everyone's looking for the guy," Richard says. "Like . . . *everyone*. People from out of town, all over. Chaps, Goblin. Farther than that even. This shit is scary."

It's true: Samhattan doesn't feel like Samhattan anymore.

Stewart looks to Dana's gun. "Where'd you get it?"

"Dawn Pawn."

"Seriously?" Brandon asks. "They sold you that? You're underage."

He reaches for it and Dana pulls it away.

"You sure it's not a toy?" he asks.

"Fuck you," Dana says.

"Seriously. They wouldn't sell you a real gun, Dana. They can't. Does it even go off?"

She brings it forward again. The boys gather closer. Little Richard shakes his head.

"That's a relic," Emily says. "The kind of thing you put on your mantel, but don't actually use." Then, "War reenactment shit."

Dana reddens.

"It's got a place for bullets, doesn't it?"

Emily acknowledges it does.

"But be careful," she says. "You don't want it blowing up in your face."

They go quiet. Thinking of faces. Tammy's and Melanie's.

A police siren blips from out on Fallow El Street. The friends peer around the brick side of the building as a group, see a squad car has pulled over a beat-up sedan out in front of the high school. The long-haired man in the driver's seat rolls down his window. Looks like he's unsure why he's been pulled over. The cop exits the squad car and walks slowly to the vehicle. Halfway there his hand hovers above his holster but he doesn't draw the gun. He gives the driver's door a wide berth and bends at the waist as he asks questions. The driver shakes his head no, looks confused, then adamant. The cop points up the road, but the ballers have no idea what he's saying.

"That's how little their leads are," Natasha says. "Pulling over randos and asking if they're the killer."

"Most killers are caught in stupid ways," Dana says. "Expired plates, running red lights, stealing a pack of gum from a gas station the same night they killed someone."

The cop steps back another foot and the driver's door opens. The man looks upset. He can't be that much older than the ballers, maybe in his late twenties, tops. He walks to the back of the car and the friends think he's going to place his hands on the trunk so the cop can search him, but no, he opens the trunk.

"Whoa," Natasha says.

The cop keeps a safe distance, but close enough to see what's inside. The man pulls out a blanket. The cop spots something, leans in, reaches in, removes what looks like a joint, the way he holds it between his forefinger and thumb.

They exchange words. The cop smells it. Hands it back to the man.

"Maybe he was drunk driving," Stewart says.

"Her arm was removed," Dana says.

A basketball rolls between the group and they turn to see a little girl has come to retrieve it. Older kids play on the concrete court thirty yards away.

"You got a good handle?" Natasha asks the kid. Natasha who can't dribble without bouncing it off her knee.

The girl looks to Dana, to Kit, to the others.

"Can you dribble?" Dana asks.

The girl nods.

"Show us," Dana says. She has the gun behind her back.

The girl picks up the ball and dribbles once between her legs. It rolls to the grass.

"Yeah, you're gonna be just fine," Dana says.

Another quick siren sounds and the group gets back to the brick corner and sees the cop back in his car, the driver starting his. They both pull away. The cop looks in their direction as he does. The friends duck behind the building.

"No sign of a break-in," Emily says. "In either case."

"No sign of anything at all," Natasha says.

"Why us?" Kit says.

They hear another siren.

It's the same cop. This time he's pulled over a nicer car, but an equally surprised man behind the wheel.

"They're gonna pull over every fuckin' man who passes through town," Natasha says. "Wasting their time."

"Why do you keep bringing this up?" Emily asks. "Why are you so sure it's a woman?"

Natasha shrugs.

"I just think she's smart. Smarter than the cops."

They watch the officer ask the man to step out of his car. Watch him follow the man to his trunk. Watch as the man opens it and, less than a minute later, closes it again.

"What are the cops even looking for?" Brandon asks. "It's not like a body is missing."

"They're looking for a weapon," Dana says. "Something to help explain what was done. They're looking for a vise. A mallet. A fucking huge hammer."

"Do they have any leads on a weapon?" Richard asks.

"No," Dana says. "They don't have any leads at all, dude."

"But they want one bad," Natasha says. "Because if they can't determine what weapon was used, then they're gonna have to deal with what's left."

"What's that? What's left?" Richard asks.

Natasha watches the synchronicity of the driver getting back into his car just as the cop gets back into his. Their doors close in unison. Natasha says: "Bare hands."

Kit shakes her head no as the back door to the school opens and Detective McGowan steps outside.

Spotted by the police, then. Called in.

"Girls," she says. "Come on. We are well past serious at this point." She looks exhausted. Worried. Scared. "You know the rules, and you *have* to stick to them. No gathering out of sight. Our sight. Come on. Back home. Each of you. All of you. Or I'll lock you up in the jail to make sure."

"Tammy and Melanie were both killed at home," Dana says.

The gun is tucked into the back of her waistband.

But McGowan has done police work a long time.

She steps to her and holds out her hand. Dana tries to look tough. A standoff? No. She gives in, hands it over.

"Jesus Christ," McGowan says. "You get this at Dawn Pawn?"

She doesn't answer.

"Doesn't matter for now," she says. She keeps the gun. "How'd you all get out?"

"They're not really watching us," Natasha says. "They're watching the street."

"And we all have back doors," Dana says.

For a second, it looks like McGowan might snap.

"Well, that's about to fucking change."

The ballers only stare back.

McGowan, semi-composed, says, "I'll give anybody who needs it a ride home. And I'll drive four miles an hour beside those who choose to walk. We need you to be this way for two more days."

"Two days?" Kit asks.

"We'll catch him by then," McGowan says.

"It's not a him," Natasha says.

"Right," McGowan says. "So you keep saying." Then, "If I didn't know better, I'd think you were all are starting to believe in the bogeywoman."

Kit sees it then. A dark spark in the woman's eyes. And she knows the detective is being more serious than she's letting on.

Kit knows.

Carla McGowan has begun thinking about Daphne.

o o o

Carla McGowan *has* begun thinking of Daphne.

"It's a copycat," she tells the chief of police, Barbara Pollen, on the phone in her apartment on Third. "Whoever is doing this is a fan of Samhattan's Daphne. Do you know who I mean when I say that?" She pauses. Half-expecting a guarded response. But Pollen simply says yes. McGowan notes this. "I'd never heard of her before yesterday. Seems like I'm the only one. Hear me out, please. Principal Taylor gave me a file last night, a file I'm not sure you've seen yourself, on the murdered girls Kell Darren and Nicole Welsh. Yes, you know of them, of course. What was that? And you believe that? Randy Scotts pushed them from the parking structure? He confessed to that? Well . . . I'm not so sure, Chief. Hear me out. Please. I understand, but what have we got to lose? Yes, time. I suppose so. But maybe we gain back what we've already lost if we open our minds a little bit here. Okay, so . . . Darren and Welsh kept journals. Yes, I'm sure you did. But did you read them? I don't mean to point a finger, I'm literally just trying to catch a killer. So . . . in this box there are photocopies of these journals and pictures from their bedrooms, all stuff you've apparently seen. Thing is, eventually, something interesting occurs in their journals. Both of them. In sync. As if the two girls were writing side by side, which, by way of other documents in the box, I know wasn't the case. Still, almost to the day, almost to the *hour,* Darren and Welsh began to dance around the concept of . . . Daphne. The legend, yes. So, the two girls, their experience with the Daphne story is identical: both admit to having heard the name as kids, but both say, and I quote here: 'I hadn't thought of it in years.' It's likely they got to talking about the story together and so their journals mirror one another's, but it's where they heard the story, shortly before they're killed, that's interesting: for Darren it was at a bus stop. For Welsh, outside Hi-Fi Grocery. Neither say *who* told them the story, but I think it's likely the same person. And why? Here we have this story, this slice of Samhattan history, that nobody seems to want to talk about, then suddenly these two girls get the whole story, or a version of it anyway, and within days they are both dead. In their journals, independent of one another, they admit to being afraid of Daphne. This might not constitute much if the girls weren't high schoolers. Seems more like the kind of thing a child would be scared of. Welsh writes about, and I quote, 'feeling bare hands around the house.' Yes. There's a particularly chilling entry about feeling a hand upon hers in the shower, and how she pulled the curtain aside, expecting to see her mom, but nobody else was in the bathroom. Yes, I understand. Young people are hysterical at all times, in their way. Everything's dramatic. I'm certainly not suggesting what she felt was real. But what stands out to me is: Both girls became completely obsessed with the story. Both girls started doing all they could *not* to mention Daphne by name. I mean to the day, to the hour. They both reference her in vague terms, call her 'her,' almost vigilantly refusing to write her actual name. It's a bit of a performance, how well they avoid what they really want to say. But eventually . . . they give in. Their entries go from long passages about Cynthia Cooper-Dyke and Sheryl Swoopes, then to vague mentions of *her*, then to a sort of half-and-half basketball-Daphne balance, all the way to a full-blown it's all they can confide about is their absolute fear of and fascination with Daphne. The journals are near mirror images of each other in that their obsessions grow at exactly the same rate. None of this is mentioned in the interviews with either of their parents, nor is it accounted for in the police reports. No, I'm absolutely *not* saying it was lazy work. It's completely justifiable that nobody took the Daphne stuff too seriously, but if you read these journals like you would a novel, let's say, you really see how involved these two ballers became. What am I saying exactly? Well, here's my current theory, though this is liable to change: I think whoever told Darren and Welsh about Daphne was doing more than just making small talk. I think he was likely an unstable man who deeply related to the story he told them. I think he staked them out first, knew they were friends and teammates, then talked to both, then moved in on both too. I think he was thinking, *I* can be Daphne. *I* can be the Samhattan bogeyman these two ballers fear. *I* can touch legend by way of *imitating* legend. You see? And I think he's still around now. I think we have a copycat who has come out of hibernation and is doing it again. A man in Samhattan, *being* Daphne."

McGowan listens as Pollen responds, but the chief is only reciting the usual playbook. Protect the girls. Find clues. Arrest suspects. Pollen doesn't sound particularly taken by this theory. McGowan knows it's because she hasn't read the journals. Not with McGowan's eye anyway.

"But there's a catch," McGowan says. "No human being can crush a person to death with their bare hands. So what's the next best thing? Well, tossing them from the parking structure is certainly one. The toxicology report says they'd been drinking, yes, but it was also inconclusive as to whether or not any drugs were used. So maybe they were. A fan, a *super* fan, disturbed for years and now feeling relevant and empowered by these girls, their fears, he *drugs* them, slips drugs into their drinks, drives them to the top of the structure, and shoves them off. Because, if you pay attention to the story of Daphne, you know it's all about too much thinking. About her. So this fan, this copycat, he plants the seed, believes it's growing (which the journals prove is true), and he carries out the closest killings he can to the type that would've been found in the myth itself. And these new cases? Something creative happened here too. Obviously, something was used. This is *not* bare hands. I need to think about who might *like* Daphne. Because whether or not you want to believe it, there *are* people who rank their favorite serial killers, their favorite urban legends, their favorite famous deaths. And almost all of those people are wonderful, contributing members of society. But in a city this size, simple math tells you there's gotta be some loose screws. And while I'm not saying I've solved something here, I am saying I want to explore this idea, this direction, immediately. So, with your okay, I'd like to start looking for fans of Daphne. Tonight. *Now.*"

But Pollen doesn't give McGowan the okay. Rather, she insists McGowan stay the course, to think *inside* the box, to stay vigilant and not be seduced by colorful loose ends. Pollen even goes so far as to give examples of past cases that should've been simple to solve, had law enforcement looked under their own noses.

Look under your nose, Pollen says. Not into the consciousness of a city.

After McGowan hangs up, this phrase sticks with her. Between the excitable inarticulation with which Chuck Larson mumbled his story and the obvious relief (and fear) on Janice Taylor's face when she handed over the file box, it does feel something like Samhattan is one communal consciousness, and the story of Daphne . . .

Suppressed.

Despite not receiving approval, McGowan leans forward on the couch, removes her phone from her pocket, scrolls to the death-scene photos of Tammy Jones, sets the phone on the table, picks up a pencil, and writes on an envelope for a credit card she's apparently qualified for:

What is a copycat killer if not a fan?

Look for fans.

Find a fan of Daphne's.

○ ○ ○

Outside in the street, in their squad car, the cops look at their phones. They've been out there all day, and, now, all night. Kit wishes they made her feel safer, but in both unbelievable cases, the killer left no trace of forced entry or any evidence of any kind.

It feels like, if she blinks, she could get killed.

And she can't stop thinking about Daphne.

Is Daphne going to kill me?

Nighttime makes thoughts like these inescapable.

She sits at the head of her bed, her back to the postered wall. Large, glossy pictures of WNBA stars frame her. There's Sue Bird making a sweet pass. Diana Taurasi in her orange Phoenix Mercury jersey. Lisa Leslie, dunking for L.A. These women feel most protective of all. Kit wishes Elena Delle Donne and Brittney Griner were standing watch in the driveway instead.

These thoughts of basketball, coupled with those of Daphne,

have Kit imagining the seven-foot woman in the post under the basket, wearing all denim. Kit has the ball and she's afraid to throw it down to her, fearing the woman will catch it, swing her elbows, show Kit her face.

"Stop it," Kit tells herself.

But there's no stopping it now.

She's heard of fear fatigue but has never really lived it. It's exhausting, worrying like this. It plays tricks on the mind. Makes you angry for being scared. Then angry for being angry.

She opens her computer and googles *Daphne Samhattan Michigan Obituary.*

Because if she can't stop herself from thinking about her, she may as well study.

Yet no results show. Unrelated Samhattan facts. Obituaries, yes, but nothing about Daphne. One Daphne does pop up: a Daphne Foster, who resided at 977 Muriel Way. She was eighty when she passed. And judging by the one photo, she was closer to five feet than seven.

"Myth," Kit says.

Fine. As it should be. Every city in every county in every state has a local legend. Hell, even some streets have legends the people on the next street don't know about.

This should make Kit feel better. It doesn't. Because sometimes new information, or coming to a conclusion, tells the truth in an indirect way: it's not the information itself but how you *feel* upon receiving it. Does Kit feel confident about writing it off as a myth? Does it feel right? Or does some deeper instinct tell her Daphne is real?

None of this feels right. Like glancing behind a curtain, seeing there this *name,* realizing it was always there and that she *knew* it was there but never thought to peek.

As if the entire city, Kit included, ultimately ostracized this outsider: deciding, subconsciously or not, never to speak of her again.

Kit looks to her journal. It's funny: she's never considered herself a writer, yet she does it almost every day. She identifies, first, with being an athlete. And like most girls her age, the two worlds don't entirely mix. Who has time for everything? Either you focus on your body or your mind, and Kit's fantasies never include the written word. Yet it helps. Always has. And whether she feels like writing or not, when she forces herself to do it, anxious thoughts can't quite touch her until she's done.

The concept of the Coming Doom is long gone. Doom is here. It's a constant hum now. And justifiably so: too much has happened in recent days. Success on the basketball court. The deaths of two teammates. Questions by the police, parents, friends.

It's a wonder she hasn't cracked.

Or maybe I have . . .

But her thoughts are interrupted: static voices from the police radio outside. The officers below must have their windows open. She moves quick to her own. Kit wants to hear this.

Outside, it's dark. The streets extend into individual black horizons. Kit eyes the officers.

Are they prepared? Would they be able to stop whoever comes?

Because she *is* coming, Kit thinks. And with the thought, that heat at the base of her neck.

She can't make out the words on the police radio. The tone of the dispatcher's voice could go either way: emphatic calm or a calm deadly seriousness. No way to tell.

She considers shouting down to them. Flat-out asking them for any news. Is Natasha okay? Is Dana? How many officers from Chaps are here to help? Any Goblin police? Chowder?

You're thinking too much.

Sure, but when is she not?

Back on the end of the bed, she does take her journal. And she writes. And while it doesn't quell the anxiety, it feels like the right thing to do. Above her desk (and above her desk drawer, yes, where pills await, yes, pills that, if she takes enough of them, could make it so she doesn't care at all anymore, isn't scared), flat to the wall, is her vanity mirror. It's shaped something like a heart, and Mom got it for her when she was much younger and Kit has always gone back and forth on it: it's the kind of mirror that a kid would have in her room, yet it's also a landmark of her own, a fixture in one of the only safe havens in Kit's life: her bedroom.

And in it, now she *does* see a writer. Not a child, not a little girl, but a woman, with strong features, in shape, her hair pulled back, some wisdom in the anxious face above the tank top she wears. Her hand moves across the page with elegance, grace, not too different from a piano player, she thinks, and for the first time in her life, Kit thinks: *You could do this forever.*

Writing, she means. And the act of putting real emotion, real fears, on paper. It's something she's never even explained to Dana, her closest friend, never even tried to describe the sensation of a second person, a friend, the journal, in the room with her, the moment the pen touches the page. Like she's truly *talking* to someone, a person who would understand her more than any doctor ever could, certainly more than the doctors she was sent to following her unfathomably panicked call to 911. Who calls 911 on themselves? And for the reasons Kit did? But never mind that now, forget it, because the journal is open, Jolly is listening, and Kit pours it all out. The horror she feels, the doubt in her assumptions, the lack of faith in the police outside, the worry for her parents and what finding their daughter crushed might do to them. It's awful, every bit of this nightmare Samhattan is experiencing at once. It's cruel and it's unfair and Kit just wants it to go away, oh Jolly, don't you see? Is there anything you can do? And isn't it kinda *right* that the city is going through this? When something is suppressed, it eventually comes out. When something is ignored, it eventually makes noise. And the sound is louder than any sound you can make, and the entire world is eclipsed by the bad decision you made (here, the whole city made, yes: Kit *believes* Samhattan and all who run it have intentionally buried the myth of Daphne).

There is nothing to be done but to wait for that noise, that unearthing, and, in this case, for Kit, to write.

She sees herself in the mirror again. Lean. Her fingers that are so fluent with the basketball, gripping the pen, expressing herself. Her shoulders are even with the posters on the wall behind her. Her legs are crossed. One sneaker held suspended above the carpet, the other flat to the floor. And beside that second shoe, tucked just under the bed, close enough to be seen, clearly, in the glass, a face looking directly at her.

"Hello, girl," the man says.

Kit leaps up. The journal falls to the floor. The entire world feels blurred, like it's moving too fast, like it's unreal, like this isn't happening.

But she knows it is.

"Help," she says.

She says it quiet the first time. A sound a shy person might make. Someone who's had half their voice destroyed by bare hands.

The man under the bed grips the box spring as Kit reaches the open window. As if he's going to crawl out now.

"HELP! SOMEONE'S IN HERE WITH ME!"

Below, in the drive, they move. Squad car doors open and close rapidly. Fast footsteps up the sidewalk. Mom and Dad, too, barreling up the stairs.

"SOMEONE'S IN MY ROOM!"

The eyes under the bed don't leave Kit's own.

"You shouldn't have done that," the man says.

"MOM! DAD! HELP!"

And he *is* sliding out from under now. And Kit sees his bald head, his dirty jacket and pants. His bare hands using the bed frame for leverage.

"You shouldn't have done that."

The bedroom door crashes open. The sound scares Kit into another scream. Mom and Dad rush in, the police behind them.

One of the officers draws her gun. Trains it on the man, still on the floor, not quite standing yet, not quite in reach of Kit.

"Don't move," the officer says. And the man does not move. But he doesn't look at the officer, either.

His eyes remained fixed on Kit's. His lips almost a smile.

He raises his arms above his head.

"Take me in," he says.

"Do not move," the officer repeats, even as the second officer steps even closer, handcuffs drawn.

"Don't shoot," the man says. "I have no weapon. Only my hands."

Yes. Bare-handed.

Mom and Dad are in the doorjamb, looking to Kit as though across a chasm.

This is him, their eyes betray. *This is the killer in our daughter's bedroom!*

The cops cuff him and drag him from the bedroom before Kit can move. The journal lies open on the floor. She feels violated. She has been. Every object of her room no longer safe, nostalgic, no longer her own.

It feels like he will always be here. In this room. In the glass.

Mom and Dad are suddenly beside her. She didn't even see

them move. They're asking her questions. Checking her for wounds. Outside in the street, the officers drag the man to the car. He complains. He laughs. He says the words "bare hands."

Lights go on in neighboring homes. People step outside to witness.

"What . . ." Kit says. "Who . . ."

The man is yelling now. He says:

"Daphne's on her way!"

He spits on a cop. The officers jam him into the back of the squad car and slam the door closed.

Kit at the window. Shaking. Can't speak right. Can't believe what she's seeing, hearing, thinking.

"Did he . . ." she says.

"They got him baby," Mom says. "They got him."

"Did he say her name?"

She looks over her shoulder, to her journal, as if the pages that bring her so much solace might turn on their own, might answer her, might calm the unbearable anxiety upon her.

Engines rev below.

Dad hugs her as Mom goes to the window.

"They got him," Mom says again. Then, "Jason? How did this happen?"

"Calm down, Kit," Dad says. "You're okay. Thank God you're okay."

But why did he tell her to calm down? Does she look crazy? Is her entire body visibly shaking?

Is she having a heart attack in front of her parents?

"Call 911," she says.

Because she's dying. Of course. Because this must be what dying feels like.

Hello, girl . . .

. . . Daphne is on her way.

Involuntarily, Kit remembers a thing she read about dogs, how some are embarrassed to die in front of their owners. Some run away when they know it's the end. But they don't run from death. They run from becoming the spectacle. From the indignity of death before witnesses.

Mom is now searching the closets, searching the halls.

Kit can't move. Can't make a decision. Keeps hearing the man saying Daphne's name.

Then Mom is back in the doorjamb.

"Do you smell that?" she asks. Then, "Smoke."

And Kit thinks of Natasha's story. Thinks of Daphne in denim, dead behind the wheel of her muscle car.

"He's not the killer," she says. Her voice doesn't sound like her own. Sounds like an older woman, a woman who's been through more than any teenager deserves.

"They got him," Dad says. But Kit sees it. As Mom and Dad exchange a glance. Uncertainty there. They want it to be true. They *want* it.

Kit wants it too.

But there are too many thoughts, too many feelings, to believe a single one.

"He wanted to see Daphne," Kit says. "He wanted to watch her kill me."

Her mind's in pieces: the man from beneath her bed in the bleachers, Daphne strangling people midcourt. The smell of the man in her room. The bald head beneath the bed, in her hands, as she shoots, as she asks the rim a question.

"Is Daphne going to kill me . . ."

Daphne with the ball down low. The orange of the ball against the blue of her jeans. Daphne doesn't turn and shoot, doesn't face the basket.

She crushes the ball in her bare hands.

"HE WANTED TO WATCH HER KILL ME!"

But it's not his perversion that freezes her. It's not even the fact that somehow he got in.

"He knows it's going to happen," Kit says. And her voice is the engine of an old, dying muscle car.

"No," Dad says. Even as Mom continues to check closets, behind doors. Even behind the posters of Kit's heroes.

Kit says, "Daphne is on her way . . ."

And she thinks of that perfect orange rim in the Samhattan High School gym. Thinks how no rim has ever lied to her. And that one, of all the rims in the world, never would.

"He knows, Dad . . ."

"No, Kit . . ."

"She's on her way."

"No."

"He knows."

o o o

Kennedy Lichtenstein has already graduated Samhattan High School. But because the rule for the summer basketball league is age (under eighteen) rather than high-school status, she was allowed to play with the team in the summer league after receiving her diploma. Kennedy *is* now eighteen years old. Her birthday is today.

She doesn't really care about sports. Then again, she doesn't really care about a lot of things. Money, movies, cars, boys. She thinks love is a form of mental illness (she's lost more than one friend to love), though she does like songs and poems about it. She's never been in love herself, and she's in no hurry to find it. She has friends, a solid core she's known since she was a kid, some of whom she's meeting up with tonight. Her circle has always existed on the true fringe, not where the burnouts smoke joints, not where the thespians put on shows, but where the rest of Samhattan can hardly see them, in the corners of the city that aren't corners at all, the high school halls, even the bedrooms of the homes they grew up in. Still, Kennedy has never felt like an outsider. What she does feel, when asked by others (including the unnecessary therapists she's been assigned many times), is content. When she considers her own worldview (that is, mindfulness over gratification), she feels warm. She likes who she is, she knows she needs work, and she's excited to do it. She sings, she writes occasional poetry, and sometimes she intentionally does nothing at all. To Kennedy Lichtenstein, everybody is a rough draft, and as long as they come from a place of kindness, their story will be written well.

And basketball? Well, it's all right. The sport itself isn't a big deal to her. She enjoyed having a touchstone after-school activity on dreary days, but, like the rest of Samhattan High, the other players rarely acknowledged her unless it was with a deliberate degree of sympathy. She played her senior year, but only got into a game once, when the team was down seventeen points with forty-six seconds to go. She didn't touch the ball in those forty-six seconds. Kit Lamb (who hit that baller free throw to win the summer league, that was fun) tried to get Kennedy the ball in her debut, gave her a soft enough pass she might be able to catch with her elbows. But the players from East Kent weren't paying attention to the fact the Samhattan fans were cheering Kennedy's first and only appearance, a show of solidarity she thought was pretty cool. One of the East Kent Carolers stole the soft pass and brought it the other way for a missed layup. It was nice of Kit to try.

The crowd gave Kennedy a standing ovation anyway.

Because Kennedy Lichtenstein playing basketball at all was a big deal to them.

Because Kennedy Lichtenstein was born without hands.

Hands, bare hands, have been a real topic lately. But hands are something she's never known, and so, in a way, she doesn't miss them like most people think she would. That said, every day she witnesses more efficient lives than her own, with the oft-taken-for-granted luxury of ten fingers. It's all right, she tells people when they get personal enough with her to ask. She doesn't begrudge anybody the caution they use when bringing it up any more than she would herself for asking someone born without eyes. Kennedy understands curiosity. And she doesn't mind being one herself. Way she sees it: the way technology moves these days, she'll be getting a set of bionics before she reaches twenty-four. That is, if she even wants them.

Right now, intentionally immobile in the shadows along the gates to Samhattan's centerpiece graveyard, she looks to the ends of her sweatshirt sleeves, tied up at their ends, and would have it no other way.

There once was a time she regularly searched videos featuring prosthetics, and progress in the field, but she quit doing that three years ago. The day will come, she tells herself, and when it does, it'll be huge news. She'll know what the news is because the people in her life will be smiling before they reveal it. Sometimes she fantasizes about that moment. Other times, not so much. The amazement at how she's learned to do things her own way isn't exclusive to others: Kennedy wows herself all the same.

Like right now as she hops the fence into the cemetery.

There's nothing to it, really, though none of her friends have ever quite got the hang of it. You just use your elbows like you do the tips of your shoes. And now you've got four points of leverage to climb. Arms tucked tight to the body, you've got a more efficient roll over the top. And almost all Kennedy's landings are clean.

Tonight, she's the first of her friends to show. Birthday or not, she always is. And she's been sneaking into "Town Square" for at least eight years. A lot of Samhattanites do. It's a rite of passage for those born under the slate sky. But while some locals are tired of the police presence (the cemetery is searched somewhat routinely), Kennedy thinks it's worth the risk. She's often wondered if the cops aren't lenient with her; others have been arrested, but not her. And while she's not a fan of preferential treatment, in this instance she'll take it. It's not uncommon to observe headlights gliding along the square late at night. Some are cops. Some are not. But, once you get deep enough between the stones, the trees obscure the city, and you forget all about that.

"Besides," she says, "they're busy right now."

It's true: the Samhattan police are occupied these days. Yet there are no cops stationed outside her home. Even now: overlooked. But it makes sense, she thinks. It's not easy to see the corners of a round world, she knows. And she gives the department the benefit of the doubt on this one: having skipped school with the very people she's set to meet up with tonight, she missed the team photo. This means, of course, Kennedy isn't *in* the picture that was taken from the wall of Tammy Jones's bedroom. This, coupled with the fact that she is no longer a student at Samhattan High, and Kennedy Lichtenstein is persona non-thought-of. For that, she feels a little outside the experience. A location she is familiar with.

Upon the path now, the gravel white in the scant moonlight that breaks the canopy of trees, she thinks of Beck Nelson, the underclassman who texted her that the other ballers were talking about (of all people) Daphne.

Kennedy's a Samhattanite through and through. She was born here, raised here, could walk the streets with her eyes closed. Seeing that name in the text, she had to admit: it chilled her. Not because she believed in some brutal ghost story but because Kennedy just heard the name recently, for the first time in a long time. It's a name from her past, but Kennedy isn't one to forget. In fact, she prides herself on knowing the city's history, the new restaurants in town, the successes of any locals. You didn't have to be part of the daily grind to pay attention to it. Yet this name . . . and the sense that she'd long overlooked a topic specific to her hometown, feels wrong.

And what's more, Beck Nelson confirmed the information Kennedy was given only days before Tammy Jones was murdered:

Sorry to bring it up. We're not supposed to think of her.

It's the reason she's come early and alone to her own birthday party. Kennedy wants to clear her mind of that name.

Daphne, she thinks but does not say.

It's a trick she learned from Patricia Maxwell at Third-and-Fourth-Eye Books. Patricia, a class behind Kennedy, is wise beyond her years. She recommended (then sold) a book explaining (in rich, smart detail) how a person chooses what they think about. *Your Mind, Your Land* blew Kennedy's mind, indeed. It described bandwidth of thought like it was real estate, and says the landowner gets to choose what's built there.

Not a bad philosophy, Kennedy thinks. And better: a tenet of the book was *never to run* from a thought but to endure it, let it live, then let it die. If you're scared? Be scared. Don't be angry at yourself for being scared. Jealous? Be jealous. Don't be ashamed. As the author put it: a lot of uninvited guests claim that bandwidth, that land, if you don't make a few rules.

Kennedy is scared right now. And she allows herself to be.

For her, the name Daphne isn't quite as vague as it is for, say, Beck Nelson. And while Beck told her about the sleepover, about Natasha Manska's story (a sleepover Kennedy didn't attend), Kennedy didn't tell Beck what she'd heard.

And why not? What stopped her?

It was almost as if, being a Samhattanite, she'd had it drilled into her head *not* to speak of Daphne, even with someone who was doing most of the talking.

Walking the graveyard gravel now, she recalls the time her mother scolded her, fifteen years ago: *If you ever speak the name Daphne, I will spank you blue.*

Yes. A story you weren't supposed to tell. Weren't even supposed to think about.

A story everybody wanted buried.

Yet . . . Zach . . . at work . . . only days before Tammy Jones . . .

A shift at Hi-Fi Grocery meant more money toward heading west. Now, graduated, that's where Kennedy longs to be. *My two favorite things to hear from the mouths of my friends,* she's known to say, *are (1) I've quit my job, and (2) I'm moving somewhere I've never been.* This is also true of herself: if there's one thing Kennedy respects, it's new phases. Plans for a new life. The nerve to attempt it all.

Kennedy Lichtenstein wants to see the world in full.

Still, Hi-Fi is good to her. For now. It's paving the way for those dreams. Giving her options. Giving her money. Money that will eventually be exchanged for a bus ticket.

But good as it's been, Hi-Fi is also where she heard Daphne's name for the first time since she was a kid.

In fact, she read it before she heard it. Written in black marker on the wall in the breakroom, the letters chilled her, bringing back that formerly buried memory of her mother's serious face. She'd been up front at the registers when her co-worker Zach Gold suddenly appeared at her side, breathless, insisting she come with him. He physically pulled her by the arms, even as she tried to write this urgency off as Zach's dramatic nature. What could be so important? Kennedy has long known Zach Gold is in love with her, which may be interesting, which may be flattering, but she has no plans of dating and there's not a chance in Samhattan she'd settle for anything right now. She has plans, after all.

Where are you taking me? she asked.

Zach hurried her to the back of the store. He took her through the plastic saloon doors, down the concrete hall to the breakroom.

Did you see *this?* he said, pointing to the wall by the microwave.

Kennedy saw it then:

DAPHNE LIVES

She read it again. The way it was written, she thought maybe it was the name of a band.

Okay, she said. *So?*

But she'd felt it. A brief chill. That name . . .

This is bad, Zach said.

But the zeal with which Zach took his bagger job didn't help his cause: it almost came off as funny.

Yeah, funny how scared he was.

Do you know who did this? he asked.

How would I know?

She saw a dark spark in his eyes then. Not only had he recognized she wasn't taking this seriously, he saw an opportunity to explain why she should.

So, he told her the story of Daphne. And as he did, Kennedy started thinking of her mother, scolding her, after having picked her up from Meegan Elementary.

Zach's story was long and involved and he knew details Kennedy could never have known. She'd never dreamed there was this much to know about this name, a name that had been lodged so far into her subconscious, she was surprised she recognized it at all.

And then, something unexpected: there in the breakroom,

skinny Zach Gold nervously pointing to the name, talking a mile a minute about how he didn't like it, how it shouldn't be there, how people weren't supposed to talk about Daphne, how people weren't even supposed to *think* about her, Kennedy found herself *interested* in the story. She noted the careful, almost regretful tone Zach took when he got to the part about the seven-footer killing without any weapon, only using her . . .

Bare hands.

Kennedy looked to her own lack of hands, then thought (not for the first time) that some people took theirs for granted. If more people understood how precious their hands were, they wouldn't do bad things with them. She studied the letters on the wall as Zach used words like "dangerous" and "crisis" and said they had to "contain" this. But Kennedy didn't understand. Contain what? Zach was talking as if Daphne were a disease. He was sweating and his voice cracked with anxiety and his expression wasn't so different from that of her mother's, that day.

A Samhattan myth, okay. One she should've known more about. Okay. But Kennedy happened to be keyed into the mind-as-real-estate idea, and so it bothered her how much room Zach's story was taking up in her head.

It stuck with her for the duration of her shift. His urgency, his passion, his belief.

Still, this Kennedy could live with. She could also handle the idea that something a little weird happened at work. Zach had gotten all worked up over some graffiti in the breakroom. But the part Kennedy wasn't prepared for was how the name, brought to her attention, then examined within, made her feel.

It almost tickled the mind, that name. Bare fingers on the brain.

Who wrote it on the wall?

Later in her shift, alone in the breakroom to eat, the words looked like they were written in spider:

DAPHNE LIVES

She sat facing the microwave counter, the writing in view. She thought of those other two words too:

Bare hands.

It was almost ridiculous, right? Almost . . . too inviting. How could she not be immediately interested in the legend of a woman who used her hands, the very things Kennedy Lichtenstein did *not* have, to kill? Kennedy studied the wall as she ate. The words were spectacularly ugly. Almost like the letters were rendered with ink at the tip of a greasy finger. And the wall was stained, too, with employee meals, messes made over months. As she stared, she internalized. The name, yes, but the story too. Kennedy was no stranger to living life on the fringe. She wouldn't dream of existing anywhere else. From the fringe you had a great view of what really mattered. You recognized drama. Futility. Kindness and intelligence too.

Did Daphne see truth out there? In her day? From her fringe?

Later, when Kennedy punched out for the night, as she took her time card from the slot, she saw, on the wall behind it, the faded impression of those very same letters. Though smaller, the impact was twice as big:

DAPHNE LIVES

Someone had tried to scrub these away. She could tell. Zach was already gone for the night and even if he wasn't, she didn't think it was a good idea to show him.

Or did he know? And a stranger, more curious thought: Did he write them himself?

Now, walking the gravel road that splits the cemetery into two equal halves, the sky dark, it's easy for Kennedy to examine how powerful the name became in just a few days' time. She started looking for it in other places and finding it. First, at work: Behind boxes on the shelves in back. Under a register. In a staff bathroom stall. Then, in the bathroom stall of a bar on Sixth Street. In a dressing room at Just Jackets at the mall. And each time she found it, Zach's story got a little more real. As if Daphne, the woman, grew another inch with each unearthing of her name. The night Tammy Jones was killed, Kennedy had started rereading the book about mental real estate, *Your Mind, Your Land,* using the Daphne story as an experiment, attempting to make physical room in her head, to "evict the thought" rather than accepting it as her burden. But it seemed the more she tried, the harder it stuck. And the longer this went on, the deeper Daphne's roots descended, until it seemed Daphne owned this land as much as Kennedy did. By the time Melanie Jack was killed, Kennedy had fallen deep into self-examination, wondering, in an almost scientific way, why she couldn't stop thinking about Daphne.

She even bought a jean jacket of her own.

She wears it now as she passes far enough into the cemetery so that the dark trees have become solid dark walls, and the city of Samhattan, her hometown, is erased. Kennedy doesn't consider herself neurotic, though she recognizes this as a neurotic moment in time. She knows other ballers from the team have issues of their own; it's one of the perks of living on the fringe. From here, she sees. She also understands that right now they all have every right and reason to be afraid.

Two ballers have been killed. And if the rumors are to be believed, bare hands were used on both.

Kennedy looks at the cuffs of her jean jacket, rolled up to her wrists. The deeper shadows accept her, and she knows her friends will get here soon. She wants to stop thinking about Daphne by the time they do.

She knows she won't.

And more: No, Kennedy wasn't at Dana's the night Natasha told the others the story Zach told her, but she heard enough the day they were all questioned by Detective McGowan to know the name is no longer only on her mind alone.

It's everywhere in Samhattan.

As she walks the cemetery, confident in the tools she was born with, trusting in the person she is, she thinks of the lessons from the book.

Your Mind, Your Land

Yes. She believes in this because she must. With all her heart she believes she is capable of focusing on what she decides to focus on and not what the world tells her she should. It's how she's lived her entire life: *outside.* Like Daphne. Maybe. Yes. Even the city police overlook her as they stand guard outside every other baller's house. Even while being part of a team, Kennedy has retained her autonomy.

Your mind, your land.

Indeed.

She hears her friends now. Her lifelong friends whom she has been hiding all this from. There's the rattle of the fence. Do they hop it the way she taught them? The way she does it? The gravel crunches behind her. But when she looks back to where they should be, they're not there. All the better. The cemetery shadows and the deep pockets of trees. The dead, buried here at the center of town. What a concept. She wonders if she'll miss that out west. Will she frequent graveyards there? At night? On her birthdays?

Growing up in Samhattan does things to a person. Kennedy knows. And sometimes she takes pride in this.

She reaches her favorite part of the cemetery, and so she stops walking. It's where the city lights just make it through the branches and gift a thin white beam upon the excess dirt beneath the heavy trees. She's reached the far end of the cemetery now. The most private of spots. Her mind, her land. Here where the excess dirt is kept. She hears her friends upon the gravel. She wants to touch the earth tonight. Wants to remember her eighteenth birthday, this part of it, alone.

She bends at the waist and touches the dirt with both wrists, the cool, dark earth that she believes will eventually be used to bury the next Samhattanite to die. She closes her eyes and hopes it's not another baller.

I'm gonna miss you, Samhattan, she thinks, with intention. *I'm gonna miss your gray skies, your macabre city planning. But most of all, I'll miss your corners, your pockets, your fringes. I know them well. And to me, they are home. So, thank you for your borderlands, your edges, your outer rim . . . for hosting me for eighteen years.*

She's up again. She looks to the dirt at her handless wrists.

But there are hands there now.

"Hey," she says. Her friends are here. The smell of smoke and alcohol tell her they got a head start on the party.

Happy birthday, Kennedy Lichtenstein.

One of them is pressed up behind her. Their arms against hers. Their hands her own for a moment. A memory. A present.

"Shell," Kennedy says. And for a moment she loves her friend Shell in the same way she thinks Zach Gold loves her. In a crazy, young way, she wants to bring Shell with her out west. Wants to bring everyone.

New land out there. New mind. New life.

Daphne Lives

"Aw, Shell . . ."

She leans back into her friend, looks to the hands, and almost laughs at how big they are. Do hands always look so big, so clumsy, to those who have them?

She inhales the aromas of smoke and booze. The smell of youth in a cemetery at night. The smell of an eighteenth birthday begun.

Kennedy thinks of Zach Gold. She doesn't mean to, and she wants him off her land. But he's pointing, in her mind's eye, he says:

That's also the smell of someone listening to music in their car long after the sun's gone down.

"Shell?"

The hands extending from her rolled-up jean jacket sleeves are big. Yes. Too big. Large enough to palm a basketball in each. Large enough to crush those basketballs too.

Kennedy makes to turn, to face her friend, to hear the word "surprise" in the way only Shell can say it.

But the hands come up. Too fast. And even as they clamp to her face, even as they grip the sides of her skull, Kennedy thinks it's fascinating, the sensation of hands, these hands, any, being her own.

She does not say *help* or *please*. Instead:

"Daphne."

Even as the hands begin to pull her head apart.

As they do, she imagines that land stretching, imagines a break in the sky over her mind, *her* land, and she knows now *this* is how to get rid of an unwanted thought, *this* is how to get that name out of her head.

She hears the rattling of the fence, her friends no doubt hopping where she did the same. But she has time for only one more thought:

The story of Daphne is wrong.

No outsider would do this to a friend on the fringe.

Then, an unfathomable sound. Her mind. Her land.

And even as Kennedy's cracked head falls to her favorite part of the cemetery, it occurs to her that Daphne is no friend.

And never was.

And the words written in the breakroom seem to crawl up the

messy walls, spiders after all, they crawl everywhere in Hi-Fi Grocery, then out the front sliding doors to all of Samhattan.

Daphne Lives

The last thing she feels is sorrow. Not for herself, but for the city she was saving up money to leave.

As Kennedy Lichtenstein dies, she fears for all who call Samhattan home, and for all who know its legends by name. And she thinks,

This is not excess dirt . . . this is not my grave . . .

. . . it's hers.

○ ○ ○

Kit Lamb's Journal—Don't Think About a

Don't think about a blue raven.

Isn't this what people say? That it's impossible not to think about whatever you're told not to think about?

Don't think about a blue raven.

But you did, Jolly. You did.

Do you know that if Melanie or Tammy had died in any ordinary way, I'd think about their deaths every day for the rest of my life? Do you know that one day I'd be walking the streets of a city and I'd enter a restaurant and as the host asked me how many I'd think,

One. Alone. Just me. No Melanie or Tammy because they died back when we were in high school?

But . . . don't think about band patches on the wings of a blue-jean raven . . .

Here: Don't think about the deaths of two friends.

And definitely do not think about who killed them.

Is this fair?

I'm angry, Jolly.

I'm thinking of a blue raven. It flies from one side of my mind to the other and it perches on ledges I didn't know I had.

There was a man in my room, Jolly. Under my bed.

Far as I know the police still think it's him, but they'll find out soon enough. In fact, Mom and Dad are talking about something serious downstairs and I think one of the cops from the driveway is in the house with them down there, and so maybe something happened tonight and if so, then I guess it wasn't the man from under my bed after all.

JOLLY, guess what?

I'm thinking of the blue face of a blue raven.

It's got long black hair and it smells like the bar and its feathers are denim and it flies from one end of my mind to the other, the sound of its wings like the sound of jeans hanging on a clothesline in a storm.

What sound does anxiety make, Jolly?

They're talking about the cemetery downstairs. I don't wanna know what happened. I'm afraid to look at my phone. I don't wanna see a text from Dana saying Natasha was crushed, a text from Natasha saying the same about Dana.

No new messages. Not yet.

But I'm thinking of a blue raven.

Are you?

It's tall, Jolly, so tall, and the more you think about it, the more it flies. DON'T, they say. DON'T THINK ABOUT A BLUE-JEAN RAVEN.

But that's all I can do.

That's the future, isn't it? I wasn't hysterical when I said she's going to get me. I know she is. I'm small, weak, meek. She's a seven-foot bird with a taste for blood and she plucks us from the dirt like bugs.

I can't do it. I'm not strong enough to survive this. If she attacks . . . WHEN she

OH NO

OH MY . . . NO, NO

I just heard the name "Kennedy" from downstairs. Oh no, Jolly. No, please no. What did Kennedy Lichtenstein EVER DO WRONG TO ANYBODY IN HER LIFE? Oh my God, Jolly. Please no.

That's the news. Has to be.

Oh no.

I look under the bed. No one there, but there was a man who wanted to watch me die.

I look out the window. Red and blue (jean) lights swirling. Everything is police now. EVERYTHING.

Did Kennedy get hurt? Is that what happened?

I'm afraid to find out. I'm afraid not to find out. I wanna take enough pills so I can't think about anything ever again.

Hey . . .

I have pills in my desk, Jolly.

I can knock myself out.

Should I?

Oh God, please say Kennedy is okay. Oh God, I'm too afraid to ask.

I'm thinking of a blue raven. It flies from one end of my mind to the other and I can't hear it coming until it's already right up on me and I don't want to know any more and I don't want to try any harder and I'm walking to the desk because I don't deserve this and Melanie and Tammy (and please NOT Kennedy please) DIDN'T DESERVE THIS and the bird is not going away, Jolly, the blue-jean raven is literally not going to go away, not so long as we tell ourselves:

DON'T THINK ABOUT A BLUE RAVEN

o o o

"Jesus Christ, Nat," Quincy Manska says. As Natasha's mom, she says this a lot. "That's a heavy story." She's been staring at the grass for some time following what Natasha told her. But there's more in Quincy's face than simply internalizing the words. It's clear she has thoughts of her own on the subject. Natasha wonders how clear those thoughts are.

"What do you know about this?" Natasha asks. Because she has to. Because Quincy looks like she's figuring out an invisible Rubik's Cube.

"I don't know for sure," Quincy says. It's weird; she usually speaks with total confidence. It's a trait Natasha's inherited. "But I know that's not the right story."

The two are in the backyard. Dad is inside on the phone, debating with other parents about the man caught in Kit's house. The police believe the killer is a man. Most Samhattanites think the man under Kit's bed is the killer. Yet the police are still out front.

It used to be they were a phone call away. Then in the street. Now in the driveway.

"What do they know that we don't?" Dad asks. "Why haven't they made an official announcement? The man was *under Kit Lamb's bed*. What more do they need?"

"How the fuck should I know the real story?" Natasha says. She's impatient. Scared. Not least of all because she wasn't expecting her mom to react this way. It almost feels like, by telling her mom the same thing she told her baller teammates, she activated something in her. Like she wound up a talking doll. How long has her mom known what she's about to say? And why does it feel like, not only is this the first time Quincy is going to say it but that the alcohol she grips tightly is more responsible for the telling than the fact that people are dying?

How long has Quincy wanted to tell this story?

And why was she scared to tell it?

Yet . . . it's more like Quincy is *marveling* at her own thoughts. Her memories. Whatever she knows.

"I never tied the two together . . ." she says.

"What, Mom? The two what?"

Her mom is the one person who gets under Natasha's skin. Natasha acts tough with her friends. And in a way, she *is* tough with them. She's funny, crass, speaks her mind. But there's something about Quincy Manska that drives her nuts. Dad says it's because they're alike. But Dad can piss off.

"Do *you* know the real story?" Natasha asks.

Quincy does the thing that shuts Natasha up. The only thing.

She looks at her like she's dumb.

"Yes . . . maybe," Quincy says. She's wearing a white nightgown, got a tall vodka-cranberry in hand. Quincy Manska is the smartest person in most rooms. To Natasha's dismay, they both know this.

But Natasha respects the hell out of it too. Especially when push comes to shove. And right now, it has.

"So . . ." Natasha says. "Talk to me. Please."

Because Natasha is done playing around.

Quincy breathes deep, makes a face Natasha has never seen her wear before. Looks like the face one might make before leaping from a cliff, having told nobody of the decision to do so beforehand.

Yet she looks at peace with her decision to speak, if only because there's no other choice now.

"If I have all this right," she says. "And I'm just putting it together . . . then she wasn't any saint. Get that idea out of your head right now. This isn't the story of some poor eccentric woman who ran into a bunch of closed-minded conservatives. Daphne was . . ." She marvels again, seems to be piecing old broken memories together. Yet she becomes convinced of them as soon as they are restored. "Daphne was evil."

"What do you mean? You knew her?"

"I can't believe I'm saying this but . . . I know I'm right now. Nat . . . I crossed paths with her when I was a little girl."

"What? What the fuck? Mom, how much do you know about this? How real is—"

"You wanna hear the story or you wanna practice your curse words?"

It's like Quincy is trying to be herself. Trying to be funny. But Natasha sees fear in her mother's face. And it's horrifying to witness.

"Go ahead. Sorry."

Quincy goes ahead: "There used to be a candy store on Willoughby. The kind of place little shits like me begged to go. There was nothing like Sandy's Candy when you were growing up. We're talking bright-pink façade, gold-trimmed windows, displays to make those under four feet tall salivate. You had to be beneath this height"—she held up an arm—"for it to sink into your soul like religion, and whoever was in charge of marketing ought to be shot for subliminal warfare. I didn't leave my grandparents alone about Sandy's. I dreamed of Sandy's. Sometimes I even pretended I wanted to visit other places in town just so I could get a clean *look* at Sandy's. Even on the days I was told no, I still needed a fix. A glance at the gilded boxes in the windows. It got to the point where people in Samhattan were worried about Sandy's. Felt like a pusher had moved in. Or like a topless dancer was parading about town, tassels twirling. It was just too much, Nat. Tailor-made. We were nuts for it the way people are nuts for television shows, only you couldn't just turn on the set and tell the kids to shut the fuck up. Nobody was shutting up about this place. And so . . . your great-grandparents, God bless them both, took me there regularly. And while it was small enough to roam free inside, it was also designed a bit like a maze; short rows upon rows of technicolored packag-

ing, all glossy plastic, the ceiling lights no doubt angled intentionally, the whole place with an unforgettable otherworldly glow.

"But, most important, the rabbit suits.

"Man-sized, mind you. In the four corners of the shop, these
giant pastel rabbits had individual characteristics; one was cross-
eyed, another was winking, one was candy blue, another caramel
brown, another sugar pink. When I think now of who was in
charge of Sandy's (there was no woman named Sandy), I think of
those fucking rabbits. I think of where they stood, so that at about
the exact moment you got completely lost in all that confection,
you found yourself facing one of them. They weren't *quite* under
the lights: they were positioned to be partly in the shadows, so that
there was a sense the rabbit was in motion, too, or had just arrived
at the same time you did. This was breathtaking stuff for a little
girl. These sentinels guarded the candy, see? They were the good
guys, no matter how bad they looked. My grandparents laughed
about how cruddy they were, their matted fur, their cracked-egg
eyes. My God, I can still see Grandma touching the arm of the
green one, her head inches from the fat tongue hanging from its
crazy face. I can still see Grandpa pretending to be afraid of the
pink one. The more I think about it (and I haven't thought about
this in quite some time), these images are iconic to me. My grandparents laughing in unison the way they used to, the reason everybody to this day talks about them like they were Romeo and Juliet."

"Mom. Daphne."

The name hangs in the break in Quincy's narrative. A sense that
Natasha has unknowingly brought a shovel to a grave, unearthed a
story she had no intention of revealing. And Quincy, just as
shocked to be telling it:

"One afternoon, Grandpa took me to Sandy's alone. Grandma
was getting her hair done up the street at a place called Samhattan
Hair. Nobody ever accused our hometown of being creative with

the names. She was talking a mile a minute the moment she sat down, and Grandpa and I looked at one another across the waiting area and he winked and I knew we were going to Sandy's without even asking for it. We snuck out and hurried up the street and the moment we stepped inside, those bells chimed, and I bolted to the closest aisle, leaving Grandpa in my dust. Well . . . after enough turns, I got lost. Switchbacks come to mind, as if the register at the center of that store was at the bottom of a mountain."

Quincy seems to be remembering as she's speaking. There's no humor here. No levity. It looks to Natasha like she's weighing whether she wants to know how her own story ends.

"You okay, Mom?" Because she has to ask it. Because she's never seen her mom look exactly this way before.

"It was the cotton-candy-blue rabbit," Quincy says, eyes now locked on her glass of vodka. "I came racing out of a row of yellow packages and came to a skidding stop, a couple feet from Big Blue. You know how they say cats and dogs know when something's wrong?"

"Yeah."

"Yeah, well, I could tell right away it was different."

"What was?"

"The rabbit suit. It was . . . fuller. Taller. The ears were mashed up against the ceiling and they looked more like hyena ears, folded at the top. Usually the face rested about Grandpa-high. But that day . . ."

"Oh fuck," Natasha says.

"What's worse: The midsection was showing. I'd never noticed before the legs were separate from the belly; I blindly, childishly, justifiably assumed it was all one body, all one *real rabbit*. But under those shitty lights, there was a human belly showing, above where the legs began. There were other breaks in the suit too: Gloves not quite touching the arms. Feet not touching the legs.

And the neck. Oh, the neck was the worst of it. Seeing that human neck, knowing that behind that manic mask was the face of a human being. A person big enough to touch the ceiling was inside that suit. And crazy enough to wear it."

"Jesus."

"Christ."

Out front, beyond the yard's wood fence, the police radio crackles. Natasha watches her mom closely. It's like Quincy is literally gaining energy as she speaks. Like she's revving up an old engine.

Why hadn't her mom told her this before? More important: Why does it seem like she forgot to?

"I'm remembering things, Nat," Quincy says. "As I'm telling them. It's like . . . everyone told you to forget about a mean motherfucker from your past and you were just young enough to listen to them. Yet here she is . . . stepping out of the fog on my past. And I see her and I know this was no dream. Nat . . . there was just one person in town tall enough to touch the ceiling of that candy store."

"She was real then," Natasha says.

Quincy doesn't seem to hear her. Plows through the question.

"I took off. I ran back the way I'd come, past stacks of vanilla fudge in yellow boxes, and took a hard left into the sours aisle. This was typically where Grandpa would be. He had one sweet tooth and one sweet tooth only: sour. But he wasn't there. Nobody was. And I took a left, got lost again, found myself amongst the Peeps. You know what? That store music, or any music like it, still makes me nervous to this day."

Quincy takes a gulp. Plows ahead.

"I took another left. And another. And another. And I came to that blue rabbit again. Seven feet tall at the shortest. That belly, those wrists, those ankles, and that fleshy neck. In those days, children didn't have the same variety of entertainments you grew up with. If there was one game I knew, it was Hide-and-Seek. And I sure as hell knew when someone was hiding."

"From who?"

"How could I have known? But I know now. I *remember,* Nat." She laughs. Almost angrily. Almost relieved too. "This is what I meant when I said I hadn't tied the two stories together. And you're going to think me terrible for not doing it sooner. But news didn't travel like it does today. These days, I'd shout for help. But then? How could I have known a seven-foot woman in a jean jacket had been spotted breaking into a house where a newborn slept soundly? How could I have known the Samhattan Police were actively looking for the very woman I saw hiding in a blue bunny suit in the darkest corner of the candy store? And that's not the worst of it. Because your great-grandfather called to me then. *Quincy!* He said. *Where the hell did you go?* And as I opened my mouth to holler back, the rabbit moved. It raised those blue paws toward me and I froze."

"Fuck, Mom."

"You gotta understand. The woman on the news. Daphne, yes. And the woman in the store. I just didn't think . . . I ran. Again. I took a left instead of a right and a right instead of a left and I was sweating and I was close to tears, and God as my witness, Nat, I ran into another little girl, lost in the rows of candy. She was my age, I remember that. I asked her how we get to the front of the store, but she didn't know. We both stood up on our tiptoes but couldn't see over the shelves. *I'm gonna go that way,* I said. *You wanna follow me?* She didn't. I told her good luck, she went her way, and I went mine. I wouldn't see her face again until I saw it on the Samhattan Nightly News."

"Fuck. Mom!"

"Same hair, same look in her eye, as if she'd had her school picture taken the very day I'd seen her. MISSING, they said. Brea Delany. Last seen entering Sandy's Candy Store. And whether or not I thought to connect the two, the person in the rabbit suit, those paws coming at me, with the girl I had seen, the girl gone *missing*, whether or not I tied it all together *then*, I sure as shit haven't done so since. In fact, I've thought of Sandy's Candy a hundred times, and a hundred times I've felt queasy with the memory of those small rows, those tall shelves, the shadows in the corner of the store. But not once have I thought I was somehow witness to something as horrible as I now realize I was. And not once did I think of the woman Daphne breathing inside that suit."

"Daphne was a . . . kidnapper?"

"Who knows what else she was."

Natasha doesn't know what to say. Her mother doesn't mince words. She doesn't lie.

"Who told you the story you heard?" Quincy asks. There's an edge to her voice. A dark spark in her eye.

"This guy Zach at Hi-Fi Grocery," Natasha says. "Last I went."

Quincy takes another gulp of vodka and it's clear to Natasha she's clearing her throat for the end of this story.

"Turns out Brea Delany was the little sister of one of Samhattan High School's top athletes."

"Wait. Mom . . . what are you saying?"

"Well, turns out Brea's older sister played—"

"Don't say it," Natasha says. She puts her hands over her ears. "Don't fucking say basketball, Mom."

"Twenty-two points a game. One of the best seasons in Samhattan High history. On her way to that anyway. But when the police couldn't find anything to pin on Daphne, Amira Delany and her friends took matters into their own hands."

"Why did they think it was her?"

Something like tears well in Quincy's eyes. She doesn't cry; it's the ice of her memories thawing.

Natasha stands up.

"Jesus, *Mom*. Are you telling me you're responsible for what happened to Daphne? You told the police about her?"

Quincy squints up at her.

"When the fuck did I say that? There was a security camera in the back of Sandy's. Clear as day the seven-foot rabbit took the little girl out that way, stuffed her into her muscle car. Drove off like a phantasm back to hell."

"The basketball team," Natasha says. "The fucking *team* killed Daphne."

"They did."

"And what happened to the team?"

"I don't remember, Nat. I barely remembered everything I just told you until you brought it up."

The police radio crackles again, this time with more urgency. More clarity too. Natasha looks to the house, through the house, it seems, to the police out front.

"Town Square," the dispatcher says.

"Something happened at the cemetery," Natasha says.

They get up and move to the fence for a closer listen. As they peer over, the officer speaking into the CB turns in her seat, blocking their view. But they still hear her when she says:

"This while the man's in custody."

o o o

Detective McGowan sits across a small metal table from the man pulled out from under Kit Lamb's bed, Peter Lords. The man's voice, twiggy, thin, is as out of place as his enthusiasm. Lords has a boyish quality McGowan wasn't expecting and is a little bit disgusted by. The least he can do is act the part of the criminal he is.

The news of Kennedy Lichtenstein's death, carried out in the same way as Melanie Jack's and Tammy Jones's, and ruled to have occurred while Peter Lords was in custody, means Peter Lords is not Kennedy's killer. But Melanie's? Tammy's?

McGowan has found a fan of Daphne. That's crystal clear. But is he the right one?

Or the only?

The interrogation room here at the Samhattan Police Department is nicer than the one in Chaps, where Carla McGowan physically assaulted a woman accused of burglary, a suspect she was entirely sure of. In that room, the table was plastic, stained with coffee rings and ashes. The floor that table stood upon was cracked and the lone overhead bulb buzzed like a single large fly. The woman was on video inside the electronics store after hours. She was the only person on tape and McGowan was long tired of loopholes sinking sure things. Truth is, she was tired of *proof* in a general way. Sometimes things were just obvious. Clear as Kansas skies. Sometimes you had to acquiesce to common sense, a thing that felt lost to her, sucked up into the vent and devoid of the bureaucracy of law enforcement. It had been some time since she trusted the system, any system but her own.

Yet two days after blackening both the suspect's eyes, the Chaps Police Department received an anonymous tip that the robbery had been an inside job, and that the woman was a middle-aged and homeless runaway from Illinois, coerced into the store (and onto that video) at gunpoint by the actual perpetrator.

McGowan had been *so* sure . . .

"I'm gonna ask you until you answer, Peter," McGowan says now, sitting under a quieter light, in a cleaner room. But feeling a lot like she did that day. That is, close to the line. "Who else loves her?"

Lords has already been questioned inside out. Why he was in the Lamb house (*to watch Kit die*), what connection he has to the ballers (*none*), what he knows about the chances of Kit Lamb or any other Samhattanite being targeted in any way.

This last answer is consistently the same:

Daphne.

The deaths of Kell Darren and Nicole Welsh are similar to that of Belinda from Chuck Larson's story in the car. And all three mirror the current tragedies.

Is Samhattan really so inept, as a city, as a whole, that only the detective spotted the similarities?

"Who else loves her?" McGowan asks.

Lords smiles fondly. As if he likes the word "love" when used in reference to Daphne.

"You're afraid to say her name," he says. It's quite sudden and boy-ish, and McGowan imagines slamming his face to the metal table.

"Three girls dead," she says. "Speak. Now."

"*Everybody* loves Daphne."

McGowan thinks to get up. She's wasting time. This man is as vague with her as the city has been. Yet as Chief Pollen asked her just minutes before McGowan entered this room, *when* would have been the right time to bring up Daphne? The woman has been dead for nearly thirty years. Does McGowan need to know the details of every closed case prior to her arrival?

And is the detective sincerely weighing the elements of a local ghost story?

"You're glad we're all thinking about her," McGowan says.

Lords nods yes. McGowan knows he is. That's how the ghost story goes. The one she was never told.

She taps her shoes. Her fingertip on the table. Thinks of that night in Chaps. Can still see the innocent woman's face bruising beneath her fists.

"Why doesn't she come after you?" she asks.

McGowan is playing into the man's fantasy. How else to get him to talk? Is there a clubhouse for fans? Are there meetings? Can Peter Lords give her a list of people who have pledged their hearts to Daphne?

"I wish she would," he says.

And she sees in his eyes he means it.

"Friends, fellow fans, I need names," she says. Her voice is as unstable as it was in that Chaps interrogation room.

"I told you—"

"We'll let you go for breaking into the Lamb house if you give us names."

She knows Pollen has stood up on the other side of the glass. The chief is no doubt on her way to the interrogation-room door.

"Give us names, Peter. And we'll let you go."

The door opens behind her.

"*Now,* Peter," McGowan says, her eyes locked on his.

"Everybody in Samhattan loves—"

But he doesn't get to finish the sentiment.

And McGowan's hand hurts before she even realizes she's leapt across the table and hit him.

An officer has her by the shoulder. He's pulling her toward the door.

"Peter . . ." McGowan calls, even as an officer checks the man's bloody nose. Even as Pollen yells inches from her face.

"Peter . . ." McGowan says.

She's holding onto the doorjamb. Refusing to be taken from this room.

Peter wipes blood from his nose. Says:

"Zach Gold."

The officer stops pulling her arm. Even Pollen faces the man.

"Who is Zach Gold?" Pollen asks.

"He's part of the metal scene in Samhattan," Peter says. "There, I gave you your name."

McGowan doesn't look to Pollen. With no trace of guilt or wrongdoing in her voice, she says:

"I lied."

Then she's out of the room. In the hall. Thinking: *Zach Gold.*

Peter is yelling about his rights, his voice muted as the door closes, as McGowan moves quickly up the hall. Chief Pollen moves just as fast behind her.

But she only hears two words.

Zach Gold.

Pollen can reprimand her until she's blue in the face (Daphne was blue in the face; they found her that way in her muscle car, McGowan read). McGowan is going to solve this case.

Pollen grabs her hard by the arm.

"What the *fuck* do you think you're doing?" Pollen says.

McGowan doesn't hesitate. She pulls away and continues up the hall.

"Fire me," she calls over her shoulder. "Send me to jail. But give me time to find Zach Gold first."

And as she exits the station, she thinks of the remaining girls, the ballers who no doubt are thinking of Daphne more than she is, more than even Peter Lords is, imagining her like a denim-clad wrecking ball swinging slowly toward their homes, their bedrooms, their lives.

And McGowan no longer walks fast.

She runs.

o o o

Kit Lamb's Journal—That Time

Hi, Jolly.

I'm going to tell you about the time I called 911 on myself.

Are you ready?

Deep breath.

Maybe put some music on.

Okay . . .

Mom and Dad were already asleep and I was downstairs in the living room. It's where we keep all the records. Dad had taught me how to use the record player a few years back and I went down there alone sometimes. A lot, actually.

There was a sweet spot on the volume knob where it got loud enough to feel, but not loud enough so that it would wake them up. I tested this out a bunch. I went up and down the steps a dozen times before I found the spot. Even after I did, I made sure a few more times. The last thing I wanted was one of them to come down and ruin the moment for me. I guess you could say I was meditating. If you wanna use words like that.

So here's the thing: after a while it became my safe spot, listening to music downstairs alone. Imagine that, Jolly. Some girls sneak out to get wasted and some just want a corner of the round world to themselves. You know . . . maybe, MAYBE, I was already being chased back then, but I didn't know it yet. I mean, after all, what was I safe from in my safe spot? What was I fortifying myself against?

Well . . . it arrived that night.

Have you heard the album Pretty Hate Machine by Nine Inch Nails, Jolly? Don't make fun of me if everyone's heard it. I don't know music like a lot of kids do. I know what feels good and what gets me excited for a game and that's about it. Some kids at school talk about music like it's a secret club, right? If you don't know so-and-so you're *not allowed in. Well, that's fine. That's their religion, I guess, just like basketball might be considered mine. But that album . . .*

Dad and Mom never played it for me before, but for whatever reason it stood out that night.

Maybe it's because the title sounds like a strong wall, right? Like you could build a pretty hate machine and you could sit in the cockpit and drive it all over town, crushing everything in your path. I felt a bit like a pretty hate machine myself that night; all full of beauty and rage and like the two ends of the world were touching. Like I was wrapped up in the whole world, right? You need good music in a place like that. So, I put it on and I sat on the couch and the first song came on and I had to get up and test the volume all over again. I went upstairs and no, you couldn't hear it up there BUT . . . it sounded louder than the other albums usually did. I think it's because I felt it more.

This is the night I realized some songs, some albums, some games, are louder than others. Even if they're played at the same volume. I mean . . . I could HEAR the singer's meaning. Does that make sense? Or, how about this: I could hear how much he meant what he was singing. Some people call it passion, but I think passion can be faked. Some people open their mouths and they sing and it's amazing whether or not they mean it and other people have to find that lever inside to grip as they sing, to give them the leverage, but if they lose their handle they'll go mad, they'll go insane and I heard all that in the man Trent Reznor's voice that night.

I was shaking inside with it. I sat back on the couch and closed my eyes and just listened. And every time I opened my eyes, I kept expecting to see Mom or Dad sitting on the couch next to me, their eyes closed, too, because if they DID hear this music they would have no choice but to come downstairs and join me in listening.

Something was happening inside me, Jolly. Something real big.

"Terrible Lie" and *"Down in It"* made me feel like I was electricity, like I was IN the band or at the show or like . . . like I was one of the instruments they played! Insanely, I believed I knew the members better than I knew myself, which suddenly felt like NOT AT ALL. How was it possible I was relating to something I'd never heard before? This SOUNDED LIKE ME, yet I hadn't ever heard it. So, who had I been before hearing it? And all while this album was sitting here in the living room, evidence of something like me, and I had no idea.

I felt like I needed a guide. Someone to say, HEY, KIT, THIS IS YOU, HELLO, THIS IS YOUUUUUUU

You pretty hate machine, you.

"Sanctified" blew my mind. I didn't care about waking Mom or Dad anymore. I turned it up a little and just . . . FELT it. I sank into the couch and I sank into the song like people sink into baths. YES. JOLLY! It was like I was taking a bath in water that CAME FROM ME. Not from tears, but from sweat. You know? Eyes closed, sweating now, heart pounding, thinking THIS IS ME AND I DIDN'T KNOW THIS WAS ME AND HOLY SHIT THEN WHO AM I?

But it wasn't quite there yet. Panic.

Looking back, I'd say it was in the kitchen maybe, sitting at the table, waiting to get up.

What's worse, Jolly? Realizing you don't know yourself? Or realizing it didn't matter because you could be anyone you wanted to be?

This is it, Jolly. This is when things got scary.

It was during *"Something I Can Never Have."* A phrase, not in the song, popped into my head. This was it:

YOU CAN DO ANYTHING YOU WANT WITH YOUR LIFE

Hold up: Remember that magnet I told you about? The one Dad put on the fridge? About how everything you want is on the other side of fear? Yeah, there are a LOT of those magnets in the world.

Quotes, all tryin' to sound smart and all about life lessons, how you gotta treat others like you would be treated and all that. And when you hear these phrases, you just . . . you just IGNORE THEM. Right? Who thinks "You can do anything you want with your life" and actually . . . believes it?

It's just a phrase. A string of words. A magnet.

Right?

Well . . . not always.

That night it was change.

That night it was revelation.

"You can do anything you want with your life."

Even now, the words frighten me. Though they're not new to me anymore. THAT NIGHT they came like an envelope under the front door. Like God had bent at the waist and whispered it in my ear.

You can do

anything

It's the first time I remember feeling that heat at the base of my neck. And my first thought was that someone touched me. Right? Like a ghost had laid a hand on me.

I turned to look. I TURNED TO LOOK, Jolly!

And I wouldn't say nobody was there because . . . who knows? Do you? SOMEONE had to have delivered that message to me. SOMEONE chose then to tell me, just me, Kitty Lamb, that hey, you can do anything you want with your life.

ANYTHING

I bet it just sounds like words to you right now, Jolly. I bet it sounds like one of those phrases. But the phrase didn't just travel from one ear to the other. It wasn't just wind in my head:

It took root, buddy.

ROOT

Hey, Jolly, do you know the power of the word . . . anything? What *a word, right? ANYTHING? Ha. I could've walked to the kitchen and grabbed a knife and killed Mom and Dad. I could've become a killer that night. I could've left the house and started walking and never looked back and started a whole new life that, years later, I would tell strangers about, I would tell them about the time I just left the house and didn't turn back. ANYTHING. I could start studying psychology. I could start building things. I could marry, love, kill, eat, hide, run, sing, swing, punch, laugh, scream, mimic, kick, drink, move, walk, dance. I could DO anything and by doing anything I would be knocking over the first domino on the way to BECOMING anything I wanted to be. It's impossible to explain to you what this felt like unless those words take root for you too.*

Do you know that you can do anything you want with your life?

Is it easier if the words are smaller?

You can do anything you want with your life

You wanna be a musician? A doctor? A baller? Sounds like a nice revelation, right?

Right . . .

Here's the thing: it became truth too fast.

Like the death of close friends.

TRUTH TOO FAST

My PERSON was bursting with the fact that, while I sat on this couch in the middle of Samhattan, Michigan, I COULD be any-where. Why not steal a hundred bucks from Mom and Dad and walk to the bus station and just . . . go? It had nothing to do with loving them or hating them or hating Samhattan or anything like that at all.

This was new thinking. New me.

All at once.

And so WHY NOT leave the house and go wherever the phrase took me?

But in that moment I couldn't even stand up, let alone make a decision. The heat had risen from the base of my neck to my ears and the top of my head.

I felt like I was gonna die from revelation. I believed I would DIE from this truth. That's how little room I had FOR that truth, at that time, that time. Were my eyes open or closed as I sat on the couch? I can't say for sure. I can still see the record spinning, can still hear the songs, so loud, too loud, gonna wake up all of Samhattan with this revelation, right? If my eyes were open, I was seeing only the future. About a thousand futures.

Root
it took root
it became truth
the
moment
I thought it.
Oh, Jolly.
Ha

Can you imagine it? Not all truths are the same size. Studying for math, 18 divided by 6 is 3, but that's not how the numbers worked with the truth I suddenly had inside me.

Hey, realizing every path is open to you and will remain open to you for the rest of your life isn't just encouragement.

It's horror.

I was flooded: if me, why not Mom? Why not Dad? Were they already doing what they wanted with their lives? How about our teachers? Their parents, their friends? All of Samhattan? Was the entire city doing what they wanted with their lives?

Because . . .

they could.

I had to get up. I couldn't take it anymore. I was going to die with

it. *My blood was moving too fast for my body. I remember thinking
that. The music didn't sound like songs anymore: just this FEELING
and the feeling was that some truths are cold. TRUTH. Sudden, absolute, truth. The kind that changes your entire mind at once, and
everything you thought was real . . .*

was not.

*I was scared. Overwhelmed. I couldn't sit still. I walked toward
the record player, walked back to the couch. Over and over, feeling
like an animal in a cage. What was I doing in the living room of this
house if I could be anywhere in the world?*

*A revelation like this is horrifying because it comes with pressure.
You see? You can't realize something like this and then not do anything about it. And here, I couldn't even decide if I should turn down
the dial. What if I turned it up and Mom came down and asked
what I was doing and I told her I could do anything with my life and
she said okay what do you want to do with it and I said I wanted to
be a coach and she said okay then be a coach and THEN I got stuck
on that path because I said it because I was too scared to say I don't
know? You see? I didn't want to commit to anything because there
was everything!*

Yet I knew if I didn't do something I was gonna die about it.

*I hurried to the kitchen. I found Mom's phone on the counter
where she always leaves it and I called the police. I did it without
asking myself why I would, without thinking this might be the wrong
thing to do, this might make people ask you if you're okay for the rest
of your life.*

*I called 911 and when the woman at the other end said, "What's
your emergency?" I said:*

I can do anything I want with my life.

*She asked me to repeat it and I did but by then I wasn't able to see
straight, I could barely breathe, I thought this was it, you know,*

death, as Mom and Dad slept soundly upstairs, me, Kit, Kitty, gonna die down there in the kitchen, die from potential.

Had the record stopped spinning? Was that silence in the house?

I was about to stop too. All of me. All at once. Under the weight of this.

Crushed.

The woman asked if I'd taken drugs. Asked about LSD. I said no. She said someone was on their way. Did I need to sit down? I couldn't. Did I need some water? I couldn't complete a task so enormous as that.

Then she said something I'll never forget. I knew she was trying to be nice, to make me smile while I waited for an ambulance to come rescue me from this truth. She said:

The mind can be a scary place. You can think anything into being.

I hung up on her. I stood, frozen, rooted, in the kitchen. I suppose I waited, but there was a side of me that didn't remember calling at all. And her words rattled inside me, up and down, all over, YOU CAN THINK ANYTHING INTO BEING. And when the ambulance pulled up in the drive and the paramedics knocked on the door, when Mom and Dad came downstairs, confused and scared, I was on the couch again, eyes closed, nodding my head along to the record (was it on?), no longer hiding in the cockpit of my pretty hate machine, but driving it now, all over Samhattan, all over the world.

I kept my eyes closed as my parents opened the front door. I listened. I didn't respond. Then: hands upon me. The paramedics. None as powerful as that first hand, the hot one, still upon me, that showed at the base of my neck and worked its way to my mind.

All these questions, Jolly! And so much worry! And me, short of breath, I kept saying the phrase over and over, wanting it to take root in everyone else in the room because, despite how scary it was, despite how outside myself I felt, I KNEW IT TO BE TRUE.

You can do anything you want with your life.

Mom was real scared. Dad got angry. The paramedics asked if there were any drugs in the house. Heavy ones, they said. Mom and Dad said they had some grass in their bedroom closet. Dad went to check if I'd smoked some. If I'd eaten some. But I think they knew I hadn't. I think they saw something in my eyes that day I've never really seen in anybody else's.

Perception, Patricia Maxwell from school would no doubt call it. And she'd be right. Reality is just perception, ain't that so?

They walked me out of the house. The whole street was watching, and I heard the question asked for the first time, as a neighbor kid asked his mom:

Is she okay?

ME.

Was I?

In the ambulance they hooked me up to some monitors and talked about sedatives. I told them the ambulance was a pretty hate machine and we could drive it anywhere in the world we wanted.

We could get far, I told them, in a car like this one.

The paramedics said they wanted to take me to the hospital. Just to be sure. Mom and Dad argued over it. I barely heard them. It was just words, suddenly, these two, an argument that would mean nothing soon. What were these words compared to the ones I'd believed that night?

Finally they agreed. We went. I spent a few hours talking to a doctor who was worried something was up with my nerves. They checked my heart rate, my pulse, my breathing. And the whole time I was sitting on that hospital room bed, I was thinking:

Whatever this was that's come tonight . . . it'll come again. Something this powerful doesn't only put on one show, doesn't only play one game.

Yet horrifying as that sounded? I also accepted it. This new me, right? Now this girl who believed she could do anything with her life. Well, she also knew that, while she could take any path she chose, she wouldn't be alone out there. Nope. Check it, Jolly: wherever I went, this thing that happened to me that night . . .

. . . it would follow me.

So, while I could smile about doors opening, I could howl with gratitude for being shown the way (Patricia might've put it that way), I was also now tied forever to this monster, this demon, this witch.

And her name?

ANYTHING

It's a big word, Jolly. And it comes with big pressure. No, I wouldn't be alone out there, but I WOULD be out there. Because this wasn't the kind of thing you could turn your back on.

I told the doctor this and he laughed and he said,

I don't think I've ever had someone call 911 on themselves for this exact reason.

Mom and Dad laughed then, too, and we all shared a smile, but it was in the room with us.

ANYTHING

The woman who answered the 911 knew about it too.

Does Detective McGowan know about it?

I hope she does. I hope she knows she can solve anything she wants to.

Yep, it was there with us in the hospital.

Call it whatever you want.

Panic.

Attack.

Free-floating anxiety.

Truth.

That day I called it: anything.

But I don't know, Jolly. I think it may have had a name, after all. One the whole city has been too afraid to say out loud. Too afraid to even think.

Like I said, it's horror. And sometimes a whole group of people can agree to ignore a truth without even opening their mouths.

A whole city can suppress the story of one of its own.

In those days
I called it
anything
but
these days
I know it as
Daphne.

○ ○ ○

Jan Holt drives worse than she normally does. Emily, in the passenger seat, grips the dashboard with every sharp turn through the streets of Samhattan, even as she's gripped in return by visions of the police questioning her mother next. Mom's always been a bad driver. But right now, Emily's grateful they haven't killed someone. And here, trying to avoid murder themselves.

"We're leaving," Mom said when word of Kennedy Lichtenstein came through. The whole exodus happened within minutes of the news. Emily packed a bag as Jan instructed her how little she needed.

"We're leaving till this is over," she'd said. "And anything we forget, we'll buy out on the road."

The road. Yes. Emily Holt, the Samhattan High School girls' basketball team's starting center. It's a role she worked hard for, spending hours on footwork and boxing out, catching the ball high and "staying tall" despite a proclivity to drop the ball to her waist, to hold it at her hip like a gunslinger. She's put in the time. Cherishes how far she's come. Cut as a freshman, she got into two games her sophomore year. While Kit Lamb and Dana Berger were heralded from the start, Emily had to work her ass off. It didn't hurt that she grew five inches before her junior year. Now she's about the size of Mom, who drives the Blazer through the city streets at midnight as if the news were about her own daughter.

Emily gets it. And she agrees. Why wait around to see who's next?

"You're too young to know about Randy Scotts," Jan says, making a hard turn on Fifth Street, a shortcut to the highway but one most Samhattanites avoid. "It hasn't felt this dark in Samhattan since he was alive. A bona fide serial killer. A mailman first."

"I know," Emily says. "He took people's lips."

Jan eyes her quick. A glance to make sure her daughter is okay with what she just said.

"Yep. He did. They found a trunk full of mouths when they caught him. And for a few weeks, nobody smiled in this city."

Men sit on shadowed stoops, others stumble up Fifth like they're walking from one end of the bar to the other. Emily hasn't been down here in a long time. Just driving through makes her a little nervous.

Daphne isn't the only Samhattan legend, and a lot of news comes from Fifth Street.

But the city seems to be mostly asleep. Indoors anyway. And Emily and Jan are leaving town. First Tammy, then Melanie, now Kennedy. Yes, time to go indeed.

"Even when they caught him and killed him and buried him," Jan says, "it took some time for us to feel safe again. We'd spent so long seeing him in every corner, behind every door, that he'd taken on this ghostlike quality. He may as well have been a demon to us.

And so, what did it mean that they caught him? You can't catch a demon, you understand. A ghost can slip through the bars of any cell, slip right out of a pair of cuffs. Some things are hard to accept at first because they go against what you've come to believe. It's like that now. Feels the same. Everything's completely on edge. And I always said if something like that ever happened again, I'd leave Samhattan and take you with me."

"I'm glad we're going."

That look again. Just making sure.

"We'll get a hotel outside East Kent. Spend a few nights. Check the news. Once they catch whoever's doing this, we'll spend an extra few days or so away, get our heads together, let the reality of it all sink in."

"What about your job?"

Jan shakes her head no.

"No job is supposed to keep you from protecting yourself. What good is putting food on the table if those about to eat are dead?"

"Mom!"

A man steps out into the street and Jan slams on the brakes. His blue suit looks at first like denim to Emily. He squints into the headlights and for a second it looks as if he's reaching into his jacket for a gun. Jan puts the car in reverse. She's prepared to back up as fast as she arrived. But he only pulls out a cigar and, shaking his head, lights it without moving.

Jan honks. Puts the car in drive.

"Think this guy is scared?" she asks. "He hears about you girls getting picked off one by one and he thinks it's funny."

The man raises a fist, lifts his middle finger, and finally moves.

Jan drives. Flips him off as they pass.

"Who do you think is doing it?" Emily asks.

They haven't discussed much of this, as Jan and Emily Holt are both practical women. Someone is doing this. Until they know who it is, why speculate? At the same time, Emily's peers are suggesting something far less practical. And it's nowhere near lost on her that the horror began after the night they all spent at Dana's, after Natasha told them the story about Daphne.

"Don't know, don't care," Jan says. "Only one piece of news I'm waiting on, and that's that this is over."

As Jan makes a hard right on Governor Road, Emily tries not to think about the story, the legend, the name. But just like when she watches a show about alien abductions, it's hard not to at least temporarily believe in the possibility of alien abductions. When evidence is presented in such ways . . .

Her teammates were crushed.

Even poor Kennedy Lichtenstein, who was about the most down-to-earth girl Emily ever met. One could explain this all away with science (or, if you're Jan Holt, you might say the reports of the girls being crushed by bare hands are exaggerated and when the news says "crushed" they just mean "beat to death"), but Emily hasn't been able to fully commit.

Natasha did explain (in her own vague way) how easily something like this could spread: one teammate gets killed, the rest think of Daphne. Daphne then comes for the rest.

See? Something real practical in all that too.

"Less than three miles," Jan says. "Then we're out."

She's wearing a coat, the windows down. Emily has hers in her lap. They each have one packed bag in the backseat. Mom brought a cooler with some snacks but didn't stop to add any ice. It's okay. Emily isn't hungry. She isn't anything, really, other than scared.

"There's a HoJo on 85," Jan says. "Your father and I spent a night there in the early days."

Emily's dad died seven years ago. It's been a long, often dark, trip without him. Jan, she knows, loved him deeply.

"But you both had places in Samhattan," she says.

"Hey," Jan says.

Emily wants to smile. Normally, an innuendo like this would make her outright laugh. Mom and Dad stayed in a hotel when they didn't need to. What for? Emily knows what for. She suddenly wonders if they're heading to the very place she was conceived.

The highway's in sight. The top of the trucks using the concrete overpass.

Ahead, a woman in what looks like a nightgown crosses the street at a slow walk. She's barefoot. They may have turned off Fifth Street but there's more to Samhattan's underbelly than a few blocks.

Jan slows the car. Emily looks out the passenger window. In this concrete pocket by the highway, the warehouses are closed up for the night. Barred windows. Dented steel doors. Some streetlamps light up the cracked sidewalks, but there's a lot of darkness.

The side street they drive on is slim, and the woman now in the middle of it takes up more room than she should.

Emily thinks of Kennedy Lichtenstein, the one time Kennedy got into a game, when Kit Lamb sent her a pass and that asshole stole the ball and went the other way with it. Emily wants to kill that girl right now. Wants to grab her by the sides of her head and—

"*Move it,*" Jan says. Probably loud enough for the woman to hear, as the windows are still down. But the woman doesn't move it. She raises a hand and points at the car. "Oh, come on," Jan says. "What is this?"

But Emily is focused on something else. The woman isn't just pointing; her eyes are wide, her mouth open. She's talking.

Emily turns around, looks out the Blazer's back window. Hard to tell if anything's back there.

"She's probably high on PCP," Jan says.

"I don't think she is," Emily says. She isn't sure why she said this. But she doesn't like the woman, the pointing.

Emily looks out the back window again.

Nobody here but them.

Jan honks.

"*Come on!*" she yells, this time for the woman to hear.

But the woman remains where she is. Pointing.

Emily leans her head out the window.

"Hey, don't," Jan says. "Woman like that could throw a needle at you."

Again, Emily might've laughed at this on a different day. But she wants to hear what the woman says.

"What?' Emily calls. "What's wrong?"

"Emily . . ." Jan says.

She can't hear the words. It's a loud whisper at best. She pulls her head back into the car, looks out the back window.

"I can't drive around her," Jan says. She's right. Either direction is too narrow.

She honks again. Holds it longer.

The sound of the horn coupled with the woman's indistinct voice makes Emily feel sick inside. Whatever this is, it's wrong. She remembers a time when she and her dad got stuck in an elevator in Chicago. The feeling that, had they just not taken that particular elevator, they could've avoided the harrowing forty minutes it took to fix it. The understanding of how one decision can walk you somewhere you don't want to be and leave you there.

The woman still points at the Blazer.

"She needs a hospital," Jan says.

Emily thinks of the way Natasha described it, like it was a disease, just *thinking* about the woman, how it spreads, girl to girl, baller to baller, Samhattanite to Samhattanite.

"Go around her," Emily says. She looks out the back window again. "Hurry, Mom."

"I can't."

But maybe there's room. Just maybe. So she starts driving, slowly, toward the right of the woman.

"See?" Jan says. Then, "Hey, move please!"

The Blazer is almost level with the woman, the woman who isn't moving, as Emily looks out the passenger window and sees someone on the sidewalk, less than a foot from the car. Someone so tall she can't see their face.

"Mom," she says, meekly, more to herself, unable to muster the courage to speak any louder.

But Jan is talking out the open window to the woman, telling her it's dangerous to be in the middle of the street at night, asking her to move so they can get by, calling her names.

"Mom . . ."

The figure on the sidewalk reaches into the car and grips Emily Holt by the shoulder.

Strong hands.

Smells of smoke and booze.

"MOM!"

This time with volume.

Jan turns to see her daughter yanked hard to the side of the car. She steps on the gas. It's the first thing she thinks to do. The Blazer is passing the woman, the woman who looks to the passenger door, to something outside it, against it. Jan doesn't think to hit the brakes. She grabs Emily by the arm and pulls.

"Emily! What's going on?"

Because nobody's there. Nobody she can see.

"MOM!"

But Emily can see. And smell. And feel. She hears, too, the jean jacket rippling with the motion, the breathing that sounds more like exhaust pumped into a closed garage.

Emily is yanked hard against the passenger door.

Jan floors it. But Emily is already half out of the window.

One hand on the wheel, Jan tries to pull her back in. Her mind is reeling: the barefoot woman in the street, the Blazer in motion, Emily fighting something Jan can't see.

"Emily . . ."

There's a killer in Samhattan. The girls from Emily's team are being targeted. It's night. The woman in the street saw someone. Emily is struggling with someone.

Jan slams on the brakes but Emily doesn't fly toward the dashboard. She's pulled further out of the car.

Both hands free now, Jan pulls her daughter back with all she's got. Trucks move on the overpass.

They're so close.

"Dammit, Emily! Sit still!"

Because there's nobody else here. And for a moment, it seems her daughter does sit still. She's back in her seat. Eyes ahead.

But the look in those eyes tells Jan that whatever's happening, it's not over.

"Mom . . ."

When she was half out the window, Emily saw her face. Saw the makeup Natasha spoke of, Natasha who knows nothing about this woman because if she did she never would have told her story.

It's Daphne.

Practical Emily knows this for a fact.

"Emily?"

Because Emily isn't moving. Her eyes are wider than Jan's ever seen them. Even as a little kid, Emily wasn't afraid of the same things other kids were. She didn't mind the dark. Didn't mind the basement. Didn't mind ghost stories.

What scares her now?

"Emily?"

Jan thinks to drive, but there's a sense, a feeling, that her daughter is somehow rooted to this spot. Like someone has a gun trained on her and if Jan moves this car an inch, Emily will die.

"Daphne . . ." Emily says.

And she sounds practical, even now. The realism Jan is so proud to have instilled in her daughter.

Jan does not ask what Emily means. She only asks:

"Where?"

Yes, she's asking Emily where the Samhattan myth is standing. Where exactly is this legend so she, Jan, can stop her.

And when's the last time Jan Holt heard that name? It feels like it's been shot out of the past, her past, the city's past too.

Emily doesn't move, she can't, but she looks hard to the right, far as she is able.

Then the right side of her face caves in. Like papier-mâché. An aluminum can crushed in an unseen fist. Nothing there to make it happen. No pressure, no vise. As if Jan is watching Emily removing her helmet on Mars.

"Emily!"

Jan reaches for her daughter just as the left side caves in, symmetrical now. But not really. And now Emily doesn't look like Emily anymore. Her eyes long ovals, ugly shapes, her nose the width of a hand.

Jan can't move. Can't take her eyes off her daughter.

And sees nobody beside her.

It's like balling up a piece of paper from there. As Emily's head shrinks in size, crushed into garbage, as Jan screams and the woman in the street cries out (and runs; somewhere in this nightmare Jan hears footsteps racing away from this scene).

Jan floors it.

But this doesn't stop what's happening. As she drives fast, as she cries out, Emily's right shoulder caves in. Her left. Like her daughter's made of cardboard. Crushed in the recycle truck. She sees (and hears) it all. Sees Emily's fingers compressed, her chest go suddenly concave, her thighs flattened to the seat.

Jan doesn't know when she started screaming but she hasn't stopped. And she's driving too fast. Too sharp a turn, so that she's no longer traveling toward the highway but rather toward the brick façade of one of the gray Samhattan warehouses, this concrete valley before the highway, the way out, the way they were heading, she, Jan, having made the right choice, dammit, the decision to leave this city, the people here not having been this scared since Randy Scotts, since a city worker went home to home, removing the lips from unsuspecting Samhattanites; *the way out,* this was supposed to be the practical thing to do.

She looks to the passenger seat just before the Blazer smashes against the side of the warehouse. Emily has been reduced to a crushed pile of features, and in that mess, an approximation of a face she knows so well, a face she loves, looking back at her, an expression, formed haphazardly by what remains, a look that says:

Does the name ring a bell?

And Jan thinks, in the one second before the Blazer is crushed against the wall, and her along with it:

Yeah, but we all agreed never to speak it. Without actually making a pact, silently and as a city, we all agreed never to say Daphne again.

o o o

McGowan never got the address from Chief Pollen. But these things are easy to find these days. A brief (but frenzied) search online showed her where the young man Zach Gold lives, the man Peter Lords specifically cited as being a fan of Daphne's.

Why did Lords say his name? Is he the killer? What did McGowan see in Lords's eyes?

It's difficult to say, now, as she pulls to the concrete curb, Gold's address painted on the concrete, 373, the black and white chipped, the flakes long ago swallowed by the storm drain beneath it. There were many things going on in the eyes of Peter Lords, a man crazy enough to break into a house that was under police surveillance, crazy enough to hide under the bed of a young woman whose friends are being killed, insane enough to claim front-row seats for what he believed to be a murdering ghost. But, while Lords is insane, he's all McGowan has right now. And while she believes Pollen is already starting the paperwork to remove her badge, she's not going to ignore the only lead she has. There's a word for what she's doing, where she's gone, what she's become. She's heard it used in relation to herself before:

Rogue.

Carla McGowan does not have a warrant to search Zach Gold's house. In fact, she didn't even request one. She saw the sun come up as she drove here, believing her phone, her gun, and an address to be all she required to continue this case. Young women are being killed, nightly. McGowan needs to put a stop to this. As simple as that sounds, she won't let herself think any bigger.

She puts the car in park and catches a glimpse of herself in the rearview mirror. She looks like hell. Older. Crazier. She understands that whether or not she solves this case, this will be her last in Samhattan. In fact, she may be charged for what she's done and what she's about to do.

She gets out of the car. The sun's just come up and it's hot and her head hurts like she's hungover. Her jacket feels heavy, her boots feel heavy, even the gun in her left pocket drags down toward the street.

Rogue.

She feels it. The disconnect from the police force. A sense of living under the radar, above the law. That's fine. Because it has to be. And don't people like Barbara Pollen know the law is man-made? And that the police and its detective are here to protect and to serve? And if citizens are being killed, crushed . . . what is law if not ending this?

The yards are small here, barely any grass out front. The sidewalk is cracked and the trees are thin. The sun beats down upon the black roofs and gives the neighborhood a sense of having its own ozone layer: McGowan hasn't felt this hot in a long time.

If Zach Gold answers his door, she will first point her gun at him and demand he let her in. If he doesn't answer, she will kick his door down and question him all the same. And if he tries to run? She will shoot him.

Rogue.

But who has gone rogue? Christ, even if Daphne was just a myth, a bedtime story, it's something that should've come up *sometime.* Over lunch, at a police party, driving the streets with a colleague, in a meeting, on another case, on the phone. If there's one thing McGowan has learned while moving from city to city, department to department, it's that the most sensational cases come up in conversation. For law enforcement, those cases are the city's history. More than the accomplishments of its citizens.

McGowan removes the gun from her jacket pocket at the foot of the stone porch steps. Let the neighbors see. Let the neighbors talk. Maybe one of them will tell her something, willingly, on their own, something they've wanted to get off their chest for a long time. No more playing by the rules here. No more quiet paperwork and questions asked in soundproof rooms.

It's time to get loud.

She climbs the steps, gun trained on the door. She knocks with it.

"Zach Gold? Detective McGowan, Samhattan Police."

Her voice is tired yet loud in the quiet early morning. Up the street, a door opens and closes. A car engine starts. Someone beginning their day, even as McGowan continues her long night.

"Zach Gold? A few questions, is all."

She listens close for movement. Upstairs, downstairs, inside and out. She understands she could be standing on the front porch of the very man who is killing ballers from the high school and so he may not behave favorably. He may shoot at her from inside the house.

She knocks again.

Up the street, a Samhattanite yells to another. Someone is taking too long to get ready. McGowan looks to Gold's driveway and sees there is no car. This scares her, briefly, not because she hadn't thought to look there first, but because it might mean he's somewhere else. Killing. Maybe McGowan's CB is about to announce exactly what he's up to as she stands impotent at his door.

"Mr. Gold?"

Peter Lords cited this man. Why?

McGowan tries the handle. It's locked. She knocks again. Tries the door again. Locked. She looks up and down the street once, trains the gun on the doorknob, and fires.

The sound is so unbelievably loud that it temporarily wakes her from her lawless stupor. For the duration of two breaths she sees clearly what she's doing and what she's now done. There's no coming back from this one.

Rogue.

"So be it," she says. Then she kicks the splintered door wide open.

No sound of quick movement deep in the house, no sudden feet on the floor. No clicking of a second gun either. But McGowan keeps hers up all the same.

"Mr. Gold? A couple questions, is all."

Daphne. You a fan?

She's through the front living-room area now, pointing the gun to the four corners of the kitchen. She kicks open the pantry.

"Zach Gold?"

But he isn't here. And by the looks of the open bedroom window, she didn't need to shoot the doorknob off either.

She studies the bedroom. A mattress on the ground. No sheets. Just a yellow blanket. No posters on the walls. And the stuffy smell of a single man who doesn't clean up often.

She steps quickly to the closet. He could be in here. Could be armed.

She kicks the flimsy doors in, gun chin-high.

Only two articles of clothing hang on the chipped, wooden bar.

"Fuck me," McGowan says.

A pair of jeans folded over the hanger's bar and a jean jacket on its shoulders. There was a lot of talk about denim in the journals of Kell Darren and Nicole Welsh.

McGowan takes the clothing. Warrant or not, these are coming with her.

Through the living room again, she reaches the front door. But something in the living room has caught her eye.

A big, fancy smart TV.

The nicest thing in this place.

She finds the controller on the arm of the couch, turns the TV on.

Then she sits on the couch and removes her phone from her pocket. The photos of Tammy Jones are still the first that show. She closes these out and opens her notes.

Because this might take a second.

On the screen that takes up eighty percent of Zach Gold's living room is a thread. A chat he hadn't closed out. A conversation among like-minded friends that seemingly goes on for thousands of words.

But the word that stands out immediately (and shows more often than any other) is:

Daphne.

"Where are you . . ." McGowan asks.

Her CB crackles and she grips it, almost afraid to hear the news. "Detective."

It's Chief Pollen. McGowan doesn't respond. Only reads the words on the big screen.

"McGowan. Meet me at the Wild Stallion."

McGowan doesn't respond. Only begins to make sense of what she's reading.

"I'm not taking your badge," Pollen says. "I'm gonna help you solve this fucking case."

McGowan looks to the CB. Brings it to her lips.

"McGowan here," she says. "How soon can you get there?"

o o o

Kit can't stop thinking about Daphne.

Tammy, Melanie, Kennedy.

Maybe more? She doesn't know. Won't let herself know. Yesterday, Natasha wrote the team (those who remain) on a group thread. Said she had "more of the story to tell."

Kit turned her phone off then. Hasn't turned it on since.

The anxiety she feels now is new to her. It renders the stuff she writes about in her journal meaningless. If she catches herself in a mirror, in the window of a storefront downtown, what she sees is what she believes she will look like the day she dies.

This is next-level anxiety. As if she's reached a plane few people have endured.

There's strength in that, she thinks.

She feels it, in every pocket of her body, every joint, each cell of her piqued brain: there's nothing she can do. No way to vanquish this anxiety that, if she's honest with herself, has been growing since she made the game-winning free throw with a second to play. Yes, Kit Lamb was changed that day and has been changed every day since. And it's not for the better, no, as life force, it seems, is evaporating, even as the police force stands sentry in her drive, the same drive she learned to dribble upon, fetching the ball whenever it hit the cracks and did not bounce her way. Dead, yes, already, walking dead, at only seventeen years old. The sky in Samhattan has always been gray, but today it feels like ash, her own ashes, rising from the crematorium, her useless body burning in the casket, the eulogies still ringing in the funeral home:

Kit Lamb, who shouldn't have asked that question of the rim:
Will Daphne kill me?

Still: strength in this.

No way of getting out from beneath it. None she knows of. No strategy, no resistance.

Yet . . . alive. And while she can't outfight Daphne . . . maybe she can still beat her.

This is why she stands at the front door of Third-and-Fourth-Eye Books in downtown Samhattan, only forty yards from the entrance to the cemetery where they found Kennedy Lichtenstein crushed. If there's one place that might know the workings of mind over matter, this is it.

Wearing "family time" clothes—that is, jeans, penny loafers, and a T-shirt (the opposite of what the ballers typically wear: she's attempting to distance herself from everything Daphne)—she enters Third-Eye and smells, up-close, for the first time, the patchouli that hovers about the sidewalk outside and has since Kit was a little girl. A bell doesn't sound as she enters, rather, a series of wind chimes rise in scale, augmenting the sense this is all a cruel dream.

Nobody greets her. This surprises Kit. She's long imagined a bookseller surrounded by cats. Eyes behind thick glasses. An intelligent voice asking how she might be helped.

Because Kit needs help.

And again: strength in that. In looking for it.

The store is dimly lit, partially by candle, and the thick, glossy books are shelved in a semicircle around a blue rug with an enormous yellow eye stitched into it. There is no couch, no chairs, but Kit can tell the spot is designated for readers. The bookmarks upon the pupil tell her so.

The door closes behind her, the chimes sing in reverse, and Kit steps deeper into Third-Eye for the first time in her Samhattan life.

"Hello?" she calls. And this small, everyday question sounds complex.

Is Daphne going to kill me?

Swish.

"Hello?" she calls again.

Maybe they want you to make yourself at home in a place like this. Maybe they think it's up to you to become one with the place, introduce yourself to it, make friends with the space first. A couple weeks ago, Kit would've laughed at her own thoughts.

Not today. Today she enters the store a changed woman.

"Oh!" someone calls out. "I didn't hear you come in! I was using the blender in back."

It's Patricia Maxwell from school. Kit isn't sure what to make of that. Maybe she expected it. Maybe she sought Patricia out on purpose. Or maybe she's afraid to see a young woman her age, even as young women their age are being killed.

"Hi," Kit says.

"Kit Lamb!" Patricia says. "How awesome."

But Patricia knows about the killings. Because everyone in Samhattan must.

"I need help," Kit says. And it sounds like what it really means.

Patricia steps out from behind the counter. A purple shirt above high-waisted jeans. A mass of brown hair framing her eyes that always seem to be processing.

"Well, this is a good place for that. Glad you came." Then, "Do you have something specific in mind? It's okay if you don't. That's probably the best way to enter a bookstore."

Kit shakes her head no. Even this small act seems directed by Anxiety. Two bare fingers holding her face by the chin.

"I'm actually looking for books on how not to think at all."

"Interesting," Patricia says. "Anything particular you're trying to block out?" She shakes her head at her own question. "Wait. What I meant to ask was, what kind of thing are we talking here? A memory? An idea? An impulse? An urge?"

"A ghost," Kit says.

"Wow." Patricia's countenance becomes more serious, more empathetic, at once. "I'm so unbelievably sorry about your friends. Sometimes I think no words are better than any."

"I just need to block some thoughts."

"I get it."

"Is there an expert here?"

"Me."

"But you're . . . my age. What could you know?"

"Well," Patricia says, stepping to the rug and sitting cross-legged upon the eye. "It's what I dedicate my time to. Just like you dedicate yours to making good passes. Right? You know how to do that because you practice. Same here." She pats the rug, asking Kit to join her.

In this bookstore, Patricia's hair and clothes look less witchy than they do in the halls of Samhattan High School. In fact, Patricia looks like salvation to Kit. Like someone who may yet be strong enough to open doors.

Kit sits cross-legged, facing her.

"A common mistake," Patricia begins, "is to try to bury one thought with another. That's like putting a blanket over a dead body in bed." Then, "Shit."

"No. I think I get what you mean."

"Okay. Good. Yeah. What you need, what you *want*, first, is to *clean the room*. You, my friend, Kit, you need to meditate. What do you know about it? Hopefully nothing."

"Why hopefully nothing?"

"Because then there's less shitty information to clean up. A bare room is a lot easier to work with."

"You make it sound like my mind is an actual place."

But Kit's begun thinking this way too. And she knows she's let Daphne in.

Patricia looks serious when she says, "But that's exactly why you're here, Kit. Because it *is* an actual place. With all the consequences and potential of any room, anywhere."

"Do you think you can think something into being?"

Patricia smiles. "That's the only way anything *is*," she says. "It has to be thought of first. Then? Then it comes."

Kit looks to the rug. The candle flames upon the dark bookshelves flicker, have her thinking of the impermanence of life.

"But you can't imagine nothing into something, right?" she says, with hope and fear both.

"Sure you can."

"Like what?"

"Like relationships. Right? Love isn't visible. No emotion is. In fact, your entire worldview is unseen. Even by you."

"But I see the world."

"Yes, you see the world, but you don't see *how* you see the world. The lens."

Tears well in Kit's eyes. She can't stop them and she doesn't want to bring her hands to her face. Doesn't want to underscore how scared she is.

"Wait," Patricia says. "I don't mean to pry, but are you trying to get away from a specific person?"

"Why do you ask that?"

"There's an actual person you're trying not to think about. And it isn't one of your friends."

"Yes. That's right."

"Okay. Is it the person who hurt them? You don't have to answer that. But I think it will help in terms of discussing what to do. How not to think about him."

"Her."

"Really?"

"Yes."

In this place, the answer feels like irrefutable fact.

"Listen," Kit says. "I need to . . . erase this person from my head. Whatever that takes. Even if I was standing next to someone who knows her. Even if someone said her name. I need to *not* think about her . . . *at all.*"

"That's next-level stuff. You're talking hardcore compartmental-ization."

"What?"

"I'm not even sure monks can do *that.* The mission shouldn't necessarily be to forget the person, it's more—"

"Yes. That is the mission."

Kit knows how desperate she must look. She sees the concern in Patricia's face. *She's gonna stand up,* she thinks. *She's gonna say, hey give me one sec, will ya? Then she's gonna go back behind that curtain and call the cops.*

The same police she snuck past to get downtown today.

"The problem with *that,*" Patricia says, "is that it's literally impossible not to think of something if you're told not to. So . . . don't think of a cross-eyed bull."

"Oh, I know. I wrote about this in my journal."

"You keep a journal?"

"I do."

"I love that. And also . . . you thought about a cross-eyed bull, didn't you?"

"Yeah." But . . . kind of. What she really thought about was Daphne.

Patricia smiles.

"Now, I'm not saying the cross-eyed bull is your spirit animal, but if you found room for the bull in your head, then you've just proven to yourself it can be done."

"How?"

"Because, like any thoughts we have, the bull can take up more room. If you want him to."

"I want him to."

"And you didn't cover up what's worrying you. You simply . . . thought of *something else.*"

Kit feels momentarily defeated. What Patricia says might've been interesting before Natasha told her story. But not now.

"Even if I got rid of her," Kit says. She points to her head. "She's gonna come back."

"Come back?"

Kit looks over her shoulder, to the store's front door

"Listen," she says. "I don't think I'm strong enough to do this."

Patricia slides across the carpet to her, takes her hands in her own.

"You *are* strong enough, Kit. For literally anything you want to do. You literally are strong enough. It's all perspective. Everything. Okay? You need to accept that, to *know* that first. Okay?"

"Okay." And it's the first time Kit isn't afraid to hear words similar to those that found her calling 911.

"Good. Let's start there. But it can't just be a phrase, you know? It can't just be something to say. The belief that you can defeat this thing must be real to you. The philosophy itself. Are you in a bookstore right now with Patricia Maxwell from school?"

"I . . . I am."

"Good. Can you beat this thing?"

"I don't know."

"That's fine. You don't have to know that. Not this second. But eventually it has to become as obvious and as real as the fact that you're sitting in a bookstore with Patricia Maxwell from school."

"Okay."

"Close your eyes."

"I don't know."

"Mine will be open. And either way, if someone enters, the chimes will let us know."

"Okay."

Kit closes her eyes.

"Now . . . don't think of nothing. That's impossible. People try to imagine a white sheet of paper but then they start seeing the paper's edge, the table the paper is on, the room the table is in, a person sitting in a chair at the table."

Kit opens her eyes.

"I thought you were trying to help me."

"I am. Sorry. Close your eyes. Okay. Good. Now . . . what do you like? What makes you feel good?"

"Basketball makes me feel good."

"That's outstanding. I don't think you could've picked a more perfect subject."

"Why?"

"Because there are so many moving parts. So many players to pay attention to. The ball constantly moves. Dribbling, passing, shooting. This is great. Motion and moving parts, fluidity, not like hypnosis, but not entirely unlike it either. Who do you want to pass the ball to?"

"Sue Bird."

"Okay. Pass the ball to Sue Bird. Who should she pass to?"

"Um . . . Dana."

"Great. Are you in the Samhattan gym or are you thinking, like, a stadium?"

"I had us outside."

"Great. You're in the park. Garland Park. You pass the ball to Sue Bird. She passes the ball to Dana. Dana passes to Rebecca Lobo."

"Wait."

"We've got books on sports too."

"Really?"

"Sure. Now, Lobo passes back to you. Is it windy?"

"No. Well, yes. A little."

"Shoot the ball."

"Okay."

"Did you make it?"

"No."

"Interesting. Where's the ball?"

"In the grass."

"All right. Go get the ball."

Kit, eyes closed, goes to retrieve the ball. Sue Bird and Dana and Rebecca Lobo stand quiet. In fact, the whole world is quiet. All of Samhattan is like a movie set, seconds before the camera rolls.

"Do you have the ball?"

She doesn't. She looks to the grass and doesn't see the ball. She looks back. The other three are waiting.

She hears a car engine come to life.

Someone is awake in this silent Samhattan after all.

"Now do you have it?"

Patricia's voice comes from a distance, soft.

"No. I can't . . ."

"Can't find it? That's fine. How about you join the others on the pavement again. Let's hand you a new ball. Sue Bird has a new ball."

Kit looks to Sue Bird and sees, yes, she has a ball. Only, it's not a ball. It's Tammy Jones's head.

"Fuck."

"Don't worry," Patricia says. "You're probably mixing images up by now. It's hard to maintain an inner vision. The details get fuzzy. Your mom becomes your dad. All that."

"I don't think I can stay here."

"You can. You can control this thing. This thing being *you.* Is Sue holding a ball?"

Kit looks again. Yes. A ball. But the ball bulges.

What's inside the ball?

"Yeah."

"Great! Go to her. Go to them."

Kit does. She feels the pavement beneath her again. Feels a cool breeze.

Sue Bird tosses her the ball. She catches it, passes to Rebecca Lobo. Lobo to Dana.

"You're back in action," Patricia says. "Whoever has the ball, have them shoot it."

Dana fires an awkward shot that cracks off the side of the backboard.

The car engine gets louder.

"Who shot the ball?"

"Daphne."

"Who?"

"Dana. *Dana.*"

"Did she make it?"

"No."

"Have her go get it this time. Let her search the grass."

Dana walks to the grass. Beyond her, a navy-blue muscle car pulls up to the far edge of the park. The driver's door opens.

"Oh no," Kit says.

"No, it's okay," Patricia says. "It's absolutely common for the person you're trying to avoid to show up. Is that what's happening?"

The driver's door opens with a grating crack.

"Does Dana have the ball?" Patricia asks.

Dana does not. She only stares across the park, to the giant woman in denim who walks slowly her way.

"I can't stop her," Kit says.

"You don't have to stop her," Patricia says. "You just need to render her useless. Okay?"

"How? *How?*"

Patricia squeezes her hands.

"Change her. This is *your* fantasy, after all. Wanna change her into a tree? A basketball? A punching bag? This is yours, Kit. Your world. Sic the bull on her."

Kit tries. Daphne momentarily becomes a tree. Switches back. She's closer now.

"Dana!" Kit says.

"She'll be okay," Patricia says. "Just have her pick up the ball."

The idling car growls. Heavy guitar riffs rise from the open door.

"Fuck," Kit says. "She's too strong for me. Too big."

"Nothing is," Patricia says. "Nothing in the—"

But her voice is lost to the roaring car, the roaring music. And the thudding of Daphne's black boots across the grass.

"I can't stop her!"

Her huge hands are made into fists. Her stringy hair hides most of her face but Kit catches a glimpse . . .

KISS makeup. But no cat. No stars.

Demon.

"Dana!"

"She's fine," Patricia says. "And you're doing it. You're—"

But Kit is trembling, *shaking* where she stands in her vision. She looks to see Sue Bird and Rebecca Lobo far away, their backs to her, walking away from what comes.

When she looks back to Dana, she doesn't see Dana at all. No grass. No park.

She's in the living room of a Samhattan home.

"Wait . . ."

"What is it, Kit?"

She sees a woman, Beck Nelson's mom, sitting in a big chair in front of a television. Kit met Mrs. Nelson at last year's season-ending banquet. Mrs. Nelson told her Beck admires her. Talks about her at home. This home.

"I'm not at the park anymore," Kit says.

"That's okay. Sometimes the setting switches on you."

But this feels worse than that. Kit has never been to Beck Nelson's house.

"No," she says. "This isn't right, Patricia."

"It's *all* right. Whatever you think about, it's—"

That same engine revs outside the Nelson home and Patricia's voice is drowned. The front door opens behind Kit and she turns and sees Beck, sweating, wearing shorts and a jersey, carrying a basketball.

"Hey, Mom," Beck says.

Mrs. Nelson smiles.

"Beck," Kit says. But they don't hear her.

Beck shuts the door.

"The police are nice," Beck says.

"They didn't mind you shooting baskets?"

"No. I think they wanted to shoot too. I shot it well."

Kit believes it. Beck Nelson is science-minded. She talks about basketball like pool players do their angles. A year younger than Kit, she's already older in ways Kit doesn't think she'll ever be.

Beck tilts her head to the front door. She sniffs the air.

"Do you smell that?" She asks.

Kit thinks Beck smells her. Somehow smells Kit in this house.

"I don't think so?" Mrs. Nelson says.

Beck looks back to the front door. To the pitch-darkness of the corner where the two walls meet.

"Smells like . . . alcohol," she says.

"Oh no," Kit says. "No, no, no, no . . ."

From elsewhere, miles, Patricia speaks: "It's okay, Kit. It's—"

The engine revs again. A blue muscle car big enough to accommodate a seven-foot woman who spends a lot of time listening to music in there.

"Do you see that?" Beck asks Mrs. Nelson. She's backing up. Toward Kit.

"See what, dear?"

But Beck is scared of something in that dark corner of the home. She lifts a finger.

And the finger is crushed.

"BECK!" Kit screams.

Beck screams too.

Kit reaches for her, takes her by the shoulders, turns her around to talk to her, to tell her they have to leave this house.

Just as Beck's shoulders cave in.

Mrs. Nelson screams.

And her scream mingles with the engine as Kit watches the darkness materialize, transform, from floor to ceiling.

Daphne isn't only visible now, she's facing Kit.

She lifts her bare hands as wind from an open window pulls her greasy hair aside, showing Kit her face.

In full.

No makeup at all.

"GET AWAY FROM ME!"

The wind chimes above the store's door rattle the scale, a piercing arpeggio that rips Kit from her vision, even as Patricia releases her hands.

Kit opens her eyes, wide, spinning to face (*Daphne*) the door.

"*Get away from me!*" she yells again, falling to her back, hands in front of her face.

The man in the doorway looks to Patricia.

"The hell's going on in here?"

It's a man. Just a man. The basketball court, the park, the car, the music, the Nelson home, the bare hands, the face, all . . .

. . . gone.

Kit imagines a new series of texts on her phone that remains off.

Beck Nelson . . .

"We're in the middle of something," Patricia tells the man. She looks to Kit. "You okay?"

"The last time I looked like *that*," the man says, pointing a finger at Kit, "was at a co-op in East Lansing, 1995. I took too much."

Patricia crouches, holds Kit's face in her hands.

"Well, it's a start," she says. "And nobody says it's easy."

"I can't do it. I can't stop thinking about her."

"But you *can*," Patricia says. "And you will. And I'll help you. But first . . . I need to do my job for one second here."

She rises, greets the man. Kit sees the remains of the Nelson house in her memory. As if the yellow eye she sits upon will never see anything else ever again.

Then she's up. Even as Patricia tells her to wait, Kit rushes to the exit. The man is describing a book, Patricia is asking him to hang on, and all Kit hears are those chimes, descending as the door swings closed behind her, as she flees the store.

And the whole world seems to descend with the notes.

"Stay away from me," Kit says. She trembles as she moves through downtown Samhattan. As everyone she sees is a thought away from death. One thought, repeated, over and over. A woman. A name.

A face.

Kit hurries. But where to? When the monster lives where the mind's walls meet, where can she possibly go?

Yet despite the paralytic anxiety, despite the unfathomable odds, she does.

She goes.

And somewhere deep in her head, her own voice continues to say:

There is strength in this.

o o o

Barbara Pollen's hair remains mostly blond, despite her sixty-six years. It's pulled back tight enough into its trademark ponytail to give her face a windblown look; the chief of police always appears to be moving against something. McGowan recognizes it as a hallmark of a lifetime in law enforcement. So is the pint of pissy beer in front of her on the booth table. To say nothing of the empty one beside it.

McGowan doesn't even consider employing small talk as she slides in across from her superior.

Pollen is not in uniform. McGowan steels herself for a revelatory conversation. But she starts first:

"I've got four kids who call themselves the Vann Guards. Was on the TV at Zach Gold's house. And if you remember, Zach's was the name Lords gave us."

Pollen frowns down at her beer. McGowan's never known the woman to avoid eye contact before.

"I didn't request a warrant because—"

"Shut up, Carla."

McGowan does. The two women have set their phones close to their right hands. As if guns on the table in the Old West. As if loaded.

"They call themselves that because that's her last name," Pollen says.

"Who?"

"Daphne Vann."

McGowan's dealing with a lot right now: The fact that her superior isn't chastising her for breaking into a young man's house, for starters. The fact that she has in her notes the names of four people she needs to question *now*. And this . . . this almost too-easy talk about Daphne.

"She was a bad person," Pollen says. "A kidnapper. All seven feet of her, though I wonder if that's an exaggeration. I never measured. She lived alone. She made no friends. She held no jobs. Whether or not she was born here, I do not know. But you don't have to be born somewhere to become part of the local fabric. And *that* she most certainly has."

"Do you—"

"I haven't thought of Daphne Vann in close to ten years. And it must've been close to that before that last time I did too. The journals you read, I read them. I suppose she must've crossed my mind then. But I have no recollection of that. Just as I imagine I'll have no recollection of this conversation we're having not long after it ends."

"What are you saying?"

Pollen looks her in the eye now. It's not a pretty feeling. Whatever the chief is going on about, it's something much more complex than warrants and procedure.

"You're not from here," Pollen says. "You're still new. For that, I think maybe you can do something about it. But I don't know. And so it's possible I'm giving you the green light to go kill yourself. It's possible I'm killing you by talking about her, by giving you more information to chew on, more thoughts, until all you can think about is that terrible woman in her jean jacket, always a little closer in your imagination than the last time you thought of her, always closing in on you."

"What did she do exactly?"

McGowan wants to know because a superfan, a copycat, would likely do the same.

Pollen slides her phone across the table.

"The photos are up. You need to see these."

McGowan takes the phone, lifts it, but pauses. She thinks of the images from Tammy Jones's bedroom on her own phone.

What might she see here?

"The problem with being so tall," Pollen says, "is that there's no costume to hide behind."

McGowan touches the screen. The first photo is of a kitchen sink. A swirl of dark colors and unrecognizable objects beneath the faucet.

McGowan zooms in.

"You got any trauma in your life?" Pollen asks. "Anything you don't intentionally ignore, but ignore all the same?"

"Jesus," McGowan says.

She looks away from the phone. Looks to Pollen's half-drunk pint of Pabst Blue Ribbon beer.

"I've got trauma like that," Pollen says. "A camp counselor. A woman. Did things with me she wasn't supposed to do. Maybe it's why I got into police work. But it's funny . . . I almost never think about her. And when I do, she sort of comes downstairs in the house in my head, shows herself, and then heads back up. Then I just . . . don't think of her again. Most of the time I forget there's even a second floor."

It's body parts in the sink. Small arms and legs. The fingers give it away:

A child.

McGowan braces herself for the next photo. Swipes.

"Samhattan has one of those too," Pollen says. "And her name is Daphne Vann. And the entire city only thinks about her when she comes downstairs."

The second photo is worse than the first, if such a thing is possible. It's small hands in water yet to be boiled in a pan on a stove.

McGowan tries to look away again, but she can't. The door to this particular slice of madness has been opened. And she needs to see what's inside.

"I'm the chief of police," Pollen says, "and I've never once told someone not to talk about her. I've never once been told the same. Yet . . . here we all are . . . covering it up. But what do you call it when everyone just does it at once? And always? What do you call a cover-up that nobody planned, nobody enforces?"

McGowan swipes to the next photo.

It's of a bedroom, she thinks. Whether or not it was Daphne's she doesn't know. Is this where she kept the kids she took? The small, scattered clothes indicate yes. But the empty bottles of Rich and Rare, the ashtray on the windowsill, say no.

"I can't recall a single time in my forty years on the force, having to tell someone to keep quiet about Daphne. I can't recall a single time she was even brought up."

"Chuck Larson told me about her."

Pollen laughs. But it's cold.

McGowan swipes to the next photo. Has to look away immediately.

"Maybe he talked about her with me too," Pollen says. "Maybe he did, and his words sunk into the same swamp those thoughts about my camp counselor do. Or, more likely, you triggered something in him. Just as you did with me on the phone. All that talk about the journals. The two basketball girls writing about Daphne. Most likely you *reminded* Chuck about Daphne."

Ordinarily, McGowan would have so much to say now. So many questions. But the current photo is tattooing itself on her consciousness. Even as she closes her eyes.

It's of a tiled floor in a filthy little house. It's of what looks like a wig on those tiles. It's of the slightest profile of a nose, letting you know it's not just hair, but a little head, facing the other way.

"And Janice Taylor too," Pollen says. "Either you or the current events reminded her of Daphne, and she held on to the idea just long enough to find that box about those girls. Just long enough to hand it over. I bet if you called Principal Taylor up right now, she'd barely remember what you're talking about." Pollen snaps her fingers close to McGowan's nose. "Carla? You listening?"

She is. But she's also seeing the most heinous crime-scene photos she's ever seen in her life. And an unseen part of her is already exiting the Wild Stallion Bar and Grill.

They call themselves that because that's her last name.

To be fans of this . . .

"A whole city silently agreed to move right on from that." Pollen makes a small gesture at her phone in McGowan's hands. "But there's more. And it's worse. Do you believe in magic, Carla?"

"I don't know, I—"

"Your mother or father believe in magic? What are you . . . Irish and Cuban, right?"

"Yes."

"A lot of magic between those two. Did you grow up with it?"

"No."

It's hard to believe it's her own voice answering the question. That orange-and-yellow tiled floor . . .

"Well, I didn't either. But in moments like these . . ."

"What are you saying, Barbara?"

Pollen takes a long pull of beer. Doesn't wipe the suds from her lips when she answers.

"There's a video next." She nods toward the phone. "Watch it."

McGowan swipes, bracing herself for the worst of it. But this isn't footage from inside the home. This looks more like . . .

"Is this a costume shop?"

"Like I said earlier, no costume big enough to conceal a seven-foot kidnapper."

At the right of the screen is a large blue rabbit. McGowan recognizes shelves of candy beside it in the grainy footage. It's a security camera, she would recognize footage like this anywhere.

"What am I . . ."

But she spoke too soon. A little girl enters the frame. Looks up the length of the rabbit. Seems to ask it a question.

There's a pause. And in that pause the entire bar seems to go still. As if, in step with the crazy stuff Pollen is saying, all of Samhattan holds their breath for this next part.

"Oh no," McGowan says.

Because maybe it was this little girl's head on that tiled floor.

The rabbit moves fast. A huge blue paw over the child's face.

Drags her violently off-camera.

The video ends there.

"That's Brea Delany," Pollen says. "The last little girl Daphne stole. Send yourself all that if you need to. That was Daphne Vann who took her."

"She went to jail then?" McGowan asks. But somehow she knows this isn't the case.

"Someone got to her before we did," Pollen says.

"Chief . . ."

"You got any trauma in your life, Carla?"

The way she asks it, it's like she isn't aware she's already done that. McGowan tries to process all she's heard. The idea of a cover-up without any actual covering up. An entire city deciding to send that trauma back upstairs into a room they forget exists.

McGowan sends herself the pics. The video.

"You have my blessing," Pollen says. "That's why I asked you here. To tell you as much as I know before I stop . . . thinking about her again. Because I will do that. And so will every other Samhat-tanite, the moment they can. You ever hear the phrase 'it's in the water'? Yeah, well, this is our water. This is our communal trauma, Carla. And maybe, just maybe, because you're not from here, be-cause you never quietly ignored this terrible bit of history, because you're not *scared* of Daphne . . . maybe you can beat her."

McGowan sets the phone on the table. Thinks of that pan on the stove. Thinks of the kitchen sink.

"But she's dead," she says. "You said someone got to her before you did. Who?"

Pollen shrugs. But this time it feels more like an intentional cover-up.

"A relative of a victim?" Pollen posits. But again, it feels to McGowan like the chief of police knows. Or once knew. And decided to forget.

"Either way," McGowan says. "Dead."

"Well, that's just it, isn't it? Some people grow up with magic. And some of that magic is the sparkly kind and some of it isn't."

"You don't really think . . ."

"All that matters right now is that my job is to protect the people of Samhattan the best I can. I've succeeded at that much more often than I've failed. And right now . . . I believe you are the best line of protection these people have."

"It's a copycat," McGowan says.

Pollen looks like she might shake her head no. But doesn't.

"Might be," she says. "And while I fear what fate awaits you, I believe it's the only fate we got." Then, "Go on now."

McGowan only stares back. So many questions. So many thoughts.

"Go on," Pollen says.

McGowan slides out of the booth. Looks down at her chief once more.

"Thank you for your blessing," she says.

"Do whatever you have to do, Carla. *Whatever you have to do.*"

o o o

Natasha texted the rest of the team everything her mom told her about Daphne. But not everybody has responded. In fact, she hasn't heard from Kit in too long. Deeply and justifiably scared about this, she told the police in her driveway they needed to check on her friend. Kit's house is easy to sneak in and out of. Natasha's done it dozens of times. There's a back door in the basement bathroom, a bizarre feature the ballers joke about whenever they visit the Lamb house. *This is for the sunbathing shits. This is so you don't shit your pants mowing the lawn.* And really, who thought to put it there? What if somebody walked in on you while you were going? Still, the older they got, the more useful the door. Natasha and Kit spent many nights up the street, in the cemetery, or just whispering in Kit's backyard. Wherever they went on these excursions it felt like a singular place, the two of them, *together,* a place in and of itself, *together,* always there. And while Natasha knows Kit uses that door to see Dana, too, it feels good having a secret with a friend.

So . . . why isn't she in on the secret now?

Where's Kit?

And while it's only Kit who hasn't responded, those who do aren't really acting like themselves. In fact, Gemma Wells's mom responded for her, asking Natasha to please cool it, to leave Gemma alone:

Nobody needs any more horror in their lives than what's already there.

Natasha knows Emily Holt and her mom tried to leave town. That's the most recent news, and the images conjured by the piecemeal story are almost impossible to process. Down by the warehouses. Jan Holt's Chevy Blazer smashed against a brick building. Emily crushed by the crash. Or maybe . . . before impact.

Natasha doesn't want to think of Emily like that. Doesn't want to think of Melanie, Tammy, Kennedy. And absolutely does not want to think of the fact that she's the one who told the others the story of Daphne. She's doing a good job imagining a dam, resisting the huge glut of guilt that will drown her if she allows it. Quincy Manska helped. She more or less convinced her daughter none of this is her fault. And while Natasha means it when she says the killer is possibly a woman, that doesn't mean she thinks it's the ghost of a seven-footer. In fact, Quincy and Natasha talked about a lot more than Daphne's backstory, long after they heard the news about Emily Holt. It's hard to know how much they've slept, how much they've talked, and just what they might've dreamed. But somewhere in the piqued discussion, Quincy suggested Natasha believes it's a woman because she wants it to be. Because there's a side of Natasha that wants *everything* of note to be a woman. Good, bad, ugly, doesn't matter.

Natasha got fired up about this:

I've been surrounded by powerful women my whole life, she said. *From you to Coach Wanda. From the girls I play with to the ones I play against. This isn't about what I want, Mom. This is about what I'm sensing, what I'm feeling, what I just . . . believe. The man who got caught beneath Kit's bed? Yeah. That was a man. And that wasn't the killer. Women are smarter, Mom. Craftier. And whoever is doing this is using a tool that literally fucking crushes people's bones. And they're not leaving a trace of evidence as to what that tool is. You think that's a man? No man is that careful.*

Still, Natasha doesn't know, of course. And does it matter? Housebound, all the same. And Quincy about the house, drink in hand, reinvigorating the discussion at a whim, more than once with the police officers who were once stationed exclusively outside but now sometimes stand inside the house too.

That's one of the scariest parts of all this to Natasha: the way Quincy goes in and out of remembering the Daphne story. It's as if, seconds after talking about it, she forgets again. Then, at the fridge, putting more ice in her drink, she suddenly remembers again. And with each memory, there's a momentary thrill, a woman recalling something specific to her city, her life. But that thrill dies quick. Crushed, it seems, in seconds.

Daphne.

Natasha wishes she never heard the name.

And while she won't allow the dam to break, she's never felt worse in her life. Is this horror? Is this what people mean when they use the word "traumatic"? Funny how it doesn't feel immediate. After all, she's Natasha still, isn't she? She can still make a joke, can't she? Watch! She'll go make one to the officer by the front door now. Just watch him laugh. Yes. Just a couple Samhattanites going about their days, far from being able to recognize what this experience is going to do to them in the long run. Far from experiencing the PTSD, the unchecked anxiety, the fatigue. Teammates are being killed daily. The entire city is on edge. Dad won't let Natasha put the television on because the news is literally only about the ballers. Natasha's own face has been broadcast, as team photos and pictures from games are used nightly. She saw herself for a second before Dad swiped the controller away. She saw a video of her (Natasha herself!), dribbling the ball like an ogre, like Frankenstein, up the right sideline before pulling up for a baseline three.

Maybe it was a good thing Dad turned it off. She missed that shot bad.

A joke. Kind of. Self-deprecation anyway. *See? Still got it.* Despite the death, the anxiety, the fact there's not only a killer but one who will eventually come for Natasha too. Because she's tried, oh yes! She's *tried* to come up with other ways Tammy and Melanie and Kennedy are linked (and Emily now, too, Emily Holt; and wasn't there a suggestion of Beck Nelson in one of the responses from one of her teammates' mothers in the text thread?). Yes, Natasha's looked everywhere for an uncommon bond. Did they all have dark hair? No. All the same age? No. And so many more makeshift, hopeful connections in an effort to tell herself she is not on the killer's radar, she has nothing to *do* with the events unfolding, she's not the killer's type.

But no. There's nothing.

And so . . .

What to do but pace? What to do but wonder what this is doing to her? Because this *is* trauma; you'd have to be made of ice for it not to be. Natasha has pretended to go through the few books on the shelves in the house. She's even pretended to be interested in what she sees online while truly trying to stay away from anything Samhattan-related. And now, right now, as the police stand sentry in the driveway, as Mom and Dad occupy themselves in their own efforts to manage their own trauma, she pretends to find calm in what she does.

Which is sitting on the end of her bed, reminding herself none of this is her fault.

Right? Right. Because to believe in Daphne in that way is to believe in a lot of things.

Ghosts.

Demons.

Witches.

Cities that are curs—

A sudden knock at her door and she doesn't pretend it didn't scare her.

"Jesus. Yeah?"

"Natasha."

It's one of the officers. Why? News? Is it Beck Nelson, after all? Is it Kit?

"I checked up on your friend," he says through the wooden door. So, yes, it's about Kit.

"And?"

"And no word yet. They said they'd check."

"You came to tell me that?"

Silence from him for a beat.

"I'll let you know as soon as I hear."

"Yeah. Okay. Good idea. Probably smarter to come with news than nothing. The last thing I need is more nothing."

Silence. Then, his footsteps receding up the hall.

Natasha checks the thread on her phone.

Kit hasn't responded. Worse, Kit still hasn't even read Natasha's messages.

Is her phone off? Is that how Kit's dealing with her own trauma?

Natasha writes the others, asking if they've heard from Kit. She isn't answering her phone, she tells them. Isn't reading any messages. Has someone called her parents? Is she okay?

Is Kit freaking out?

Why isn't anybody as scared about Kit as she is?

Down the hall, movement. Like a shoe falling to the carpet.

"Mom? You good?"

It's not hard to imagine Quincy falling onto her bed. Or onto the floor for that matter. Natasha has witnessed both.

She gets up, leaves her bedroom. No officer anymore in the hall. She hears a carpenter's bang from downstairs and thinks, right, that came from downstairs and so she passes the extra bedroom her parents use as an office and takes the stairs down.

"Mom?"

Quincy isn't in the kitchen. More banging. From below. Natasha checks if the officers are in the living room. They've been there before. She hasn't asked why. Do they come inside when the news gets worse? Do they get closer to Natasha if they hear the killer is doing the same?

Banging. The basement. A hammer on wood.

She goes to the basement door, opens it.

"Dad?"

"Yeah."

"What are you doing?"

"Trying to fix this fucking table leg, but it's driving me insane."

"Okay."

She hears him shuffle across the concrete floor before his head appears at the bottom of the steps.

"You good, sweetheart?"

"No."

"I'm sorry, Nat."

"I know."

Natasha thinks of trauma. Who could've known it'd be like this? Nobody told Natasha about the elastic state of being where you can tell you're gonna eventually have to do a lot of work, inner battles will be fought, but you haven't started fighting yet.

"Is Mom with you?" she asks.

"No."

"All right."

"Wanna hang out?" Dad asks. "You look like you're feeling restless."

"Restless. Yes. People are dying. Hard to get proper rest."

Dad smiles. It's the way he smiles when he's imparting a lesson without speaking it. His way of saying *I love you* precisely when Natasha needs to hear it.

"You gonna fix that leg?" she asks.

"Well, if I don't . . . we'll just have to eat three-legged dinners from now on."

"Gross."

"I heard they're not bad."

"I heard that's an imbalanced meal."

Now Dad almost actually laughs. He wipes sweat from his forehead with a rag.

"You, young lady . . . you need a stage."

"Haven't you heard? I'm one of the stars."

Oh. She didn't mean to allow a shudder into her voice with that last one. Dad heard it.

"God, Nat. This is just awful."

"Yes."

Tears? They might come. It's okay, she thinks. Been a lot of them lately. They're practically her closest friends these days.

"But we'll get through it," she says. Because if he says it first, there won't be any stopping the flow.

"Are the police outside or in?" he asks.

She suddenly realizes her dad is fixing the table downstairs because if he doesn't do *something,* he'll go crazy with the waiting. Just like she is.

"Out," she says. She considers asking if he's heard any more news. "I'm worried about Kit."

"Why?" Dad starts to climb the steps. To go to her. As if Natasha has news.

"No, no," Natasha says. "She just isn't answering her phone."

Dad stops.

"Okay."

Natasha looks to his tattered sneakers. Sees Daphne looking through the steps back up at her.

"DAD!"

Dad looks down.

"What? *What?"*

But Natasha is already laughing. That was a face, yes, oh my God, but it wasn't looking at her.

It's a magazine cover. The top magazine on the pile they keep under the stairs.

"Did you think . . ." Dad starts. Then he laughs too. Even as he's catching his breath. "Holy shit, Nat. You scared me bad."

Who knew? Who knew there'd be moments in trauma when you could still heartily, full-bodied laugh?

"Scared *you*?" she says. "I think I just lost some weight."

Dad takes the rag, reaches under the stairs, and places it over the top magazine.

No more face.

Thanks, Dad.

"There," he says. But he still eyes it like it could come to life. And they both give it one more little laugh. A little less body this time.

Jesus, Natasha thinks. There's almost something comforting about trauma. Like you finally know how bad a thing can get.

"I'm gonna eat," she says. "You want anything?"

"No. Thanks. I don't wanna mess with my momentum."

"Don't want a three-legged sandwich?"

Dad smiles. Natasha heads to the kitchen and thinks how there's you, and there's your reality, and then . . . this invader. This bad thing that demands entrance into your world. And you say no because there isn't enough room inside yourself for this bad thing. Where would it fit? But after you close the door on it you realize it's already sitting on the couch.

Already in.

She opens the fridge, decides she's not hungry after all. She shuts the door and hears that soft thud again. Was it the refrigerator door? She tests it. No, she doesn't think so.

She looks up.

Ah yes. There it is again.

She was right the first time. Upstairs. Down the hall.

She walks to the foot of the steps.

"Mom?"

Mom has trauma of her own. Maybe everyone does. Maybe every living thing on Earth has some trauma they didn't invite inside.

"Mom?"

She walks through the living room, goes to the front windows, checks the two police cars in the drive. Each car has two officers. That's four cops. Watching her house. Four cops at each of the ballers' homes. Jesus.

An officer looks her way, smiles. Waves.

Natasha waves back. Feels weird. As if, by making contact with someone other than her family, other than those already deeply entrenched in her daily, agreed-upon reality, she's admitting something she's not ready to admit.

Someone has to be next.

She checks her phone. No response from Kit. Kit who called 911 on herself. That was a big deal back when that happened. It was the first time Natasha heard of someone her age having troubles. She thought it meant Kit was crazy. Called an ambulance on herself. Not because she broke a bone but because she was having broken thoughts.

Either way, Kit or no Kit, the others aren't chatting either. She guesses everyone wants to shut up for a second. Let the police do their work. Let's wait. Let's shut up and—

Another soft thud from above.

Natasha climbs the steps.

"Mom," she says. "Are you hanging pictures, for fuck's sake? You mixing drinks in a blender?"

Quincy was drinking earlier. She'll be drinking later.

Natasha reaches the top.

"Mom?"

She takes the hall to her parents' bedroom.

"Yo, Mom."

She enters and checks the master bathroom. Empty. She pauses at the walk-in closet just outside the bathroom door. She waits.

Did she hear it again? Mom couldn't be so drunk she'd be in the closet, right?

She opens it. Parts the hanging clothes. But Mom isn't passed out in the closet.

"Mom?"

She leaves the bedroom and thinks: What if I feel this way forever now? And what if I want to? What if I spend the rest of my life seeking bad situations because I'll only ever feel good if I feel bad?

Is this how Kit felt when she called 911?

She hears Quincy in the office. She enters.

A sudden thought crosses her mind: *Will I still be funny? When this is all over . . . will I still make people laugh?*

She looks past the person sitting in the office chair, looks to the window because, down on the grass, Quincy is wearing a bright-pink shirt. Caught her eye.

Mom. Outside. Dad in the basement.

Natasha looks to the person sitting in the office chair.

Her first thought is that she's wrong. This person can't be sitting, after all. She's as tall as Natasha. She must be standing.

"Oh," Natasha says. Something cold in her throat. "Oh no."

She backs up. Even as the person sitting (yes, she *was* sitting) rises to her full height. Even as the top of the woman's head touches the ceiling.

"Oh God."

Daphne is only three feet from her. She wears headphones, the cord snaking down the collar of her jean jacket, the long denim sleeves.

She's thumping her black boots to the beat she hears.

Natasha runs.

She's down the hall in seconds, almost falls down the stairs, catches herself, grips the railing, hits the first floor running to the back door.

"MOM! DAD!"

Through the kitchen, to the back door, she kicks it open, rushes to Quincy on the grass.

She grabs her by the pink sleeve. She's shaking. She thought she knew how bad it could get. She was wrong.

"She's in the house," Natasha says. "Mom, *she's in the fucking house.*"

Quincy looks to the bedroom window.

"Dad's in the house too," Quincy says.

Then they're both crossing the yard, exiting through the fence door, yelling for the police.

Both cruisers' doors open. Guns drawn, three of the officers enter the house. The fourth radios the station. Tells them the killer is here. *Right here.* In the house. The Manska girl saw him.

"Her," Natasha says. But Natasha is standing at the foot of the porch steps, too worried about Dad to go any farther from the house, too scared to get any closer.

Trauma. New. Newer. Seen upstairs in the office.

The fourth officer yells into his CB. Gives the address, talks fast. He rushes to join the others inside, bumps Natasha on the way.

And Natasha is suddenly alone.

She looks to her house. The upstairs windows. The fence door. Up and down the sidewalk. To the house again. Up. Down. The windows.

No gunshots. Why not?

No loud voices.

Why not?

Where is she?

She thinks of Dad's smile at the foot of the basement stairs. Thinks of Mom struggling to run to the driveway. When's the last time Quincy moved like that?

Across the street, neighbors peer out their windows. Two young kids watch from an open garage.

The Samhattan High School basketball team isn't just the top news in the city, it's the *only* story.

And the killer is inside her house.

Something fundamental has changed inside Natasha. She knows she will not be funny anymore.

"Mom?"

Quincy went inside. The police are inside. Dad is inside.

Daphne is too.

Dad cries out from the basement.

"Dad!"

Do the police know he's down there? Trying to fix a table for his family?

And Mom. She's downstairs with Dad. She must be. She ran to him.

Okay.

Natasha runs to him too.

She climbs the front steps. The front door is partially open, and she can see the length of hall from the foyer to the kitchen.

Where are the police?

She shouldn't go inside. She knows this.

But Dad . . .

She enters. Goes to the basement door.

"Dad? Mom?"

She hurries down the steps, sees the rag Dad left on the stack of magazines. Dad, who silently says I love you every chance he gets. Dad, who puts up with Quincy's drinking. Dad, who's put up with a daughter who hasn't shut up in seventeen years. Dad, who, with Mom, stands facing the dark, far side of the basement, their backs to Natasha.

She reaches the concrete floor. Stops.

Quincy doesn't turn to Natasha when she says,

"Go back upstairs, Nat. Someone's down here with us."

Dad holds a wrench. Mom a hammer.

And the feeling that there is still something worse to experience rises in Natasha.

She doesn't go back upstairs. She takes a step deeper into the basement and sees, beyond Dad's workbench:

Daphne.

"He's back there somewhere," Quincy says.

"If you're down here," Dad says, "I'll kill you."

They can't see her, Natasha knows. As big as the wall and they can't see her.

"Mom, *listen to me.* She's looking right at you."

Can't move. Can't make a decision. Too heavy. Changed.

Daphne doesn't move either. She stares at Natasha, her head cocked, ear flat to the ceiling beam; she's too big down here by a foot.

"All three of us are going to walk upstairs now," Natasha says, forced steadiness in her voice. "Mom . . . Dad . . ."

Quincy turns to her now. She believes her, Natasha knows. Believes her daughter is seeing something she cannot.

"Now," Natasha says.

"I'll kill you," Dad says again. But Natasha cuts him off.

"*Now.*"

Not funny. Never again.

The three back up to the basement stairs. Natasha takes the wrench from Dad, pushes her parents along. *Up. Hurry. Go. Careful. But GO.*

They go.

Natasha looks Daphne in the eye.

She throws the wrench at her and runs up the stairs. But there's an echo, a second set of shoes running: the police coming down the first-floor hall to the basement door.

Guns drawn.

Natasha's parents are up there already, yelling.

The first officer enters the basement and trains her gun on the first form she sees.

"Oh my God," she says.

It's not the person killing young women in Samhattan that she sees.

It's Natasha Manska.

Yet . . .

"Oh my God," the officer says again. "Oh my *God*."

She didn't fire. Yet the girl is dead.

An impossible shape halfway up the steps.

"Don't let them see this," she yells to the other officers. Then, to the basement: "We're coming down! *We are armed and we are coming down!*"

But it's hard to get past the thing on the stairs. Like a cardboard Halloween decoration, the limbs folded upon themselves.

And the face, flat to a wooden step, looking back up at her.

Later, when the officer describes the horrific scene over her CB, she will add a detail to the report that might've seemed trivial at any other time:

Someone was smoking and drinking in the basement. I smelled it. Smelled it passing me on the stairs.

But when she gets to the bottom, nobody's there. And despite the thorough search by herself and her colleagues, and despite the screaming of the parents, too, no suspect is found.

The first thing the officer says into her CB, her voice full of defeat, is this:

"We have to do more. Whatever we're doing . . . we're not doing enough. *We have to do more.*"

o o o

McGowan already is doing more.

She stands facing the three men and one woman like she would if they were her subordinates in the military. She's well past making good decisions. She knows this. She accepts this. What's good anyway? She lied to all four in bringing them here to the former sugar factory on Milton Street. She can hardly remember what she said, exactly, but she knows she used threats and force and even blackmail. That was all thanks to the chat Zach Gold left up on his smart TV at home. No, of course she doesn't know for certain these four have done anything deserving of jail, but they're also just young enough not to know that. Still, they know this isn't right.

They understand they shouldn't be tied to chairs with rope.

They keep saying as much.

"You're the one going to jail for this," Trina McDay says. Trina wears all black. A band name in silver across her chest. Rope across her chest too. McGowan barely hears her.

"She's gonna kill us," Evan Patrick says. "She's police gone crazy. Look at her eyes."

"You have to let us go," Bjorn Davison says. But McGowan is more interested in the band patches on his jean jacket.

They've been talking like this since she brought the fourth, Zach Gold, into the abandoned space. McGowan didn't plan on doing this. Not exactly this way. She hasn't planned anything, seen anything, or really even heard anything since leaving Chief Pollen at the Wild Stallion.

Her phone dings. Reminding her she still hasn't accepted the photos she sent herself from Pollen's phone.

"You call yourselves the Vann Guards," she says.

The four are visible in the daylight that still comes through the old sugar factory's high windows. Reminds McGowan of the high windows in the Samhattan High School gymnasium.

"You call yourselves the Vann Guards," she says again.

"We didn't hurt anybody," Trina says. Her voice is wholly contempt. McGowan briefly considers hurting the truth out of her.

There's law, and then there's four young women killed in the town you've sworn to protect.

"Tell me everything," McGowan says. Her voice is granite.

"Tell you *what*?" Evan says. He's scared. They all are.

McGowan steps to him. Grabs him by his denim collar.

"Who's killing the ballers?"

"Let go of me!" Evan cries. "I don't know!"

She releases him and pulls her gun from her jacket pocket. Bjorn shrieks and they all start begging, even Zach Gold, who has remained silent until now.

When McGowan holds the gun to Evan's belly, even Zach screams.

McGowan fires at the roof.

The four Vann Guards go silent. But even their silence shakes.

"Who's killing the ballers?" she asks.

They all look to each other, desperate. This worries McGowan. Do they not know? Can that be possible?

"Do you know what she did to the children she kidnapped?" McGowan asks.

Bjorn is the first to break.

"She didn't take kids. That's a fuckin' lie put out by the Samhattan Police because one of their own killed her."

"She ate them," McGowan says. "She ate the kids she took."

"You weren't even in this city back then," Trina says.

McGowan is surprised Trina McDay knows this. Why does she?

"No, I wasn't. If I was, she would've been caught."

There's a glimmer in Zach Gold's eyes with this. Like he'd like to see her try.

McGowan steps to him.

"Who's killing the girls?" she asks.

"Jesus," Zach says. "It's not us. This is *insane.*"

It is. Absolutely. Madness. McGowan will eventually have to let these four go. And by doing so, she's sending four messenger pigeons to the Samhattan press to tell them what she's done. She will go to prison for this. And according to the law, she should. She still understands this.

"I have photos," she says. "Of Daphne Vann's home the night she died."

"You expect us to believe police photos?" Bjorn says. "Look at what you're doing right now!"

McGowan pulls out her phone, accepts the pics and video. Shows Bjorn first.

Daphne's stovetop.

Bjorn looks away.

She steps to Evan, shows him the same.

"Fuck," he says.

She steps to Trina.

"That could be anything . . . anywhere," Trina says.

McGowan bends at the waist, lips to the young woman's ear.

"I'm sure you've visited the house before," she says. "I'm sure you've snuck inside. Maybe you even spent the night. I'm sure you're familiar with the fact that the house just . . . never seems to sell. That way they don't have to explain the stains above that stove. Or the stains all around the stove's mouth, like a toothless mouth after eating spaghetti for eight. Oh, I can see in your eyes you've seen these stains. You've prayed to her or talked to her or even tried to summon her in the very house she took those children. The same house, yes, where she was killed. You've been in her bedroom, and so you saw the children's clothing on the floor in there. You explored the basement because you're brave, Trina McDay. Because you're not scared of anything and anyone who tells you otherwise is shit. You don't trust any authority and authority doesn't trust you. You like it that way. The Vann Guards. Did you wanna see more? You wanna conjure Daphne Vann? Just think about her, right? Isn't that all you have to do? I bet you've done a lot of it through the years. Have you also thought of the families of those children? Have you thought of how heartbreaking it is that these families don't speak of their children's killer because they're afraid to bring her back?" McGowan holds a pic inches from Trina's eyes. "What do you think of that head on the floor, Trina? Pretty neat, huh?"

"*Stop it,*" Trina says.

Evan comes to her aid:

"You can't stop thinking about her."

McGowan rises to her full height, steps to him, grabs him by the back of his head.

"*How do you know Peter Lords?*"

"Jesus! Get off—"

"*HOW DO YOU KNOW PETER LORDS?*"

She holds the gun to Evan's chin.

Evan cries.

"Stop," Zach says. "Please. Stop." Defeat or something like it in his voice. McGowan can taste it; catching this killer. She's so close. "He's a crazy old man. He's a fan, yeah. So are we. Okay? We're allowed to be. But Peter's a bigger fan than us."

McGowan steps back from Evan.

"What do you mean?"

"Shut up," Bjorn tells him.

But Zach goes on: "I work at Hi-Fi Grocery. I've been there five years. That's where I first heard of her."

"From who?"

"I don't know."

"You don't have to talk to her," Bjorn says.

"From who?"

"I truly don't know. My guess is it was Peter Lords. He tried to join the Vann Guards but he's . . . too much. We stopped hanging out with him months ago. Listen. Please." Zach's eyes fill up and he can't stop himself from crying and he can't lift his hands to wipe away the tears. "I showed Kennedy Lichtenstein. It's my fault she died."

"Showed her what?"

"Someone wrote 'Daphne Lives' on the breakroom wall," Zach says. "Okay? I was told to scrub it clean. But it keeps coming back. It's everywhere back there. I showed Kennedy because I thought it was cool. I—"

"Who wrote it?" McGowan asks.

"I don't know."

"Who could have written it?"

"Someone that works there . . . I guess. Someone who goes back there."

A voice crackles through McGowan's CB.

Another baller?

"Who do you work with?" she asks.

"A lot of people," Zach says

"But not Peter Lords."

"No."

She heads for the warehouse exit, where, long ago, Samhattanites got off work, some of them worried for the safety of their children in the era of Daphne Vann.

"What the *fuck*," Trina McDay calls out. "You can't leave us here like this!"

McGowan pauses at the exit.

"You wanna be untied?" she asks.

They don't answer. She didn't think they would.

"Conjure Daphne. Maybe she can help you."

o o o

Kit Lamb's Journal—The Spirit of Samhattan

Hi, Jolly. Are you there? Do you only exist in the pages of a bound book? Or are you wherever I write?

How about on a huge rock? Do you exist here? The rock I write on?

They call this the Spirit of Samhattan. There must be hundreds of layers of paint. I bet the rock is actually only half the size, the rest . . . generations of joy. This rock is a record of wins. Good times. Celebration. Victory. Nobody goes to the Spirit of Samhattan when they lose. Nobody signs and dates the rock when they got their asses kicked.

And I'd bet nobody's ever come here when they know they're about to die either.

So, okay.

This is my will. A suicide note, though I won't be killing myself. Not directly. Still, I WILL be doing it. I may not drive the knife in, but I've definitely extended the blade. After all, it is my fault I can't stop thinking about her.

It is my fault she's coming for me.

Here:

KIT LAMB, SEVENTEEN YEARS OLD

SOON TO DIE

BY DAPHNE

The Spirit of Samhattan. Ironic name now, huh? Yeah. Here I am, trying to avoid the spirit of Samhattan so I go to the Spirit of Samhattan. I suppose I was drawn here for a reason.

Daphne.

Why hide it now? Someone will come read this rock when I'm dead. And they'll see her name and they'll start thinking about her and all this horribleness will start all over again. But what's the point in hiding, right? She's in us already.

And hey, don't think she'll stop with us.

Whoever reads this rock . . . Daphne's sticking around. And if you think about her?

She'll come

for

YOU

She'll sleep inside the citizens of Samhattan like she has all these years. This giant seven-foot woman who arrives a victim, until you realize she's not. Oh, did I mention that, Jolly? Yeah, Daphne's no outsider. Nobody who had been unfairly shunned by the world would kill Kennedy Lichtenstein. No true outsider would hurt a hair on Melanie's head. Because a true outsider respects the others she finds standing out of bounds.

Outsiders know empathy better than anybody else on the planet.

So . . . without further ado

fuck you

Daphne.

Whatever your story is, you weren't the good guy.

And hey: whoever does read this, if it's Detective McGowan or Principal Taylor, or anybody else: please check on my mom and dad. And please tell them to talk about Daphne. Really. Freely. Make sure they understand the things we're told not to talk about are the things that get real bad. Those subjects get sick. And they get confused. And nobody can make sense of them because they were never allowed to talk them out.

You know?

Tell Mom and Dad I love them too.

Please.

And now, Jolly, a thought:

I swiped this Sharpie from Hi-Fi on my walk out here. Yep. Walked right into the store, went to an unmanned register, reached behind the counter, and took it. Was it because I knew I'd come here to write you? Yes and no. I knew I had to talk to you, one more time. But I didn't know where. Then, I started thinking about that shot, right? The free throw that started it all. I thought about winning that game and how sometimes winning is an illusion because it's the fantasy of winning that counts. It's what excites you, what you think you are capable of, THAT'S what matters most.

Do you hear her? Can you see her? Can you smell her yet?

She's coming. Oh yeah. She's on her way.

Wanna know why I'd recognize Daphne anywhere, Jolly?

Because she's me.

No, not like that. Let me explain.

I've come to realize something pretty dark in all that's gone on. Something that's taken me too long to admit. I've written about anxiety (regular size now, see?), written endlessly about what it's done to me and how badly I've wanted to get out from under it. But the thing is, now that it's here? Now that it's here in its worst form? Death on the front porch?

Turns out I want it.

That's right. Turns out I want to feel this way. It's me, after all, isn't it? This panic, these free-floating fears, this horror? All me, Jolly. I can't stop thinking about Daphne any more than I can stop writing about anxiety.

Know what? Watch me now. Let's just go for it:

ANXIETY

See? Doesn't that feel good? Sure does. Because that's me and I don't know who I'd be without it. And guess what? I kinda like me. That's right. I kinda like the person I am, the woman I've become. I've gone from a pipsqueak freshman who couldn't keep her head up in the halls to being the team's second leading scorer in what feels like a blink. It used to be I didn't raise my hand in class and now I'm the first one up because I want to know the answers to my questions. I want to learn. And that constant hum, that engine inside me . . . well, shit, Jolly. A lot of that is fear, anxiety, guilt. And if those are what propel me . . .

are they really that bad?

I saw an interview with Soleil Johnson after a bad loss (and she played real bad too) and the interviewer asked how she was going to move past this game and she said something that really stuck with me, she said: You can't find your identity in the game or you'll forget who you are. You can't identify as a player first or you'll lose track of who you are. Or worse: you'll think you're nothing when you're not playing the game.

But as much as I love Soleil Johnson, you know what I think?

I think it's okay to identify with anxiety. I think it's okay to say this is who I am. And I can work on it as much or as little as I want, but this is who I am. Know what else? I think it's okay to identify as a player too. Because the pride I find in the game is so big, and the lessons I've learned about myself and my friends, all that is what shapes me. Where am I supposed to find my identity if not in what I do, in what I love?

Hey, you, reading this rock, YOU, standing at the Spirit of Samhattan, where do you find your identity if not in what you love?

Is there anywhere else in the world?

Oh, Jolly. I don't know if I could live without Daphne at this point. I don't know if I could live without the constant drum of horror. You wanna know real fear, reader o' mine? Tell yourself you have nothing

left to do and nothing left to feel. That's right. I'm Daphne because
I'm anxiety, Jolly. I'm an attack. This whole fucking time . . .

It's ME I was scared of.

How would I react?

Who would I be?

Who would I become?

But you know what's scarier than the Coming Doom, Jolly?

Thinking you know how to beat it.

And I'll tell you a secret, YOU:

I think I know how to beat it.

Because I think that's the point. I want Daphne to come

because I want

to fucking

win.

So let's see if I do.

If this is my last journal entry, the last thing I ever write, I'd like to
say thank you, Jolly. For listening to me. I'm reading the rest of the
rock right now, all our signatures, all the super-hyped stuff we wrote
the night I made the game winner. I was already nervous then. We
all were. I can see it in our handwriting.

I was nervous long before then too.

And that's part of it, right?

I was nervous.

But I made the shot.

Where can you possibly look to find more of yourself than right
there?

Are you brave?

Because isn't that what life is literally, entirely about?

Bravery?

Wish me luck, Jolly. Because I'm going to face her now. I'm going
to face the thing I've been afraid of my whole life, since the first time

I heard her name on the wind of Samhattan and just as quickly forgot it.

Because I'm a Samhattanite, through and through. I was born and raised here. And I've lived my whole life with this really big issue that nobody wants to talk about.

Don't talk about her, they say.

But . . .

Don't think about her, they say.

But . . .

Bravery.

And facing the things you were told to ignore.

So, this is it, Jolly.

Time to go address it.

Time to talk about it.

Time to look it in the face.

Here, I'll start by leaving this, big as I can:

DAPHNE

And may you, reader, never keep quiet about the things that need talking about.

It's the only way to solve them.

Okay?

Now, wish me luck.

Oh God.

Here I go.

Into the brave.

Me

Brave.

○ ○ ○

McGowan enters Hi-Fi Grocery at a fast clip. She's sweating and she's still wearing her police jacket and she's already two steps in before she tucks the gun deeper into the pocket. Maybe somebody saw it. Maybe not. Maybe the people are scared of what they see. It crosses her mind that the last time she was here was for a carton of eggs. This time: a killer. Can they tell? These Samhattanites? These people who kept and still keep mum about the woman who kidnapped children and ate them in her suburban home? Do they find *her*, McGowan, scary, despite believing in things so much worse? Like ghosts? Like the ghost of the worst person to ever call this city home? In the box Principal Taylor gave her, in the journals of Kell Darren and Nicole Welsh, McGowan read about Daphne's grave, unmarked but unmistakable, located at the deep end of the cemetery, under the lowest-hanging trees, where the girl Kennedy Lichtenstein was killed. McGowan doesn't know if what the girls wrote about is factual or not. But the girls sure believed it. They sang dark folk songs and poured red wine into the dirt and repeated her name, *Daphne, Daphne, Daphne,* in a celebratory attempt to raise the dead.

McGowan is just trying to find a killer.

She doesn't even pretend to keep a low profile. Moving as fast as when she entered, she takes the large center aisle straight to the back, where she knows the push doors lead to the storage freezers, the stock shelves, and, yes, the breakroom where the sniveling Zach Gold first saw the bogeywoman's name. She pays zero mind to the locals who back up, who step out of her way, who open their mouths to say something but do not speak. They no doubt tie her presence to the killings, know she's trying to outpace a monster in Samhattan.

She thinks of Chief Pollen talking about Daphne like she was having an episode. Saying she would likely forget their conversation soon after having it. It's difficult not to imagine these locals in the same light: Do they think of Daphne? Or is the name out of reach for them like it had been for Pollen for so long?

And what did all that mean? Pollen going on about how there

was no cover-up, how she would know, *she* would be the one to cover something up . . .

The woman looked scared. That much McGowan saw with her own eyes.

When she reaches the push doors, she doesn't hesitate, doesn't care if someone's standing on the other side, feels no need to announce herself. She kicks the doors open and comes face-to-face with the store's longtime manager, Abigail Rain.

"What's going on?" Rain says. Real shock in her eyes. She shoulda seen the sugar factory.

"The breakroom," McGowan says.

Rain, who always looks shocked, whether or not the girls' basketball team is getting picked off one at a time, looks over her shoulder as if whoever is currently in that room must be the person McGowan is sweating to speak with.

"Did something happen in there?" she asks.

But McGowan saw where she looked and she's already past her, already at the breakroom door.

Rain follows.

"Who's been writing 'Daphne Lives' on the walls?" McGowan asks her.

Two young men sit at the table, eyeing her with real fear.

"Excuse me?" Rain asks.

"I'm not gonna ask twice."

"How do you even know about that? Is that who you think is responsible for—"

"I know it is. Who's been writing it?"

"I . . . I don't know."

McGowan shoots her a look of fire and glaciers both.

"Honest, Detective. I do not know. I've tried to—"

"You have cameras."

"Not in the breakroom. That's against code."

Something flickers in McGowan's eyes. A memory of codes. Of conduct.

"But I've seen it by the microwave," Rain says. "All over the place. I make 'em scrub it off. There's one behind the fridge now."

McGowan goes straight for the refrigerator. She puts her shoulder into it and doesn't ask for help. Still, the two stock boys do.

"You gotta tell me what's going on," Rain says.

They slide the fridge a few feet.

On the wall, in black marker:

Daphne Lives

"No idea who wrote this?" McGowan asks. She faces the stock boys.

"No idea," one says. The other is too scared to speak.

Abigail steps closer.

"Look," she says. "If you find out, let me know."

"A list of everyone who works here," McGowan says. "Now."

Abigail points to the time cards racked above the time clock.

"You'll find the names of every employee there."

McGowan moves quickly. She scans the names, up and down.

"This would be very bad," Rain says. "Oh my God, this would be *bad*." Then, to the stock boys, "You two. Get." Then, when they don't move, louder. "Go on! Get!"

They do. McGowan turns to face Rain. The look in her eyes different now.

She holds up a time card.

"This one," she says. "Who is this?"

It reads:

CW

"Are you serious?" Rain says. "Of all my employees . . . that's Coach Wanda, Detective."

"Wanda works here?"

"You don't make a million dollars coaching girls' high school basketball. But there's no way . . ."

"What does she do here? Why have I never seen Coach Wanda out front before?"

"Because she works solely in stock. The freezers and the shelves."

McGowan is out of the room before Rain finishes the sentence. She's pulling boxes from the shelves, two, three, at a time.

"Same writing," she says.

On the wall, in black marker:

Daphne Lives

She moves quickly to the freezers, pulls the pin, opens the door to the first, enters, rips packages of meat from the shelves.

"Same writing," she says.

Daphne Lives

"Where is she now? Right now?" she asks.

Rain manages to say, "She quit the same day the first girl from the basketball team died. Said she was grieving." Then, "Do you need her—"

But McGowan is out of the freezer and through the staff doors.

No, she doesn't need the address.

She knows where Coach Wanda lives.

o o o

Dana needs to find Kit. Now. This second.

Natasha is dead.

There is no sense anymore, no safety, nothing is safe, and nothing feels real.

The fact that Kit hasn't responded to Dana's texts (or any, including Natasha's; and how can this be possible? *Dead?*) means Kit must've gotten killed too. There's no other explanation. Yet no news about that. And whether it's from the police, family and friends, ballers, or the actual news, every death has been reported so far. Dana is able to account for every team member but one.

So, she needs to find Kit.

Find her *now*.

Problem is, there are six squad cars outside Dana's house. A Samhattan officer in every room. There are even officers from neighboring towns: Chaps, Chowder, East Kent.

Up in her bedroom, she's alternately hot and cold, empowered and paralyzed.

It's not hard to imagine Kit unconscious. Hurt. She's not responding. Maybe she saw the killer, ran, fell, hit her head. She could be unconscious right now and nobody would know where she is. The more she thinks about it, the better this idea sounds. Maybe even the killer doesn't know where Kit is . . .

Dana paces.

Of course, Kit *could* be held captive in a Samhattan basement. *Could* be enduring torture. Could be . . .

Dana goes to the window, eyes the cars below. Looks up to the attic square in her bedroom ceiling.

"Kit," she says. "Where are you?"

Is this real life? But it can't be. A killer? Here in Samhattan?

"Daphne," Dana says.

Then she wishes she didn't. She can't stand the name. Hates what it stands for. Hates how it makes her feel.

It's like a vague, traumatic memory from her childhood . . . something her parents once protected her from . . . even just the name . . . a memory of people saying, *No, don't say that, you can say any name but that one* . . .

She calls Kit again. Texts her. Texts the others. Dana is close enough to Kit's parents to call them. She does.

Kit's dad answers:

"She's upstairs," he tells her. "She doesn't want to be bothered. Please don't write her again until this is over."

But Dana pushes. Asks him to go look upstairs. It's unlike Kit not to respond. Her dad sounds like he's trying to convince himself everything's fine. He sounds tired. Sounds scared. In fact, the fear is growing, audible to Dana. He calls out to his wife, Evelyn. She yells back that Kit is sleeping upstairs.

But Dana knows she's not. She just knows.

"Mr. Lamb," she says. "She's not there."

He sounds angry when he responds. Nearly yells at her over the phone. Dana understands she's pulled him from some mental stupor. Jesus. Kit's parents are as scared as the ballers are.

"Mr. Lamb . . ."

Movement. Voices. Sounds like he's walking upstairs. He's breathing hard. Dana paces. Listens. Hears it when Kit's mom gets close. The two of them together now. They sound so tired. A third voice. An officer? Yes. He's talking like one. Says she's still asleep. Says he checked.

"No," Dana says.

But the Lambs aren't responding to her anymore.

"I'm sorry," Dana says.

Because she is. And because she knows. She knows her friend. If Dana herself is pacing her bedroom, Kit must be pacing the entire city.

She hasn't been asleep like they thought she was. Not a fucking chance.

Then, revelation on the other end. It arrives in a hysterical scream:

"How could you let this happen?"

And an argument. Rage.

"How could I? You told me you knew!"

"*HOW THE FUCK COULD YOU?*"

Dana hears every second of it. Hears fresh voices trying to calm Kit's parents down. Hears them saying please, we need to be smart, there's no sign of a struggle, no blood.

Only, also, no daughter.

The cacophony that follows, the chaos, the palpable fear, a terrible scene painted in sound.

Dana hangs up.

It's exactly what she was worried about.

What she knew was true.

Kit is, right now, missing.

Dana leaves her bedroom, sees an officer in the hall.

"You need something?" he asks.

"Worried about a friend."

He doesn't take this lightly. He gets on his CB.

"Kit is missing," Dana says. "They can't find her in her house. She was surrounded by police too."

The cop relays this info.

"Send more," he says. "Call Goblin. Do whatever you have to do."

The lack of confidence, lack of a plan, chills her. She moves to pass him in the hall.

"I think maybe you should stay up here."

"There are other officers below."

"Just stay in your room."

"Kit was just staying in her room."

The officer lets this sink in. For as mad as what the teenager is telling him, it's also true.

Still, he's not letting her go.

"I'm sorry, Dana," he says. "As bad as things are, they're better if you stay in your room."

Dana. Like he knows her. Like he's a family friend, rather than an officer assigned to protect her from a killer.

"Fine," she says.

Because she has an idea. And no man in any uniform is going to stop her.

She enters her bedroom, closes the door, moves her desk chair under the attic square in the ceiling.

She's only been up there once before. When they first moved into the house, she pushed the square aside to get a look at how much space she had. Propelled then by images of a secret, magic world, adjacent to her very real bedroom, she pulled herself up halfway. Only, there was nothing magical about the attic. For starters, it was only three feet high, tops. And the dust could've been spider webs. And the one window was as dark as a blindfold.

She slides the square aside now, listens for movement in the hall. She waits. Can the man hear her? Surely he's been trained to recognize the telltale signs of a suspect who is considering fleeing a scene. Can he tell when the same thoughts run through the mind of a person he's protecting?

No sound from out in the hall.

It strikes her that Coach Wanda's insistence on pull-ups after every practice is about to pay off. There is no ladder, no easy way up.

Dana grips the ledge and pulls herself high enough so that she can get one arm flat to the damp boards. The smell is dizzying.

She thinks of Coach Wanda counting their pull-ups, the fierce woman's voice echoing in the Samhattan High School gym.

One . . .

With leverage from the one arm, she swings her other over and onto the boards and pulls herself up to her waist. The man in the hall had to have heard that. Still, no sound out there. And too late to turn back. She gets over the lip. Her legs now, her feet.

She's in.

And she's up.

"Kit," she says as she closes the square again, "I'm coming."

Voices outside. Beyond the nearly opaque pane of glass.

Are they discussing Kit? Is there news? Is she dead?

Dana crawls to the window.

It's dark and the wood is splintered, and she knows she's going to have to pull some from her palms. Something moves beneath her right hand. She lifts it just in time to see a spider the size of her palm scurrying out of the scant light.

Her hand covers her mouth instinctively, but she can't quite quell the groan. She's never seen a spider this big, and if she'd known it was living above her bedroom, above her *bed*, she wouldn't have stayed in this house long.

She crawls, because she has to, but doesn't take her eyes off where the spider went. Are there more? Of course there are more.

This is their room.

At the window, she sees it has one latch, an old, rusted lever she prays will turn easily.

It does.

She eyes the rooftop and the grass beyond. No cops on the roof, thank God, but yes, a cruiser in view of the lawn she'd need to drop to.

She pushes the window open, crawls halfway out, feels a tickle on her ankle.

The spider, or one like it, is on her leg.

She can't cover her mouth this time.

"Get the *fuck* off me!"

She kicks at it and it rolls, actually *rolls* across the attic floor.

Dana moves fast, quiet, out the window and onto the roof.

Below: the squad car. But as far as she can tell, there's nobody behind the wheel. And nobody in the passenger seat.

She lies flat to the shingles and inches her way to the edge. She doesn't plan to use a gutter and there is no latticework, but pull-ups aren't the only thing Coach Wanda always insists on and Dana has never been more grateful for the billion exercises that strengthen the ballers' ankles.

When she gets to the edge, she looks down, sees it's far, sees also the living-room window she'd surely land in front of.

How does one get out of a house full of police officers and parents?

How did Kit?

But she knows how Kit did it. And it makes her smile, and almost cry, thinking of the basement bathroom door that leads to the yard.

She army-crawls across the shingles toward the backyard, her belly grating against the ridge running alongside the length of the house. When she reaches the back, she sees the officer below. As expected.

She waits. She listens. No movement or voices from inside. Nobody asking where she is.

Okay.

She crawls to the front of the house again, looks down, sees two officers in a cruiser parked almost in front of the neighbor's home. They're facing the other direction, up the street. She recognizes them as two who had spent some time inside the house.

She thinks: Whenever she walked to the foyer to look out the front windows, the officers were seated on the couch in the living room, their backs to the glass. As if they assumed the men and women in the cruisers had their eyes on the front door. And the officers outside? They were all looking up the street, yes. Looking for who might be coming.

That means . . . no eyes on the front door.

And none on the front windows either.

Possibly.

Without allowing herself too much time to think, Dana swings her legs over the roof's edge, counts to three, hears Coach Wanda shouting about how no baller can play without her ankles, and drops.

She lands in a perfect semi-crouch, with her back to the front windows.

She looks to the house. Looks to the squad cars.

Wasting no time, she begins walking up the sidewalk. She'll pass one of the cruisers, but maybe, *maybe,* if she carries herself the right way, they'll assume she's a neighbor. How well do they all know what she looks like? She doesn't know who is in this car, whether or not she met them. Do they expect a young woman dressed in jeans and a Doors T-shirt to be one of the starters for the Samhattan High School girls' basketball team? Would they recognize her as an athlete?

Dana's dad talks a lot about when he lived in New York City. He said he always walked like he "owned the place." Said it's the reason he never got mugged. Dad exaggerates. But the advice resonates now.

She passes the cruiser. She even nods to the cop she does not recognize. There's a little thank-you in her nod. *Thank you for all you're doing for our city. You'll catch the killer. We believe in you. We need you.*

Thank God for you.

And he nods with a little you're-welcome in return.

Dana does as Dad said to do: she walks like she owns the place, takes a right on Red Maple, vanishes behind the Metzgers' brown picket fence.

Now, no longer any reason (no time, either) to play it cool, she runs. Sure, anybody who sees her might know her, and so the cops might be notified after all. But Dana is thinking of Kit and Kit alone.

She's not going to Kit's house. No reason. The phone call told her she wasn't there. And she isn't going to the police station, though she suspects she might learn a lot just by stepping inside that place.

No. She's heading to Garland Park. The only place in the world the ballers have ever totally been themselves. The park where they all became best friends. Where Dana and Kit combined to destroy dozens of other duos on the court. Where they perfected their pick and rolls, their pick and pops, their no-look passes and those with looks too. They once won fifteen games in a row on that court, half those games against the boys, as Kit and Dana took turns being "the heavy," the primary scorer, as the other played the true point, distributing, even if only to one. There was five-on-five on that court too. Almost the entire girls' team meeting up for summer games, games Coach Wanda didn't require of them, games they arranged themselves for the straight-up love of the sport. The sidelines (the cracked concrete) would be covered in Gatorade bottles, water bottles, towels, gym bags, wallets, phones, and keys. If something got stolen? Who cared? This was basketball and threading the needle to a cutting Kit was worth more than anything Dana ever had on her.

She runs.

Dana hit game winners in Garland Park. Kit got into a yelling match with a girl named May from Chaps on that court. They almost fought with fists. Dana and Kit still bring that up today. Even Natasha hit a crazy hook shot out there, one that brought the house down. Garland Park was more than just something to do after school. It *was* school. It was where Dana learned angles and numbers, social constructs, and how things are *really* run. It's where she and Kit learned any and all street skills they had today. And now?

Now Dana approaches Garland with a gun tucked into the waistband of her jeans.

No, not the shitty relic she bought from Phil at Dawn Pawn.

This gun she swiped from the officer in the hall of her home. When she made to step around him, with no actual intention of doing so. The officer who, right now, still might not know it's missing.

Crossing Big Spruce, she tucks up a little bit into herself. She's close to Garland now and doesn't know exactly what she'll do if an officer stops her, tries to bring her home. Doesn't even want to have a plan for that.

Kit is out in the world. *Somewhere.* And Dana, her best friend, has a hunch.

She waits for a car to pass on Michigan Avenue. She looks through the glass and sees an older man with a mustache. No seven-foot woman in a jean jacket.

She crosses Michigan. She can see the park now. Sees a handful of silhouettes sitting together on the grass. She's flooded with memories. Emily swishing a no-look *shot*. Games of PIG that became games of PIGLET that became games of THEPIGLETSON-THEFARMARESMALLERTHANTHEPIGS. Kit once blocked a shot so hard it got stuck in the fence. Dana kicked a ball out of frustration so far it almost reached all the way here, to Michigan Avenue, on the bounce. Life-and-death shit on the court in Garland Park. Truth-or-dare shit too. Questioning their futures, their drive, their friendships, their sexuality, their views on parenthood, adulthood, business, sports, entertainment, money, love, death.

A lot of those questions, of course, answered by the rims.

Dana is close enough to see none of the figures are Kit.

It's Stewart, Brandon, and Little Richard instead.

This urgency she feels is unfathomable. Is this how Kit felt when she called 911 on herself? That was a scary moment for Dana.

Ahead, Brandon slowly stands up.

Maybe they know something. Maybe they saw something. Maybe they're out here for doing what Dana and Kit have done so many times at Garland Park:

Maybe the boys are out here *dealing with it.*

"Hey!" Dana calls.

Surely they see the urgency in her step. Her posture. Her eyes.

"Dana," Stewart says. Now all three boys are standing. They look to the main roads. No doubt worried the police would ask them all to go home. But the police, of course, are mostly occupied in the driveways of the remaining members of the Samhattan High School girls' basketball team.

"Have you seen Kit?" Dana asks.

A flicker. The tiniest bit. In Little Richard's eye.

Dana doesn't hesitate.

"Tell me. The fuck. Now."

Richard looks to the others. Brandon looks to the ground. Stewart is going to say it, though. Dana can tell.

"She said she wants to be alone," Stewart says. "She's okay."

The relief Dana feels is overwhelming. Like she could collapse here, become a pile of folded clothes on the concrete.

Still. "And what the *fuck* does okay mean right now, Stewart? Tell me that." Then, "When did you see her? And where?"

"Earlier today. Outside Third-and-Fourth-Eye," Stewart says. "Look, Dana. She *really* wants to be alone. She was going off about . . . about clearing her mind. She said she needed to go someplace where she could . . . really clear her mind. Alone."

It strikes Dana how fucking obvious the answer is. But she asks anyway.

"Where, Stewart?"

"Dana, I can't say. I promised."

"We're dying, you *fucking moron*."

But Dana already knows where Kit went. And, in a sense, she's already on her way there.

Kit once called it *heaven*. She said, *For me, heaven is the gym. Sam-hattan High. It's the only place I feel faster than what chases me.*

"I'm gonna tell you where she is," Dana says, eyeing the three. "And you're gonna tell me I'm right. And if you don't, and if I turn out to *be* right, that's it for us on any level ever again. You got it?"

The boys agree.

Dana clears her throat, overwhelmed with the emotion there.

"She's in the gymnasium," she says.

Stewart nods. Brandon nods. Little Richard says, "Yep."

And Dana's off. Walking so fast, the world moving so fast, it already feels like her brief encounter with the boys happened days ago. She's crossing Buckland without looking both ways, then passing the very bookstore Stewart mentioned. The cemetery to her left, the buildings where men and women no doubt discuss the basketball team, *her* team, to her right. She can't stop for anything now, wouldn't even if the police pulled up.

Her phone rings.

Dad.

Doesn't matter.

They know she's gone now.

Doesn't matter.

She takes a left. A car honks and she doesn't look to see who it is. She starts running. Jeans or no jeans, Dana is flying now. Like she's late for class—worse, late for a game.

The building is brick orange, easy to spot. Her chest hurts with the running and she imagines Coach Wanda coaching her, pushing her, applauding her endurance. Coach Wanda, who is hard as hell on the girls but only because she wants the best out of them.

Coach Wanda, who epitomizes Samhattan more than any other person Dana knows.

The parking lot now. She's still running, the same speed, the same hurt.

"Come on, Kit," she says. "Be alive."

A terrible thing to think. Yet how could she think anything else? The reality of the last few days cloaks her, wraps itself around her, gets *into* her in a way it hasn't yet. And she feels heavier for it, thicker, like she can't possibly make it all the way to the silver side doors of the gym, yes, their heaven, yes, the site of so much glory that it must remain their glory days, no matter what they do, where they go, from here.

If Garland Park is where they discovered themselves, the Samhattan High School gym is where they showed the world what they found.

Dana can hear Coach Wanda yelling at her to keep it up, to push, to reach those fucking doors. She can hear her saying the doors are open: *look!*

And they are.

Someone's inside!

And someone is.

Listen: a ball bouncing on the hardwood floor.

"Come on," Dana tells herself. "Come on."

It's Kit, has to be Kit, please, Kit, still alive.

But when Dana reaches the doors, even before her eyes adjust to the change in light, even before she has time to feel the relief at seeing her friend (yes) alive, she sees that Kit is not alone.

Kit is at the free-throw line at the far end of the gym, lining up the shot the way she does, elbow perfectly in, left hand perfectly supporting. But the seven-foot woman who smells of smoke and whiskey, who is as out of place in this gymnasium as a black bear, is stepping toward her, arms extended, her bare hands open.

Dana pulls the gun from her waistband, takes aim, and thinks:

She's not a ghost. The bullet won't go through her. The bullet won't hit Kit. Shoot her, Dana. There's no such thing as ghosts . . .

o o o

McGowan knocks on Coach Wanda's front door. That's the thing with smaller-city coaches; nobody imagines them outside the roles they play in the community. When you see them at the bar, you call them Coach. At the store, you nod, *Hey, Coach.* On the street: *Go get 'em, Coach.*

In fact, often you don't even pay real attention to their full names.

She knocks again.

"Coach?"

See? Like that. Even now. "Coach." Not Wanda Van Horn as McGowan knows her last name to be through interviews and police reports filed in conjunction with the investigation the detective has all but left behind.

She tries the knob. It's locked.

She wonders if a bullet will be enough.

Instead, she takes the porch steps and walks along the side of the house, looking into each window she passes. The interior matches McGowan's idea of Coach Wanda the person. Spartan, simple, dull.

The backyard is half-mown. A couple lawn chairs look the worse for wear. The fence is about neck-high and there is no sign a basketball coach lives here.

No sign of a dog either.

She climbs the back steps and shoulders the back door hard enough to break it.

She's inside now.

"Coach?"

Gun chest-high, McGowan steps through the small, clean kitchen. Spartan, indeed. A table with no cloth. No dishes in the sink. The walls are bare of any paintings or pictures.

There's no sign of anybody present either. No creaking boards, no running water, no voices.

McGowan eyes the tiled floor. And while it's nothing like the pattern from the new photo in her pocket, she thinks of the small head all the same.

"Coach?"

Yes. *Coach* Wanda. Wanda Van Horn. Forty-one years old. Been head coach of the Samhattan High School girls' team for fourteen years. Grew up in Michigan. But not Samhattan.

Or did she? McGowan doesn't remember asking Wanda where she was from. It didn't seem pertinent to the line of prepared questions. But now, having faced Chief Pollen, and the look on Pollen's face as she described growing up in a city with unspoken shared trauma . . . it suddenly feels very important to her.

"Miss Van Horn?"

That's right. Use her name.

"Miss Van Horn? Detective McGowan here. I'm entering your living room now."

Then: the living room, a narrow hall, a small office, a bathroom, a bedroom. All of it undecorated. McGowan would've guessed these walls had at least one framed picture of the team. A trophy on a bookshelf. A plaque, a ribbon, an award.

If there's one thing Carla McGowan has learned through detective work, it's that people display what they're proud of. What they identify with. Who they are. Yet if she had to determine who Wanda Van Horn was by way of this illegal search, she'd say . . .

"I haven't found it yet."

Her eyes alight on the top of a set of basement stairs. The steps are carpeted, indicating finished space below.

McGowan waits. Listens.

Then she moves quietly to the top step, eyeing the distance to go.

At the carpeted bottom, already more color than anything up here. What looks like graffitied snakes upon gray brick walls. Words and names.

One of those:

Daphne.

McGowan steels herself. Keeps the gun chest-high.

She doesn't announce that she's coming down. Hardly breathes as the words on the wall get bigger, easier to read, and she sees Daphne's name in full:

Daphne Vann.

It's not even the name that chills her. That makes it suddenly hard for her to stay in this house. To *not* be out in the world, on the streets, in the homes of the remaining members of the basketball team.

Nor is it the black graffitied heart that harbors the monster's name.

It's the second name with it, bound by the + sign:

Wanda Vann.

"Wanda Van Horn," McGowan says, unable to stop herself, even as she descends the steps, even as she sees more of the basement wall she approaches, even as the black snakes become something more like strands of black hair.

Wanda Vann

Daphne Vann

A simple thing to overlook. But it feels like the reason more than one girl has died in all this. It feels like McGowan was so blinded by her impatience, her duty, that she didn't pay attention to the details of her job.

When she reaches the carpet, she already knows what she's going to see. This wall and the one opposite it show the same tendrils of black hair, growing thicker, darker, as they head deeper into the basement, until they meet at the far wall, where the head and the face are painted with enough detail to scare McGowan stiff.

It's Daphne. It's a shrine to Daphne.

This is what Coach Wanda cares about.

"Christ . . ."

There aren't many places for someone to hide down here, but McGowan keeps the gun up all the same. It takes a few seconds before she realizes she's pointing the muzzle at the face itself, the giant features rendered in blue spray paint, as if the woman this basement is dedicated to is actually there, the distance of one Samhattan cellar away.

But it's the bare hands, one on each side of the huge head, that bring McGowan to think of her own hands, and what she holds, and why. She turns to make sure she is alone down here, aiming toward the four corners of the basement, looking for hidden doors in the woman's hair, before she faces the mural again.

A single small chair faces Daphne. The kind of chair McGowan has seen in the Samhattan elementary school classrooms.

McGowan approaches, slowly, and sees Daphne's hands are not empty.

At first, because of the chaos of everything surrounding this experience, McGowan mistakes the small, colorful pieces for drugs.

But they are candy.

She thinks of Pollen sitting in the booth at the Wild Stallion. The chief of police, defeated, it seems, decades ago, by this very case.

McGowan gets closer. But she feels it: the *fear* of proximity to this woman, myth or not. It's nearly intoxicating, the blue face, the black hair, the denim collar just visible behind the huge, strong hands.

But it's the signature at the mural's bottom that scares McGowan most:

Brea Delany.

And she thinks of Pollen again. Recalls the name of the last little girl taken, the very girl on the video in McGowan's police jacket pocket.

Brea Delany.

Did she paint this? Here? But Daphne didn't live here. Did Brea . . .

McGowan reaches for the chair, to stabilize herself, to keep from falling. Instinctively, she won't touch those bricks. That face.

"Jesus Christ," McGowan says. Then she brings the CB to her lips and says: "Her name's not Wanda Van Horn. Her name is Brea Delany. Are you getting this Pollen? Brea's the coach of the girls' team."

There is no response, and McGowan doesn't expect one.

McGowan stares into the blue face. Thinks of trauma. Of her own. Of Pollen's. Of Samhattan's. She thinks of a little girl stolen from a candy store and what being abducted by a woman who planned to eat you might do to your mind.

How else to deal with it than . . . to celebrate it? Because to admit what was happening, at any age, would be to admit something worse than any local myth could muster.

". . . a girl from the team has entered Samhattan High School . . ."

It's the CB. And it's Pollen.

"Chief," McGowan says. "Did you hear me? Wanda Van Horn is not—"

But the line is dead again.

McGowan looks into the large, dead eyes. She realizes the actual perspective of this mural. It's from above Daphne's face. Looking down upon her as she sits in the front seat of her muscle car. There's a small dashboard and radio detailed in the deep background. And in those two hands, the delicious candy the artist is still, unfathomably, grateful for.

McGowan leaves the basement, slower than she'd like, backing up, unable to remove from her chest the horrible sadness of this story.

Daphne

McGowan almost falls back upon the stairs as she reaches them without turning to look.

She raises her gun.

She fires it into the brick wall, into the mural, into the left dead eye of the woman who not only did such evil in life but inspires even more in death.

The smoke rises like exhaust fumes. For a moment, it looks as if those eyes aren't dead after all.

"Brea," McGowan says.

Because she believes she's her killer. Because, whether the story is fair or not, whether the trauma inflicted upon the little girl explains the actions of the woman, McGowan's job is to stop her.

But she stops herself, one more moment down here, before leaving. She thinks of Pollen and the journals in the box Principal Taylor gave her. She thinks of an entire city agreeing to remain quiet without actually saying those words.

And she imagines, as best she can, that the woman she faces, the huge blue head on the wall, that this woman is real. That Daphne's flame is kept alive by the last little girl she took. That Wanda, no, that *Brea Delany* loved her captor so much, she remains the memory in the communal mind, *Samhattan's* mind, with Brea whispering *Daphne, Daphne, Daphne . . .*

To all she greets.

To all she meets.

And to all she coaches too.

And in this moment, McGowan thinks there are no lines, crossed or uncrossed, no law, and no breaking it.

There is only navigating the damage that has been done to you and the damage you cause.

Then she's up the stairs.

She's out.

She's running to her car, already plotting the fastest route to the Samhattan High School gymnasium.

o o o

Kit stands at the free-throw line, the same line she stood at when she made her winning shot. The tips of her shoes are so close to the paint, she wouldn't be surprised if a referee called a lane violation. But there is no referee. No other players. No crowd.

Still, a bit of a game.

Kit is asking the rim questions.

Some of them are big ones. Like will her mother live long into old age (she rattled this one in), and then the same for Dad (she missed). Some of them are small.

"Am I done growing?"

She shoots. Misses. As she steps to fetch the rebound, she wonders if the rim is telling her she's not done growing *out*, wider, like maybe she'll gain a lot of weight over time, or maybe even get pregnant. Kit thinks the rim is most likely saying, *No, you will not stop growing as a person.*

The rim tends to get philosophical like that, especially when your question isn't a great one.

The *best* ones are those with no wiggle room for interpretation. Natasha used to say that all questions are open for debate, even the color of someone's hair. Because, Natasha said, we all see the world differently. At the time, it was one of the deeper things Kit had ever heard her friend say. But she knows there's much more on her phone right now. Much heavier stuff. A thousand messages Kit will never check.

And she doesn't need to: she's already standing on the precipice of madness, the free-throw line the last fence before sanity's end. Between Kit and the rim, an abyss. And that rim sees more than the rug in the center of Third-and-Fourth-Eye Books does.

"Will it be a cold winter?"

She shoots. Misses. The rim never lies to Kit.

And she's trying. And she knows she is. But if there's one thing Patricia Maxwell taught her in the few minutes they shared, it's that it's okay *not* to clear your mind of all that troubles you. The real goal is to face it.

Kit fetches the ball, hears the glorious, never-gets-old sound of her shoes squeaking against the floor. She imagines it's what a typewriter must be like for a writer. A wood bat for a baseball player. For Kit Lamb, there's nothing like the sounds, and the echoes of those sounds, in a high school gym.

"Coach Wanda," she says, teary-eyed, "this one's for you." She lines up the shot, thinks of Wanda's instructions on how to shoot free throws. "Will I play basketball in college?"

She misses. Bad. But just like anybody who receives a less-than-flattering prediction, Kit remolds the response. Maybe she won't play college, okay, but maybe that's because she's going to go *straight to the motherfuckin' WNBA.*

She wipes tears from her face.

"Will I ever own a dog?"

She swishes this one and that's good. Means she'll live, right?

Kit and the rim. The rim and Kit.

Locked and linked.

The rim doesn't lie.

That's why it's difficult to ask the questions she really wants to ask. This prefatory exchange is only small talk between good friends. Both know the big stuff must be coming soon. Because Patricia Maxwell told Kit not to cover the bad thoughts in a blanket, to face them, to reframe it so that she, Kit, is in charge.

Even if you've thought your enemy into existence, you can keep them at a safe distance.

But to do that will require asking the rim questions about Daphne.

And accepting the responses.

Kit isn't ready for that.

"Will I own a snake?"

She swishes this too. Surprises her. But only to a point. Her mind isn't on pets, love, college. It's not even on basketball. And the longer she takes to face it, the longer it feels like she won't be able to see it at all.

She fetches the ball, returns to the line, takes a deep breath.

A lot of pros have weird free-throw-line rituals. The hitch in Kevin Durant's shoulder. The spin in Karl Malone's hands, and the fact that he talked to the ball. Some were terrible shooters and so they tried it underhand. Others took a step back from the line, believing perhaps the reason they sucked was some unlucky combination of height and distance. Or, maybe, the size of their hands. Even on Kit's own team, Melanie had a weird routine. She'd bounce the ball three times, kiss it, then usually miss. Kit's routine was more conservative. Everything Coach Wanda ever taught her about breathing, form, and gathering herself no matter what point of the game they were at.

But right now, it's time for a change. Kit must step outside herself if she's going to do what she came here to do.

She turns her back to the basket. She holds the ball about stomach-high.

"Can I think Melanie back to life too?"

She hurls the ball over her head, spins to see it miss everything. For as much as this hurts, it's what she was expecting. Sometimes you've got to gauge the rim that way. Ask it something you think you know the answer to, then take a shot with almost no chance. If it goes in? It could mean the rim is lying.

Kit fetches the ball.

She looks it over in her hands. To her, a perfect shape. Not round so much as . . . basketball.

It's time.

She steps to the line.

She steadies herself.

"Is Daphne dead?"

The name sounds hollow, like a long shaft through the center of the world.

She shoots.

Swish.

Okay, no question about that one.

She fetches the ball, brings it back to the line.

"Is Natasha dead?"

She shoots.

Swishes.

Kit looks to her phone at the foot of the baseline wall padding.

"Okay," she says. Because she's past trying to rewrite history. She's past fooling herself into believing this situation is somehow better than it actually is.

Still, she cries as she gets the ball.

She steps to the line.

"Can I kill Daphne?"

She shoots.

It's a clunker, rockets off the rim, bounces hard right.

She knows she asked an interpretable question. Just because *Kit* can't kill Daphne, doesn't mean someone else can't. And besides, how do you kill something that's dead?

"Can I stop Daphne?"

Her voice shakes. She shoots.

The ball circles the rim before rolling out.

Kit nods. Okay. This is meaningful. The rim is telling her that maybe she worded the question poorly, maybe there's a tighter way to ask it. But to *stop* Daphne? To fully *stop* her?

No.

Kit fetches the ball. Steps to the line.

"Is Daphne coming for me, right now?"

Her words echo down through that shaft.

She shoots.

Swishes.

The echo of the net and the ball striking the floor resolve into silence. Kit begins breathing harder. She thinks of Patricia Maxwell. She thinks of Natasha.

But despite the tears for her friends and the near paralytic fear she feels in every joint in her body, Kit isn't here to be afraid.

She gets the ball. She breathes deep.

"Is she close?"

She shoots.

Swishes.

Very close. Kit's old friend the rim says so.

Kit nods. Wipes tears away. Fetches the make.

She steps to the line.

"Is she right outside the gym?"

She spins the ball once. Fires. Makes it.

A sound then. From somewhere deep in the school: the crashing of a door slamming open.

Kit doesn't want to stop. Doesn't want to run. Doesn't want to stand here and die like her friends either.

She tries to control her breathing. Tries to slow it down long enough to fetch the ball.

Back at the line, she moves on muscle memory alone.

Elbow in, left hand supporting, she hears the door to the gym open behind her.

Don't look, she tells herself. And she thinks of a world without Daphne.

But this is short-lived. Kit smells something she's never smelled in any gym before: smoke and alcohol.

She doesn't take her eyes off the rim.

"If thinking about Daphne brings her to me . . ." She searches for the words, trembles at the sound of boots crossing the hardwood. "Can I think her away?"

She shoots.

Swishes.

Okay. No question on that one.

The gym provides the rebound as it often does: the ball connects with the baseline wall and bounces straight back to where she faces the basket.

She breathes deep, nearly unable to hold the ball for shaking. She barely lines up her shot.

She thinks of the Spirit of Samhattan, the rock on which she wrote her final journal entry.

She told it she has a plan.

She does.

"Daphne . . ." she says.

Because maybe all this rim talk . . . maybe it's not about asking . . . but *telling.*

"Daphne," she says again. "Leave me alone."

She shoots.

She's short. Front of the rim. The ball bounces straight back to her again.

"Daphne. You can't hurt me unless I let you."

Sweat's coming down her face now. Mingles with the tears.

She misses again. This time an airball. Nerves, yes, but worse: Kit has to fetch the ball.

Meaning she has to walk back to the line. Meaning she'll see what's coming for her. What's crossing the gym.

She hurries, gets the ball, doesn't look directly at the unbelievable shape near midcourt.

She lines up again. Tucks her elbow in. Readies herself.

The smells are close now.

Kit closes her eyes at the line like Michael Jordan once did.

She *tells* the rim what to do.

Make her go away.

The silver doors to the outside world open behind her. Kit, eyes still closed, resists the urge to spin, to engage with anything but the rim. She's so close to having this all worked out. So close to finding her own way through this.

But the door she faces along the baseline wall opens at the same time.

Kit still doesn't open her eyes, not even when she hears Detective McGowan yell: "*Shoot her!*"

Daphne is inches behind.

Make her GO AWAY, she thinks.

She shoots.

Even as Dana shoots.

Even as Kit opens her eyes, sees Coach Wanda standing a foot in front of her, sees Detective McGowan rushing toward Coach Wanda.

"Coach?"

The ball swishes.

Something huge falls to the floor behind Kit.

She turns, sees Daphne, facedown, all denim and hair, at the top of the key.

Coach Wanda grabs Kit by the throat.

"I'll kill you," she says. "If you've hurt her, I'll kill you."

But Kit is much stronger than her coach. And one kick to the woman's stomach sends her to the floor too.

McGowan kneels beside Daphne.

"Look out!" Kit yells.

Because she knows. Because the rim told her.

You can't kill Daphne.

A bare hand erupts from all that denim, grips the detective by the throat, crushes it like an aluminum steering wheel.

Dana fires again.

Daphne falls face-first back to the gym floor.

"*Daphne!*" Coach Wanda shouts.

But Dana has the gun up, trained on their coach now.

"Stay back," she says.

But Coach Wanda keeps coming, her eyes on the fallen giant.

Kit, only partially understanding what she's seeing, draws on something the very woman who screams for Daphne once taught her to do.

When you go up for a layup, Coach taught her, *and the other girl is coming toward you, extend your elbow, Kit. Knock that fucker in the chest. Doesn't matter if she was actually going to hit you or not. You'll get the and-one. You'll get the call every time.*

Kit elbows Wanda in the chest just as Dana fires.

And as Wanda hits the floor . . .

. . . Daphne rises.

And her height, her full height, is the most majestic thing Kit has ever known.

"*Run!*" Dana shouts.

Kit does. But it's not for the door. It's not for escape.

It's for the ball.

Daphne steps toward her.

"*KIT!*" Dana yells.

But Kit dives, grabs the ball, and dribbles full tilt toward the rim.

Daphne steps to the rim too. Her boots as loud as an engine.

Kit focuses on the ball. Her form. The rim.

And as Daphne reaches for her, the dirt of her bare hands visible beneath the gymnasium lights, Kit recalls every shot she's ever taken, all, one upon the other, every make, every miss.

Her right foot off the ground now, the ball on the fingertips of her right hand, she does not ask the rim a question.

She tells it what to do.

"*SEND HER BACK WHERE SHE CAME FROM!!*"

The ball leaves her hand.

And she thinks: If you can think something terrible into being, why not something great?

The ball kisses the backboard, seems to stay there too long, and falls gently through the net.

Kit lands.

"Where is she?" Dana asks. "Where the *fuck* did she go?"

But Kit knows where Daphne is.

She's been thought away. Or rather, Kit, Dana, and Samhattan have already begun thinking of better things.

"Dana!"

Her best friend is on her knees now.

Kit goes to her, slides beside her. Hugs her.

"Holy shit," Dana says. "You did it. Kit! You did it."

Tears, yes. But something else too. Something Kit has never known:

Control.

In a moment as big as this one.

They look to their dead coach. To the dead detective.

"We need to go," Kit says.

And they do. They get up. They step out the open gym doors.

As police sirens escalate, the best friends leave the court together.

Outside, Dana says, "You're the bravest person I know."

"I love you, Dana."

"No, Kit. I mean it." She stops and Kit stops and Dana looks her hard in the eyes. "You're the only person I know who did something about it."

"About what?"

"About life, Kit. About when life scared you."

"I didn't—"

"When you called 911 on yourself, when you were so scared you thought you'd die . . . you asked for help."

Then Dana hugs her. And the sirens get louder.

"We're gonna have to explain a lot," Dana says. "There will be questions."

Kit recalls the question she asked the rim on her game winner, the question that started this all.

Is Daphne going to kill me?

And the rim said yes.

And the rim never lies to Kit.

"We're alive," she says. And her voice does not shake. "And all the fear in the world . . ."

"What about it?" Dana asks. "Kit?"

The squad car is visible now from where they stand. Kit puts her arm around her friend. Says,

"Let's not even think about it."

ACKNOWLEDGMENTS

I love basketball. Always have. Every variety: the college game, high school, the driveway, the street, the gym, the NBA, the WNBA. Growing up, my bedroom walls were covered with posters of Akeem Olajuwon (no "H" to start his name yet back then), Isiah Thomas, Larry Bird. A kid in high school once called me a "walking oxymoron" because I'd wear a Celtics shirt, a Lakers jacket, a Pistons hat. But I don't blame him: he didn't realize I wasn't rooting for a particular player or team, I was rooting for the *game*. Especially the rivalry between Magic Johnson and Larry Bird. It was like the Old West. I was rooting for the *duel*. I pretended to be these players outside in the driveway. But I pretended to be girls I had crushes on too. I'd pass the ball to them. Watch them pass it to each other. There was also an Alyssa Milano poster on that bedroom wall. I grew up with the game. The first thing of length I ever wrote was an account of a tournament I played in Ohio with this incredible travel team. We'd been down eleven points with about a minute and a half to play, and we came back and won. I made a three-pointer to cut that lead to five. I also almost got dunked on, but the guy missed it. Yes, the game has been there for me my whole life. Minutes after my parents told us they were getting divorced, I dribbled a basketball three miles to my high school girl-friend's house. Talked with her and her family about it. I took mushrooms with friends in college and went and played a pickup game at the rec center. One friend shot it from half court just to see what it'd feel like. I can only imagine what the sober players on the other team thought of that. We called our Gus Macker team The Tommyknockers. We called our intramural team The Ghastly Monsters. Years later, I'd challenge Bob Pollard and Guided By Voices to three on three against us, the High Strung. Bob said, simply, "You don't wanna do that." There were days I played in cowboy boots. Called them my "Karl Malones." Played in dress shoes. Called them my "Phil Jacksons." And years later, a friend who played on that high school travel team called to ask if I wanted him to send one of my books to a lawyer he knew. That story is detailed elsewhere, but it all leads to where we are now.

So yeah. I'm obsessed with the game. I know a ton about it. And I love horror. I know a ton about it. And while I wouldn't say I "love" anxiety, I do have a complex relationship with it, and I know it well too.

And if you, reader, suffer any degree of anxiety, please know . . . you are absolutely not alone.

You know that saying, "everybody's got their shit"? Yeah, well, *everybody's* got their shit. Anxiety is a chaotic animal. Sometimes, when tamed, it can almost kinda, maybe, just maybe result in something cool. But mostly it's a messy guest. For the most part, I'll only offer empathy, but let me say one thing that's helped through the years and, who knows, maybe it'll help you too:

I had a particularly rough run of it recently. A few years back. I kept telling Allison, "I can't get out from under it." I remember that phrase. The hum of the anxiety lasted months. I tried everything. Breathing, working out, etc. Then Allison suggested I "time" the episodes. So I did. The first one, the peak of it, lasted about seven minutes. I timed the next one. About seven minutes. Same with the third. After that, it all kinda went away. Once I'd given the episode a numeric value, it had *form*.

That's helped.

And Kit's story in here? About calling 911 on herself and why? Well, while no book of fiction is entirely autobiographical, that scene is nearly verbatim from my life. Yeah, that was a pivot, to say the least. One I'm eternally grateful for.

And speaking of grateful, some thanks are in order regarding the book in your hands:

Thank you to Tricia Narwani for recognizing a novella bursting at the seams, one that needed to become a novel instead.

Thank you to everyone at Del Rey and Penguin Random House for always making me feel I'm part of the team.

Thank you, Ryan Lewis, Wayne Alexander, Kristin Nelson. We would make a good four-on-four squad. I imagine Kristin as our point.

My dad! Who taught me the game. My dad can outshoot your dad any day, any time. He was/is the real deal.

My brothers! Who were and are obsessed with it too.

Allison Laakko, who has perfect Bob Cousy layup form and inspired Kit's last layup in the book.

David Simmer, for passing me the ball.

And thank you to the coach of that travel team, Barry Bershad, for being way the hell ahead of his time.

Really, thank you to anyone I ever played the game with or watched the game with. And thank you to everyone I've ever shared horror with, whether it was watching a movie, buddy reading, a writing challenge, conversations at conventions, everything and all.

And thank you to everyone I've ever freaked out with too.

Daphne is a love letter of sorts to the game of basketball and the horror genre, both.

But, while it's not a "love letter" to anxiety, it is a correspondence.

This is me reminding anxiety that I wear all the team colors, because I am still well aware of the duel.

—*Josh Malerman*
Michigan, 2022

ABOUT THE AUTHOR

JOSH MALERMAN is a *New York Times* bestselling author and one of two singer-songwriters for the rock band the High Strung. His debut novel, *Bird Box,* is the inspiration for the hit Netflix film of the same name. His other novels include *Unbury Carol, Inspection, A House at the Bottom of a Lake,* and *Malorie,* the sequel to *Bird Box.* Malerman lives in Michigan with his fiancée, the artist-musician Allison Laakko.

joshmalerman.com
Twitter: @JoshMalerman
Facebook: facebook.com/JoshMalerman
Instagram: @joshmalerman